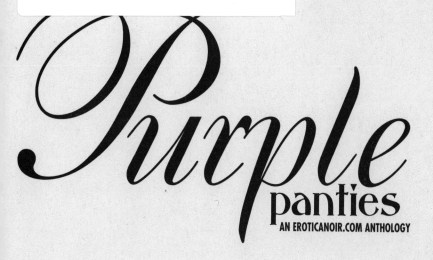

Purple
panties
AN EROTICANOIR.COM ANTHOLOGY

Purple
panties
AN EROTICANOIR.COM ANTHOLOGY

EDITED BY ZANE

STREBOR BOOKS

New York London Toronto Sydney

SBI

Strebor Books
P.O. Box 6505
Largo, MD 20792
http://www.streborbooks.com

© 2008 *Purple Panties: An Eroticanoir.com Anthology* edited by Zane

ISBN-13   978-1-59309-165-1
ISBN-10   1-59309-165-6
LCCN 2007943468

First Strebor Books trade paperback edition May 2008

Cover design: www.mariondesigns.com

20 19 18 17 16 15 14 13

Manufactured in the United States of America

For information regarding special discounts for bulk purchases, please contact Simon & Schuster Special Sales at 1-800-456-6798 or business@simonandschuster.com

*This book is dedicated to all the people in the world
involved in same-gender loving relationships.
People are always so quick to judge,
even though they fear being judged themselves.
We are given but one life and make the most of yours,
regardless of what others might think.*

TABLE OF CONTENTS

I have but one word for this book: *Hot!* No, three words: *Hot! Hot! Hot!* Yes, it is like that! When I first decided to do *Purple Panties*, a lot of my friends said, "Well, what if people think you're a lesbian!" First of all, I've often been called a lesbian; mostly by men in my past who thought that the only way I could not want to be with them is because I had to be gay. If there is one person on this earth who cares not what "hypocritical" people think, it is me or I would never have written my first book: *The Sex Chronicles: Shattering the Myth*. Secondly, if I were a lesbian, that would be my business and I would have no issues with being open and honest about it. Thirdly, I am sick of people trying to tell other people who to love, who to fuck, and, in general, how to live.

Passion and sensuality are not only universal, which is why I edited *Chocolate Flava*, *Caramel Flava* and *Asian Spice*. Passion and sensuality are also for people involved in same gender-loving relationships. Life is what it is and people have no right to judge others. Besides, if you are even reading this introduction and have an issue with the lesbian theme, why did you pick it up?

Okay, enough venting. Let me say this. I have written a lot of erotica and have read a lot more but when I was editing this collection, I realized that it is the most sensual one to date. And it is not just for lesbians. It is for women and men. In fact, I am willing to bet that men who read it will be just as hot and bothered as the women who read it. Reading a book is not going to make you eat pussy but it might just open up your mind to some new ideas. After all, women all have the same body parts and we know what pleases us; often more than any man ever will. I got a ton of new thoughts circulating in my mind after reading these stories; that's for damn sure.

I am not stopping here either. The second edition of *Purple Panties*, entitled *Missionary No More*, will be released in January 2009 so be on the lookout for it. I received so many awesome submissions that I had to split it into two books. These women are not even playing with their shit and I love women who do not play when it comes to getting their freak on. More so than the hot sex scenes contained within this volume, I truly appreciate the creativeness exhibited by the various authors, who come from all walks of life but have one common goal: being one hell of an erotica writer. The storylines and character development are nothing short of amazing. I would like to personally thank all of the contributors for allowing me to put their visions out into the world.

You might need a few drinks when you read this book, definitely a sex toy or a lover, but you are in for one hell of a ride. I want to see a lot of sisters wearing purple panties after this. In fact, visit my site, www.eroticanoir.com, and purchase them so you can make a powerful statement of your own: that you are sexually uninhibited and free from the mental chains of oppression. Make sure that you join my email list by sending a blank email to eroticanoir-subscribe@topica.com and visit me on MySpace at www.myspace.com/zaneland. Lastly, make sure you also pick up a copy of *Flesh to Flesh*, edited by Strebor Books author Lee Hayes if you have any interest in male gay erotica. I am the publisher and guarantee you will enjoy that as well. For more gay and lesbian literature from Strebor Books, visit www.streborbooks.com

Blessings,

Zane

It's All or Nothing

Laurinda D. Brown

Sitting at the intersection of Ponce and Peachtree, I found myself consumed with how I had spent my evening. The backlight from my cell phone had been blinking with missed text messages and missed calls from home. I knew most of those calls were from Walter and my grandbabies, telling me they were going to bed. Somehow, over the past several months, I'd lost concern over keeping up with their schedules. My husband of thirty years told me of his whereabouts daily, and I had grown tired of hearing the same old things, day in and day out. I often found myself mouthing his every syllable, his every word, whenever he spoke to me.

A provost at Howard University, his life didn't have much excitement. He got up in the mornings, did five miles on the treadmill, took a seven and a half-minute shower, splashed on the same Grey Flannel aftershave and cologne he'd worn for thirty years, put on a pair of black slacks and a crisp, white dress shirt with black socks, made himself a bran muffin, a glass of apple juice and a cup of black Sanka, and drove his 1973 Dodge Charger to Lot D on the university's campus. In the evenings when he got home, he'd talk my ear off about his day and his colleagues who had gotten on his nerves.

The only one who ever caught and kept my attention was Lee Matthews, a young African-American woman who'd received her MBA from Georgetown. She was in her thirties from what Walter had told me, and the administration was giving her hell about her radical stance when it came to sexual orientation discrimination in the workplace. The university's position was like the military's—*don't ask, don't tell.* Lee's attitude was that there was nothing in place to protect gays that worked for the school in the event such a problem ever arose. While she didn't come right out and say she was a lesbian, the higher-ups, including Walter, worked long hours to devise a plan for relieving this young lady of her duties.

I first met Lee in Walter's office one afternoon while I was waiting for him so we could go to lunch. She was standing at the photocopy machine in a gray pin-striped pantsuit with a pink blouse and a pearl choker clenching her neck. Her open-toed buff pink, three-inch-high slip-ons comforted the most beautiful feet I'd ever seen with toes perfected with an American pedicure. Lee wore her sandy hair in a nice fluffy ponytail that bounced when she moved. As she removed her papers from the document tray, I realized I was staring and turned shyly away. Looking out the window high over Georgia Avenue, I felt her approaching me.

"Dr. Woodson?" she asked.

I, at the age of forty-nine with four grown children, was like a schoolgirl. I had an Ed.D. from the University of Maryland that had seemed to go to waste over the years because Walter wanted me at home when the kids got in from school. I'd sacrificed who I'd worked so hard to become because my husband didn't want to be outdone by his wife. I drove what he wanted me to drive—a Black Lexus LS430, and, I wore what he wanted me to wear—Dolce and Gabbana, Versace and Prada. I looked like a million dollars whenever I stepped out of the house, and today was no exception. I was wearing Michael Kors.

"Yes?" I answered.

I'd say she was about six feet tall in her heels. She towered over my five-foot-five frame, and, as she walked closer to me, I was stricken by her beauty. Like Marvin Gaye said in "Trouble Man," I was coming apart, and the room was suddenly a little warm for me. It wasn't the hot flashes I'd grown used to, with menopause around the corner.

Extending her hand, she politely said, "I'm Lee Matthews." She firmly shook my hand and introduced herself as the new director of university advancement. "I recognized you from the picture your husband has on his desk. They need to fire whoever took that photo because you're way more beautiful in person."

Blushing, I replied, "Well, thank you, Ms. Matthews."

"No, please, call me Lee." She smelled divine. "Are you here to see him?" she asked, pointing toward Walter's office.

"As a matter of fact, I am. We're supposed to be having lunch."

Lee looked puzzled. "Today?"

"Yes, we talked about it just this morning before he left."

Lee got up and walked over to Walter's secretary's desk. "He must've been confused then. He and some of the deans are over at Catholic University for a meeting. They've been there since this morning, and, according to his calendar, he'll be out all day."

On a normal day I would've been pissed because I hated driving into D.C. from Manassas. I'd told Walter I wanted to move out of Virginia because of all the taxes we had to pay, but he was never listening to me.

"Well, I guess maybe he forgot." I was ashamed to admit he'd actually done it to me before.

Lee, flipping through the stack of papers she was cradling in her arm, headed toward the door but stopped and stole a look at her watch. "Look, I'm about to go to lunch myself, and I'd hate for you to have come all this way for nothing. Would you mind joining me? I mean, I can understand if you don't want to; since you just met me like five minutes ago."

"Oh, no, no. I wouldn't mind. I was actually going to ask you the same thing."

I laughed, collecting my purse and car keys. The moment we stepped out of Walter's office I knew I was entering a new realm.

℘〇℃

We'd agreed upon Union Station for lunch since she wanted seafood, and I wanted a good salad. In the ten minutes it took us to make it there, I'd learned that Lee had gone to Mount Holyoke for undergrad, had one brother, had interned at Marriott Hotels and had been instrumental in helping them develop more stringent diversity inclusion programs. In listening to how passionate she was about the protection of gays in the workplace and the occasional references to her "ex-roommate," I concluded she was in the life. My sister, Melba, was gay, and, before opening up to me about her lifestyle, all of her former lovers had actually been ex-roommates. I'd envied my sister for being able to have some spice in her life and for being able to do different things, and different people, whenever she wanted. In this short period of time, Lee had become something different for me. Anyway, when we pulled up the ramp to the parking garage, I noticed Lee looking around at all the cars.

"Seems a bit crowded today, you think?"

Wrapping around the curves in search of an empty parking space,

I agreed. "Yeah, it is, but I'm sure we'll find something in a sec."
Right then an Escalade, with its reverse lights on, floated from its
space. "Here we go. I told you it wouldn't take long."

Walking through the door, I glanced over the railing and saw
people entering the train station from the platform. Lee, taking
a glimpse at her watch again, walked over to the monitor and
scanned the departure schedules. Standing by waiting for her to
get finished, I was completely caught off guard when she turned
and grabbed my hand.

"Come on! It leaves in ten minutes!" she shrieked.

"What?" I said, taking off my heels as she tugged me along.

Lee didn't say anything else; scampering through the crowds.
We ended up at the ticket window.

"Two to New York City, please."

"What are you doing?" I asked.

"Hold on," she shushed.

Accustomed to doing whatever I was told, I moved aside and
leaned against the vacant counter to put my shoes back on and
catch my breath. No sooner than I had relaxed, Lee grabbed my
hand again and took off toward the platform.

"I hope you don't mind the sleeping car. That's all they had left."

"Sleeping car? New York? What's going on?" I asked. "I thought
you wanted to go to lunch."

Again, Lee didn't say anything. She pulled me through the
crowds like a Yamaha on the Beltway, and, when we got to the
steps of the train, she turned to me with my hair dripping wet
with sweat and simply smiled.

"You think I'm crazy, don't you?"

I wanted so badly to tell her yes, but my spirit, in need of this
liberty, put its hand over my mouth.

"No, I don't." I giggled, grabbing the handrail and lifting myself onto the train.

Giving our tickets to the attendant, Lee and I followed behind him as he led us up the stairs to our accommodations. I was pooped and dropped my weary bones into an awaiting chair.

With a kind but curious smile, I asked, "What are you doing, Lee?"

I wasn't one who was used to spontaneity. There was a time and a place for everything.

Standing before the mirror, wiping tiny beads of sweat from her brow, she snickered. "I decided I wanted some seafood from City Crab, and I thought you might like that, too."

Lee, taking off her jacket and hanging it up in the closet, jumped up onto the top bunk and stretched out across the bed on her stomach.

Confused at why we had to travel all the way to New York for seafood, I said, in amazement, "Dear, we could've gone down to the wharf, if that's what you wanted. There's plenty..."

"I wasn't really feeling that today, Dr. Woodson. The bosses are out of the office, so I felt like goofing off. Sometimes I think they have it in for me anyway."

"Uh, it's Meena. You can call me Meena."

"Oh, okay, Meena. You know those papers you saw me with when you came in?"

"Yes, I recall them."

"Well, that was my resume. I've been interviewing for jobs in Atlanta. Those stiff-shirts don't realize I've known for weeks that they've been plotting to get rid of me without causing a big stink. When I leave, it'll be on my own terms."

I kept to myself what I knew. "So you're going to leave? Just like that?"

"As soon as something comes through, I'm gone."

All the way to New York, Lee fired questions at me about my life, my kids, and my career I'd left behind for Walter. "So you mean to tell me you left a hundred fifty thousand-dollar-a-year job, so you could stay at home and be a trophy wife?"

"In a nutshell, yes, I did. I loved Walter at the time, and…"

"At the time?"

I'd slipped. "Well, what I meant was…"

"You don't have to explain. That's your business."

But I wanted to go on. "No, I need to say this. I have given Walter the best of me over the years, but some days I feel like I've given him all of me, and that there's nothing left for myself." Before I knew it, I was weeping.

Lee propped up on her elbows and pulled a tissue from her pocket. "Don't worry, it's clean." She laughed.

Gently, I took the tissue from her hand and continued pouring out my soul to her.

„‟

What began as a late lunch ended up becoming an early dinner at City Crab. Perusing the menu with my glasses pulled away from my face to see the fine print, I said, "Oh, the salads look nice. Old women like me have to get all the vegetables we can get."

Lee, peeping over the top of her menu, stared at me like my twenty-year-old had a tendency to do when she was fed up with me. "Will you stop it? You're not old. You're absolutely gorgeous. Now, I know you aren't going to come all this way to still eat a salad, Meena."

Sitting in a seafood restaurant at the corner of 19th and Park

Avenue with a woman who, in all of five hours, knew more about me than my own husband knew, I finally took a chance. "Okay, you're right. I'll have the Maryland Crabmeat Stuffed Idaho Rainbow Trout."

Slowly rubbing my thigh underneath the table, Lee ordered for both of us and requested the waiter bring us a pitcher of Sangria. I wasn't a drinker, but I didn't want her to know that. When the waiter left, she brought her hand back to the tabletop and gestured for me to put my hand in hers. At first I hesitated because I wasn't comfortable with holding another woman's hand in public. "Relax, Meena. No one knows us here. Besides, it's none of anybody's business what we do."

I liked Lee's attitude. Walter had always been concerned with what other people thought, and it made our outings together very uncomfortable for me. With Lee, I felt like it was right. "Okay, okay," I said, giving them to her; trembling and all.

Stroking my knuckles and the veins in my ageless hands, Lee softly asked, looking into my eyes, "You know why I did this for you?"

I'd been asking myself that for hours, and I was overdue an explanation. "Why, yes, I'd like to know," I responded, squeezing her soft hands.

"From the moment I laid eyes on you in that picture, I've thought about you. I hear Walter talking about you as if you're some type of permanent fixture in his life with no opinions, no say in anything. One day, after he and his secretary had finished talking about an event you two had attended, I asked her what you did. She referred to you as Doctor Woodson, and I was floored when she told me how heavy you were. The way he talks about you, I would've never guessed that about you. So I googled you and found out about this amazing stuff you'd done."

I was speechless. No one had ever talked to me about what my life used to be like. It was always about Walter, Walter, Walter.

"I don't really know what to say, Lee. You looked me up on the Internet?"

Quickly, Lee jumped on the defensive. "I'm not a stalker, if that's what you're asking. I wanted to know more about you, without having to ask your husband. Your work with Children's Hospital and GW should've gotten more recognition than what I saw."

"Well, at the time, Walter was up for provost, and I had to devote all of my time to him. I passed the torch to a colleague," I said humbly.

Lee had a death grip on my hands, and I was afraid for her to let them go in fear of never having someone hold them like that again. On the wall over the bar was a clock that displayed seven o'clock. Considering we hadn't eaten yet, it would be well into the morning before I got home, but I didn't care. I only wanted to spend as much time with her as I could.

"This was good for me," I said. "I needed to get away."

I searched in her eyes for an unspoken response, and I found it.

It was ten o'clock by the time we made it back to Penn Station, and we were back in another bedroom car.

"Meena, I hope you enjoyed yourself tonight. I'm sure I scared the hell out of you with my impromptu lunch date."

Once again, she jumped up to the top bunk, but this time in her heels. Her long legs were dangling over my bunk.

Chuckling to myself, I relaxed my body on the lower berth, and I sought no forgiveness for what happened next. Solemnly, I took those same hands that had trembled during dinner and removed Lee's shoes from her feet. I grabbed her pinky toe with my tongue and caressed every single toe with my lips until her entire foot was saturated with my essence. Lee slid down from the bed and met my lips with hers.

"I want to make love to you over and over again, until you scream my name like doves."

I had no idea what I was doing. All I knew was that it felt right. Button by button, I exposed Lee's bosom to me and cupped her voluptuous curves with my hands. I reclined her against my bunk and removed every stitch of her clothing until I'd reached her bare skin. Standing in the moving car as we bustled across the tracks extending north to south, I disrobed my thousand-dollar frock and lay next to her. I kissed every part of her, every part I could get to, and, in my mind, I made her all mine.

Lee, returning my affections, mounted me and rested her body against me. Motionless, our hearts beat synchronized with time. I held her nipples between my lips and softly planted my palms around her buttocks. I didn't know what I was doing, but, as she rocked back and forth in my lap moaning and whimpering my name, I knew what I had done. With my body stretched against the sheets, Lee slid between my legs and spread them; landing kisses inside my thighs that eventually landed onto the lips of my pussy. Riding a wave of lust, Lee and I journeyed into a place where our erotic souls met and fell in love.

I got home early the next morning with a barrage of questions from Walter. I told him I'd spent some time with Melba and had lost track of time.

৪০৫৪

Two months after that evening, I got a call at home from Lee telling me she had gotten a job offer from Emory University and wanted to know if I'd meet her in Atlanta to help her look for an apartment. Walter had told me she was leaving but refused to go into any details. Did they get her a job? Did any of her leads come through? I missed her and jumped at the chance and took the Red Eye out from Dulles.

Lee picked me up from the airport, and, because we hadn't seen or talked to each other since New York, I was all giddy inside. I'd thought about her and wondered where she'd fit into my life, if at all possible. We rode back to her hotel room at the Hilton and went down to Trader Vic's for a nightcap.

"Meena, I've been thinking about you every day for the past two months, and I can't get you out of my head. I want to ask you something."

Secretly, I yearned for Lee unlike I'd ever yearned for anyone. In the shower, in the tub, in the bed—everywhere, I had to have her. "What's on your mind?"

"I want you here with me."

"As in leave my family and move to Atlanta?"

Teasing a piece of ice with her straw, Lee softly answered, "Why, yes, that's what I'm asking. That night on the train meant every-thing to me. I've had lovers in the past, and none of them were ever able to do what you did."

"And what was that?"

"You made me fall in love," she said tearfully.

While Lee slept into the wee hours of the morning, I decided to brave the streets of Atlanta to think. I walked through the lobby and got a cab, asking to be driven up Peachtree and back. As we made a left on Ralph McGill and a right onto Peachtree, I contemplated my unhappiness and where it had gotten me thus far. I was nowhere. In thirty years of marriage, I'd found nothing close to what I'd found with Lee in those few hours I'd been with her. I'd experienced something I wanted with me for an eternity, and, if it meant leaving Walter, my kids, my grandbabies, and my miserably boring life, then so be it.

ℰ∞ℛ

Divine destiny is what motivates mother, daughter, author, playwright Laurinda D. Brown to do what she does—write novels and plays that portray real people in true-to-life situations no different than your average neighbor next door. Brown explains, "Growing up in Memphis, Tennessee, and graduating from Howard University in Washington, D.C., exposed me to the varied and diverse sides of human nature. It also gave me the opportunity to observe people and their situations and try to discern what made them do the things they did. I realized that people are people. My writing helped me work through my own issues, emotions and circumstances. Writing expresses my take on the world." Before Walk Like A Man—The Play, *Brown began her literary journey with* Fire & Brimstone *(Strebor Books), the 2005 Lambda Literary Award finalist for "Best Debut Lesbian Fiction," followed by* UnderCover *(Strebor Books) and* Walk Like A Man, *the 2006 Lambda Literary Award winner for "Best Lesbian Erotica." She is a featured writer in the new Nghosi Books anthology,* Longing, Lust, and Love: Black Lesbian Stories *and most recently penned* Strapped, *an urban novel about child sexual abuse and its effects on a young woman's sexuality. Laurinda resides with her two daughters in the greater Atlanta metro area where she is currently working on her explosive upcoming historical fiction novel,* The Highest Price for Passion *(Strebor Books/Atria/Simon and Schuster), release date: August 2008.*

Bread and Roses

Anna Black

"Union! Union!"

Monica Lewis lifted her sign and chanted along with the rest of the workers who marched outside the hotel. It was a hot, sweltering day. Probably the hottest day she had experienced since arriving in Tucson four months ago.

The locals had warned her about the heat but she had brushed off their warnings. She'd experienced enough summers in D.C. to feel confident she could handle one in Tucson.

But D.C. heat was nothing like this.

In a desperate attempt to feel cooler Monica had smoothed her dreads back into a ponytail. She also wore her union baseball cap to keep the sun off her face.

"Union! Union!"

Monica looked over and smiled. Mrs. Juanita Whitecloud, her plump, brown face glistening with sweat, stood near the curb, waving her sign at the passing cars. Her cardinal-red and navy-blue University of Arizona T-shirt was covered with union buttons, as was the large straw hat she wore.

Most of the cars, their windows rolled up in order to sustain their air-conditioned interiors, zipped past. But one car, its windows down, Spanish-style rap music pulsating out of its mega-speakers, slowed down for the light.

Monica moved closer to Mrs. Whitecloud.

The older woman shoved her sign at the car. "Union! Union!"

The car was full of young men. One of those in the backseat pushed his lean, handsome face out the window.

"Hey! *Abuella*! Why don't you go home and bake some *coyotas*?"

"If I do," Mrs. Whitecould taunted, "will you and your fine-looking *hijos* come over and eat them?"

The boy grinned. "I don't know. You kinda old for me. You got maybe a granddaughter I can hang with."

"No grandbabies yet. But I got a daughter."

"She fine as you?"

Mrs. Whitecloud laughed, her full bosom jiggling. "Yeah, but she's too good for you."

Before the boy could respond, the light changed and the car sped off.

Silas, who worked at the hotel as a custodian, shook his gray-haired head at Mrs. Whitecloud. "You ought to stop pimping Chenoa like that."

"I'm not pimping her. It's true what I said. I got no grandbabies yet. Chenoa's my only child. If she don't give me any, how I'm going to get any?" She looked over at Monica. "Ain't that right?"

Monica smiled. The last thing she wanted to do was encourage Mrs. Whitecloud in her campaign to get her daughter, Chenoa, married. Especially since from the moment Monica had met Chenoa, she'd been unable to stop thinking about her.

The union members marched up and down the street, waving their signs and chanting. Monica smiled. From day one she had been fighting an uphill battle to convince the hotel workers they needed a union.

Mrs. Whitecloud had been her first convert, and she had enthusiastically thrown herself into the fray, helping Monica strategize ways to organize the workers. As a result of spending so much time with her, Monica had met Chenoa, who was home for the summer from grad school back East.

Even now, standing in the hot, blazing sun, Monica felt that deliciously cool quiver deep down in her belly whenever she thought of Mrs. Whitecloud's beautiful daughter.

Chenoa. Of the black licorice hair, the smooth butterscotch skin, the succulent caramel-rich eyes.

Monica winced. Damn it. She couldn't help it if she thought about Chenoa in candy-coated images. She wanted to eat the woman alive.

Carnally speaking, of course.

"Chenoa!" Mrs. Whitecloud's voice cut through the chants of the workers. Monica quickly whirled around, bumping into Silas who was walking behind her.

He took a step back and grinned. "Watch it, girl."

"Sorry."

He slyly winked. "Keep that up and you might get me wondering if you got a thing for me."

Monica vaguely returned his smile. He'd been hitting on her since day one.

She looked over to where Mrs. Whitecloud stood next to Chenoa. What was she doing here? Chenoa had made it quite clear what she thought of her mother's union activities.

She did not approve of them.

From where Monica stood it looked as if that was the subject of their conversation, for Mrs. Whitecloud was stubbornly shaking her head. Chenoa's lovely face was set in an equally obstinate frown.

Monica went over to them. "Is something wrong?"

"No, Monica," Mrs. Whitecloud said. "There's nothing wrong."

Chenoa crossed her arms underneath her breasts. Monica couldn't help noticing how firm and enticing they looked under Chenoa's butter-yellow cotton T-shirt. She wore jean shorts that hugged her deliciously round ass and from which her long, bare legs extended enticingly.

"No, Mother. There most certainly is something wrong."

"Chenoa, don't…"

Chenoa ignored her and looked over at Monica. "Do you have any idea what the temperature is?"

Monica opened her mouth but Chenoa beat her to the punch. "A hundred ten degrees. A hundred ten! And you've got my mother out here…"

Mrs. Whitecloud moved in front of Monica and planted herself squarely in front of her daughter. "No, Chenoa. That is not fair. Monica does not control the weather."

"But apparently she controls you," Chenoa retorted.

"No! No one controls me! I am here because I believe in the union." She pointed to one of the bouquets of buttons on her shirt. "What does that say?"

Chenoa looked at the button and frowned. "Bread and roses. So?"

"And do you know what that means?

Chenoa shook her head.

Mrs. Whitecloud smiled and turned to the other marchers who had stopped to watch the row.

"She got one degree and is getting another, but she don't know everything." She looked over at Monica. "Tell Miss Smarty-Pants what it means."

Monica looked over into Chenoa's large, dark eyes and that delicious shiver had moved even lower, fluttering like the tips of fingers over her soft, inner folds.

Then, realizing with a start she'd been staring into Chenoa's eyes a hairsbreadth longer than was probably appropriate, Monica quickly looked away and at her watch. It was near the end of the time they'd been given permission to stage their protest.

Monica waved her arms. "It's almost time for us to go. Make sure you pack up any garbage."

Mrs. Whitecloud touched Monica's arm. "Ain't you going to tell her what 'bread and roses' mean?"

"Sure. But she's right; we need to get you out of this heat."

Mrs. Whitecloud snorted. "Such a fuss."

But she joined the others who were loading their union signs into Silas' van.

Monica looked at Chenoa. "We're going to stop and have a beer." She swallowed and forced herself to go on. "Want to join us?"

Mrs. Whitecloud shouted from within the van. "Yes, she can join us. Or maybe she's gotten too fancy to drink beer."

A corner of Chenoa's lush mouth curled up. "No, Mother. I'll never get that fancy." She glanced at Monica. "You buying?"

"Sure."

Chenoa shrugged her slender shoulders. "Then I'm in."

ଅର

After the bright, blistering heat, the dark, air-conditioned bar enveloped Monica like a refreshing dip into an icy pool. The union members surged around her, washing up against the bar like waves against rocks. Waving their arms, they shouted for soda, water, beers or wine coolers. The bartender, a twenty-something white boy with spiked blond hair, rushed to fill their orders.

Chenoa, her hand firmly on her mother's arm, led her to an empty table near the bar. Torn between her desire to stay as close to Chenoa as possible, yet her wish not to appear so obvious, Monica hesitated.

Mrs. Whitecloud waved her over. "Come and sit with us."

Monica went over to the table. There were three chairs. Monica sat in the one next to Mrs. Whitecloud. Chenoa was still standing.

"So, what do you want, Mother?"

"A beer," Mrs. Whitecloud promptly responded.

Chenoa rolled her eyes. "I'll bring you water first. You need to get some fluid in your body. Beer will only dehydrate you."

She went over to the bar. Monica congratulated herself for resisting the urge to watch Chenoa walk away.

Mrs. Whitecloud waited until her daughter was out of earshot. "You would think that I am the child and that she is the mother."

Monica smiled. "She's very caring. You're lucky to have her."

"Caring." Mrs. Whitecloud huffed. "More like Miss Busy-Body, Know-It-All." Then she sighed. "But you are right. She is a good daughter. It has only been me and her since her father died."

A wistful look fell over Mrs. Whitecloud's face. "It is from him Chenoa gets her looks. My family did not want me to marry him. Because he was an Indian." Mrs. Whitecloud snorted. "As if we were descended unmixed from the Spanish *hildagos* or something. But I did not care. I loved him. I loved him so much it hurt."

Mrs. Whitecloud looked keenly over at Monica. "You ever love anybody that much?"

Monica was about to answer but Chenoa had returned. She had a glass full of ice, a bottle of water and two beers. She slid one beer in front of Monica as she sat down.

"I thought I was paying?" Monica said.

Chenoa shrugged, her long dark hair moving across her shoulders. "You can get the next round."

She opened the bottled water, poured the water into the ice-filled glass and handed it to her mother.

"Drink."

Mrs. Whitecloud frowned but drank the water. The glass was half-full when she finished.

"All of it, Mother."

"All right, all right." Mrs. Whitecloud finished the water. Then she stood up.

"Where are you going?" Chenoa asked.

"If it is alright with you, Miss Nosy-Nell, I am going to empty my bladder."

Mrs. Whitecloud moved her rotund body through the obstacle course of tables and chairs toward the back of the bar.

Chenoa sighed, making the exact same sound her mother had earlier. Then she looked over at Monica. "Your mother anything like her?"

"My mother died when I was fifteen."

Chenoa's dark eyes widened. "Oh, I'm sorry."

Monica took a swig of her beer. It was cold and bitter and slid past the tight knot in her chest that always appeared when she thought of her mother.

"Don't be," she said. "I mean, I appreciate the sentiment and all but it happened a long time ago."

Chenoa's eyes narrowed. "Not so long ago it doesn't still hurt."

Monica said nothing. She didn't like talking about her mother. She didn't like talking about anything personal. But, at the same time, she wanted to make a connection with Chenoa.

"Your mother." Monica jerked her chin to where Mrs. Whitecloud was now emerging from the bathroom. "I like her."

Chenoa looked over at her mother. Instead of returning to their table, she edged her way in among the other union members gathered at the bar.

Chenoa shook her head. "She's stubborn."

Then she looked over at Monica and graced her with such a dazzling smile that it tore at Monica's heart. "But I love her, too. And, well, I wanted you to know that despite how I must have come across, I'm glad you got her involved in the union."

"You are?"

Chenoa took a drink from her beer and nodded. "When I left for grad school, I was afraid she would just go to that awful job at the hotel, get off work and then sit at home worrying about me."

She laughed. "And that's exactly what she did. Ran her phone bill up, calling me every day. But then she got involved in the union. Oh, she still worries about me but it isn't a twenty-four-seven kind of thing, you know? She has something else to occupy her mind. To make her feel important. Needed."

"It's empowering," Monica ventured.

Chenoa screwed up her face. "Yeah, I suppose so. Although I hate that word. Sounds so…yuppyish."

Monica laughed. Chenoa took another drink of her beer and Monica admired how her long, smooth throat worked as she drank. Soon the table between them was littered with beer and with the labels Monica had torn off the bottles as her state of inebriation and subsequent horniness had increased. She hadn't meant to drink so much but the more she and Chenoa had talked, the more relaxed she had felt and the more beer she had ordered.

Chenoa, however, had stopped after one beer and switched over to club soda.

Mrs. Whitecloud came over to the table. "Silas is taking me home. Are you going to stay here, Monica?"

Monica shook her head and wished she hadn't. "I need to get back to my hotel room. I've got a meeting in the morning with management." Monica stood up and swayed. She'd driven over to the bar in her rental car but she knew she was in no state to drive back to the hotel. "I'll call a taxi."

"No, Chenoa can drive you," Mrs. Whitecloud offered. "You can get your car tomorrow."

Monica looked over at Chenoa, who shrugged. "Sure, I can take you."

She rose from her chair and Monica, after making sure she wasn't going to pitch face forward onto the floor, followed her outside.

⁎

Monica slid her key card through the reader on the door. She opened the door and stepped inside. Chenoa walked in behind her. Then, when Monica saw the state of her room, she wished she had not invited Chenoa in.

Clothing, underwear, books, computer discs and an assortment of half-opened bags of cereal bars and potato chips were strewn across her bed. The desk near the window was in no better shape, covered as it was with her laptop, stacks of flyers, newsletters and boxes of union buttons.

She looked over at Chenoa and gave her an embarrassed smile. "Excuse the mess."

Chenoa shrugged. "No problem."

She went over to the bed and, surprising Monica, swept everything on it onto the floor. Then she jumped on the bed, leaned back against the pillows and looked over at her. She patted the empty space next to her.

"Well, come on."

Monica stared at her. Was this some kind of alcohol-induced hallucination?

Chenoa laughed. "Don't tell me a big-time union organizer like you is bashful."

"I'm not…" Monica stopped and drew in what she hoped was a head-clearing breath of air. "…a big-time union organizer." She pinched her fingers together. "I'm more like a flea on the humped, bristly back of the union."

"Really?" Chenoa smiled wickedly. "I thought you were going to insist you weren't shy."

Chenoa sat up and pulled off her T-shirt. She was braless. Her breasts were round and full with dusky-brown areolas.

Monica walked over to the bed and sat next to her. "What I am is confused."

Chenoa reached over and caressed the line of Monica's jaw, her cheek, the side of her face. Her voice was a low whisper. "Confused about what?"

"About…" Monica stopped. She gestured to where Chenoa lay on her bed. "About this."

"What? This?"

Chenoa gently pulled Monica's face toward hers and kissed her. It was a soft kiss, a wet kiss, a kiss that burrowed straight down to Monica's cunt.

Chenoa pulled away, her dark eyes sultry. "What's so confusing about me wanting you as much as you want me?"

Monica's throat tightened. She cupped Chenoa's breasts and stroked them. "Nothing. There's nothing confusing about it at all."

She tenderly twisted Chenoa's nipples. They hardened, becoming long and firm. Monica lowered her head and wrapped her mouth around Chenoa's breast. She slowly, attentively sucked it.

Chenoa moaned. She pulled off Monica's baseball cap and tossed it onto the floor. Then she undid the tie Monica had put around her dreads and pushed her hands through them.

"I love your hair," she whispered. "It's so beautiful. Like you."

She leaned back against the pillows, and Monica followed her, her mouth still wrapped around Chenoa's succulent breast. She moved her hand down to the curve of Chenoa's waist, just above the top of her shorts.

Moving her hands past Monica's, Chenoa took her shorts off and tossed them to the floor.

Monica stroked Chenoa's long, smooth thighs. She leaned over, her face mere inches from Chenoa's panties. She parted her lips, her breath coming short as much from her state of drunkenness as from the tantalizing aroma of Chenoa's cunt. The dark bush of it underneath the sheer lilac bikini-cut panties plumped the already damp material.

Monica pressed her lips onto the roundness of Chenoa's stomach. She kissed her, over and over, reveling in the quivering of her belly. She moved downward and pressed her nose onto Chenoa's panty-covered cunt. Slowly she breathed in the scent of her. Then gently, yet thoroughly, she slid her tongue over the front of her panties, tasting Chenoa as she did so.

Chenoa moaned, long and slow.

Unable to stand it any longer, Monica slipped her fingers beneath Chenoa's panties and pulled them off her body.

She looked down at Chenoa's cunt, a wave of dizziness flowing through her.

"I'm still drunk," Monica murmured. "But that's okay."

She lowered her head and brushed her nose and lips over

Chenoa's mound, breathing in, over and over, the smell of her; sweat and musk and soap.

Monica licked and sucked the tender lips of Chenoa's cunt. Then she wrapped her lips around her clitoris and gently sucked. Chenoa writhed beneath her, her thighs quivering. She feverishly whispered words in Spanish, her fingers digging through Chenoa's dreads.

Monica moved her wet, eager tongue deeper into Chenoa's juicy cunt. And she did as she had fantasized since first meeting Chenoa. Making low, hard sounds deep in her chest, Monica thoroughly ate that sweet, succulent, candy-coated pussy out.

Crying out, Chenoa violently shuddered and a flood of wetness gushed from her and onto Monica's tongue and lips. Monica kept on eagerly sucking and licking her slick cunt.

Chenoa climaxed again, her body trembling, her breasts jiggling wildly as she thrashed on the bed.

Once she had quieted, Monica pushed herself up until she lay next to Chenoa. Her caramel-colored eyes were glazed, her full, lush lips still trembling.

"Where…" she gasped, drew a breath, laughed and shook her head. "Where'd you learn to eat pussy like that?"

Monica shrugged. "More than a couple of bottles of beer and a few months of being horny as hell were instrumental."

Chenoa laughed. She pulled Monica's face down to hers and kissed her, thoroughly, deeply, wetly. She tasted of beer and mint and her own female musk.

Monica pulled away and took off her shirt. Unlike Chenoa, she wore a bra. Reaching around, Chenoa quickly unhooked it. Once Monica's breasts were free, Chenoa lifted her head and sucked first one, then the other nipple, her agile tongue licking them into a sweet, tart hardness, her full lips sucking earnestly.

Some of that Tucson heat must have still been smoldering inside Monica because, despite the air-conditioned hotel room, she started sweating as if she were still outside.

"Oh, baby," she moaned. "That's it. Suck 'em. Suck my titties."

Chenoa readily obliged her. Then she pushed one of her hands down the front of Monica's jeans, slid her fingers under her panties and, as she continued to suck and lick Monica's breasts, finger-fucked her to not one, not two, but three blistering orgasms.

After the last mind-blowing climax, Monica moved away from Chenoa and onto the side of the bed, the sweat pooling off her body and onto the sheet.

Chenoa rolled over onto her side and smiled at her. "So, what does it mean?"

Monica was still gasping for breath, her heart slamming. "What…what does what mean?"

"Bread and roses."

It took a moment for Monica to register the words as she continued to struggle for breath. "Oh, yeah. Well, the phrase…it first appeared in a poem in…1911 but it's mostly associated with…a textile strike in Lawrence, Massachusetts. Some say the women carried signs that said, 'We want bread, but roses, too,' but it's never been verified."

"We want bread but roses, too," Chenoa repeated softly. "I like that."

"Now, can I ask you a question?" Monica said.

"Sure."

"Does your mother know?"

"That I'm gay?"

Monica nodded.

Chenoa sighed. "No. She's so set on having grandchildren I

haven't had the heart to tell her. And, yes, I know I can still give her grandchildren but I also know she wants me to be happy."

"And she won't believe you'll be happy if you're a lesbian?"

"Yes."

Monica stroked her arm. "I can't say I know your mother better than you do, but I have a feeling she'd be a lot more open than you think."

"Maybe." Chenoa moved over Monica, her black-licorice hair falling like a curtain around their entwined bodies. "But for now, I don't want to think about that. I just want to be with you."

And, for now, that's all Monica wanted, too.

ഇൗ

Anna Black resides in the Midwest where she enjoys both reading and writing a wide variety of fiction ranging from mysteries to science fiction. She collects tarot cards and enjoys watching her eclectic collection of DVDs. She has erotic fiction published in The MILF Anthology, Cowboy Lover—Erotic Tales of the Wild West, *and Zane's upcoming anthology* Asian Spice. *She is currently working on an erotic mystery.*

My Side of Things
Raquel Moore

Have you ever had a loose secret? One that dangles inside your mouth so that every time your lips move, you fear it will fall out into your conversation? The kind that won't stay put but can't be freed 'cause you know it will change everything? Well, I got one of those and I can't bear it alone any longer. I wanna tell you everything. Exactly the way it happened… maybe with a little slant toward my side of things…but the truth nonetheless. Just listen, okay? And know that I am telling you the truth. You know, the way you would tell your girlfriend about a *tiny* little thing that happened a *long* time ago, before you two were *really* serious about each other and that really wouldn't be brought up *at all* if ol' girl you did it with wasn't threatening to make it sound like more than it really was? Yeah, that kind of slant.

It started about six months ago on the elevator, after a long day at the university. I was losing my cell phone connection while talking to ol' girl who was threatening to tell "everything," when in steps the most alluring woman I've ever met. She was dark like freshly brewed coffee, with full lips and a smile that beamed right into my soul. In one smooth motion I snapped my phone shut and dropped it in my pocket. I would have to deal with ol' girl later. I made some flippant comment about the unreliability of modern technology.

"It's not the technology," the alluring one said with a crisp British accent. "It's those among us who act surprised every time the phone loses reception in the elevator." I couldn't tell if she was flirting, or calling me out. Or both.

"By the way," she introduced herself with a hint of a smile. "My name is Sabela." We ended up sitting at the bus stop together, giggling like schoolgirls about the culture of absurdity called MTV and its blackface twin, BET. It was more than an hour later when we realized the parking lot shuttle was unusually delayed. Not ready to separate, we walked across campus to the lot together, our shoulders bumping lightly with each step. We never really separated after that.

From that moment on, I communicated with this woman almost every day. We emailed, IM'ed, texted, had lunch, brunch and sometimes just a quick coffee. Our connection was crazy. All I had to do was think her name and my phone would buzz in my pocket. My friends assumed we were already a thing 'cause usually I claim my territory early in the game. But I decided not to disappoint them. They need me to succeed so that they can maintain hope that their bland, humdrum academic lives might have some passionate flair too one day. Besides, I was working on it.

This is how it really was: Sabela was magnetic. Our thighs, shoulders, hips or hands would find each other like old friends, like they knew they belonged together and didn't care who saw. Every time she looked at me, it felt like she looked *into* me and it always sent a charge through me. A jolt that commanded certain parts of me to stand and salute. Every time. The thing is, she would never consent to a date. She agreed to a movie once but canceled. Other times she would say she'd have to check her schedule and get back to me, and each time the answer was "we'll have to do it another time because blah-blah-blah." As the kids say: she was stalling me. I was persistent because I thought maybe it was her first lesbian attraction. I've bedded enough first-timers and bi-curious types to know that past experience is no measure of present-day willingness.

My girl? Oh, Sabela didn't know about her then. I knew better than to mention my long distance "situation" up front. Geographically speaking, I was single so why complicate the matter with unnecessary details?

Anyway, for weeks I tried to get to her alone off-campus. Meanwhile the electronic intimacy was nice. It began with a three-hour discussion about our research and its relationship to our own liberation. She's from Tanzania. While her parents are progressive Africans in their views about a woman's role in society, she said they also expect her to maintain their old customs. Their desire for her to be as equally educated as her brothers allowed her to train in London. She left her village to research Natural Resource Management to help enrich the lives of her people. Stuff like clean air, water and natural habitat preservation. I write about gay people who make a healthy space for their sexuality in their spiritual life. Tell me what you think is most important in your everyday routine and I'll tell you how you define freedom. We ended most weeknights talking for two to three hours at a time. Basically spent every night together without going on one date.

Week twelve, it finally happened. She had just returned from a two-week trip home. She said "yes" for Saturday night, but only if I cooked dinner. She said I should show her what home-cooked American food is supposed to taste like. Shee-it, I couldn't have planned it better. Just the two of us breaking bread in my house, with nothing to distract us from our desires? Spicy sex was definitely in the stars. So I prepared angel hair pasta with shrimp and crabmeat in a zesty pesto sauce, garnished it with parsley, tossed a spinach salad and topped it off with my momma's blackberry pie (if that ain't American, nothing is.)

When Sabela rang the doorbell, I felt a ruffle in my stomach. I greeted her with a soft kiss below the ear. She was a magnificent specimen of femininity in form-fitting jeans and a black sleeveless top. The white shawl draping her neck had red, gold and green embroidery along its edges.

"I really like the design of your shawl," I said, caressing the fringes of the fabric.

"Thank you. It was a parting gift from my mother," she replied in a dreamy voice.

She fingered one of her shoulder-length locs and her eyes seemed to be looking at her mother. Immediately, the desire to touch her face rushed upon me. Instead I touched her hair and commented on the recent addition of cowry shells. As she walked slowly to the living room, I followed with my eyes. Below Sabela's right armpit was an armlet decorated with tiny wood squares and polished bone. The shawl fell long past her waist but with each step the mound beneath pushed against it, announcing its roundness through the veil. I had to shake my head to stave off the pornographic images my imagination created. *Dinner before dessert, playah.*

"So tell me about your visit home," I said. We were drinking cabernet on the loveseat. Jazzy notes from a saxophone player on the stereo floated just above our heads.

"It was, as always, bittersweet," Sabela replied.

"Tell me about the sweetness first." I flashed a smile. Sabela returned the smile but didn't immediately speak. I'm not disturbed by her silence 'cause she always weighs her words carefully. Then, as if I had designed the soundtrack, Brian McKnight's falsetto broke through on cue, singing "Do I Ever Cross Your Mind?" I love that song and Sabela seemed to be moved by his voice, too. So I invited her to dance. Another "yes." She wrapped her arms around my neck. The smell of coconut in her hair and her hot breath falling on my neck invited me to pull her closer. Our pointed nipples met through the clothing. Her fingertips slowly snaked into the edges of my afro. Somewhere in the distance I heard myself moan. *You touch me like you've been here before.* I pushed a hand under her shirt and ran my fingers along her spine. Her skin was so smooth. Sensing my thirst and quenching her own, she kissed me. Our lips brushed lightly at first. My tongue slowly traced the upper edge of her open lips. Then I sank into the intoxicating warmth of her mouth. Suddenly I was wading waist-deep in a stream of molten desire. Floating, yearning, swirling at a dizzying pace upon the heat and flavor of Sabela's kiss.

But she pulled away abruptly. Tried to walk away but I couldn't let her go so easily.

"It's okay," I consoled, gripping her hand.

"I know it's okay," she said, mimicking my Southern drawl. "I just need to use the bathroom."

While she was in the bathroom, I lit the candles around the apartment and set our appetizer on the dining room table. We had chilled slices of pineapples, mangoes, and peaches with a squeeze of lemon juice and a drop of whipped cream. Served in goblets.

"Everything looks and smells delicious," Sabela said as she took her seat.

"I hope it tickles your palate," I responded. I captured a slice of mango between my fingers and placed it on her waiting tongue. We ate and talked while our eyes spoke their own subtle language. Like the rest of our body parts, they were glad to be together again.

"So you're not here to stay, are you?" I asked.

"You know I came here with a plan to get the necessary knowledge and take it back home."

"Yet you've been working here for a few years. Has something changed?" My fingers danced along the smooth edges of her armlet.

"That's a perceptive question. The more I learn about myself, the more I realize that my parents' best intentions coincide with my needs. Lately I've been wondering if it's possible to be *of* the village without being *in* it."

"Does it really matter if you're living there, if your work still improves the lives of the people the way you intend?"

"It's not just that. My mother's desire to keep me attached to the 'old village' customs claims me in ways that make it difficult to…"

Her voice trailed off and her eyes took on that dreamy stare again. She fingered a dangling cowry shell near her ear. I can't remember ever wanting so badly to get inside someone's head before. *What is the story behind that stare? She has been so giving of herself, yet she remains so very private and distant at times.* Out of nowhere, a thought provoked an unexpected, rumbling jealousy in me. A tingling sensation crept from the meeting of my thighs to the tips of my nipples. To calm myself, I rested a hand on her leg.

"Do you mean you've made some priestly vow?" And then the real suspicion: "Or are you promised to someone there already?"

Sabela squirmed uncomfortably in her seat so I removed my hand.

"Not exactly," she said. "I was initiated into the sacred knowledge when I came of age. It was a gift from the women of the village. I vowed never to share the knowledge and to attend the ceremony when any woman in my family is initiated. It has complicated my life somewhat. I have committed myself to the ancestors and to the generations."

"Sacred knowledge? Can you tell me more?"

"I really like you, Marsalis."

Sabela grasped my hand and massaged between my fingers. Not sure what to make of the tinge of sadness in her voice, I instantly contemplated rejection: *Is she about to say we can't be together tonight? This conversation is killing the vibe. I know she wants me. Keep the sacred knowledge. I can be satisfied with just the carnal.*

"Why are you looking at me like that?" Sabela asked.

I decided to answer with my body. I slid out of my chair and stood on my knees before her. I pushed myself between her open legs. My hands traveled her outer thighs and hips.

"Kiss me," I said in a pleading tone.

When she bent to oblige, I grabbed her head and plunged my tongue into her balmy mix of wine and pesto. Even then, I could feel a cage of dangerous emotions flinging open. Her leg muscles flexed and released around my waist, making me want to give Sabela a preview of the expert probing that would soon take place. I pushed her gently back into the chair and brushed a hand slowly over one very erect nipple. She did not resist. So I leaned down into her lap and caressed her thighs with my face. I lifted one leg over my shoulder and, as she slid forward, I dragged my teeth over the inner seam of her jeans, roving hungrily toward her zipper.

"Wait." Sabela stiffened in the chair and took her leg from me.

"Did I do something wrong?" I sat back, resting on my heels.

"No. I just don't usually move this fast."

"Me either, baby (*okay sometimes*), but you bring something fierce out of me," I told her. "I feel like a slave to your energy right now…I know you feel it…you make me wanna bare my soul to you…make me wish I could beg in Swahili."

That made her smile. *Oh yes, you will be mine tonight.*

"Please, Sabela, trust me. I promise we won't do anything you're not comfortable with, okay? Let me love you, baby." She didn't readily respond. *But first you must be coaxed back into your comfort zone.*

"Okay, let's dance then," I said. I stood up, pulled her from her chair and led her into the living room by the hand. The soft sounds of Jonathan Butler's guitar serenaded us. The living room was darkened; except for the dim twinkling of candles. As I rolled my hips against her, I told her we would need every flat surface in the house to do all the things my mind was conjuring. I kissed her eyelids. Squeezed her ass. My hands roamed her toned curves. She unbuttoned my shirt and the next thing I remember was being on top of her on the sofa. *Sweet surrender.*

"I need to tell you something," Sabela whispered, her urgency scorching my ear.

"Whatever it is, baby, it won't change anything. I still want you."

She helped me lift her top over her head. She rested on her elbows as my tongue flicked the exposed nipples. As she began to speak again, I covered her mouth with my kiss. This is a dance we do well together. But when I opened the button of her jeans, she snatched my hand away and sat up. *Not again.*

"What's wrong, love?" I tried to sound patient.

"I just can't."

"Is this your first time?" *Maybe it does matter.*

She didn't answer. Using my failsafe seductive tone, (it has relaxed the most tightly wound of virgins) I said: "We don't have to do anything. Just let me hold you."

It failed. Sabela stood and smoothed her clothes and hair anyway. She moved into the hallway toward the front door.

"It's not that," she said.

"What then?"

I leaned close to her face and tried to block the path to the door. She moved around me and reached for the knob. I wrapped my arms around her from behind and nuzzled my face in her mesh of locs. *Still wants to be chased, I guessed.*

"I don't understand why you're fighting this. You know me," I said, feeling like an adolescent boy with a hard-on he doesn't want to have to jerk again tonight. Sabela began to relax in my arms.

"This is not about sex," I assured her as I moved us into a face-to-face embrace. "I am concerned about my friend who is clearly upset."

I think I meant it. I think I was ready to accept her explanation, once again, for why we would go no further. So imagine my utter surprise when she pulled me into a ravenous kiss. *I'm better at this than I think I am.* We groped and tore at each other's clothes until only sweat lay between us.

Back in the living room, I bent Sabela's graceful nakedness over the back of the loveseat. As I made my way to a kneeling position on the floor behind her, my nipples traveled the salty trail of her back. She spread her legs. Welcomed me. On my knees, I rubbed my face across the smoothness of her ass. I pressed my face into it. My tongue penetrated her soft, warm tunnel. Tickled the puckered edges. Charged relentlessly in and around the canal. Sabela made incoherent sounds into the cushions of the loveseat. Her knees buckled a little when my fingers moved up toward the opening of her pussy. I was meandering through the wetness, lost in the aroma and texture of it all when I realized that Sabela's clitoris tip was…*flattened?* Not completely flat, it felt like a cushy knuckle lay just beneath the skin. Still, she didn't have a whole clit. I didn't want to stop but, honestly, I didn't really know how to go on. She must have sensed the hesitation in my movements because she quickly unfolded herself and stood over me.

"Why did you stop!?!" It wasn't really a question. It was more of an accusation. She spoke in a cool, hardened tone I hadn't heard her use before.

"I am just a little surprised." I cleared my throat and gulped too loudly.

"I see." Sabela replied, her tone still cool. She began pacing back and forth in semicircles around my kneeling stature. "And *now* you want to stop?"

Sabela seemed angry. I was confused.

"Was that the initiation?" I asked, trying to stand.

But she wasn't having it. She pushed me back to my knees and—get this—stepped on my hand. She had something in store for me.

"'I'll still want you, baby.' Isn't that right?" Sabela was mimicking me again, but there was a titillating wickedness in her voice.

"You are standing on my—"

"You're a slave to my energy, right?"

"Yes, I said that. What—?"

"Quiet!" Sabela pointed a manicured fingernail in my face. "You've been luring, taunting, even coercing me into your life, into your bed. You will learn now that I only let you think you were in control of the game."

"It was not a game. I really—"

"You will only speak with permission!" She punctuated "permission" by pushing her fingertip into my forehead. The ferocity of it infused me with new lust.

"Yes, ma'am." Heat gathered between my legs.

"Don't 'ma'am' me! You will not think, act, or breathe without my sayso. Do you understand?"

"Yes."

I was dazed by the craving this game provoked. She freed my hand and helped me up.

"Now get over here and serve me."

On command, I harnessed my curved black dildo to my waist. Sabela pressed her bare body against the sliding glass door in the den. Told me to enter her from behind. We rocked slowly at first and then built momentum until each stroke caused a sloshing, slapping sound. Sabela clutched the cold metal locks for balance as her breasts flopped against the pane. By force of habit I slid two fingers over the cushy place where her clit used to reside. Her sharp fingernails cut deep into my wrist to chastise me. Even in pain I knew I couldn't stop thrusting.

"Not without permission," she reminded me. "Now back off me," she ordered.

I slid the dildo out of her wetness. She spread her sleek body across the long, rectangular coffee table.

"Take that off and get that book you were telling me about yesterday," Sabela demanded.

I retrieved *Woman, Thou Art Loosed* from the shelf. My clit throbbed as I watched the book's rounded edges glide through her pussy lips. Against her un-clit. Back and forth. She glossed it with her juices.

"Are you ready for real knowledge?" she asked, tossing the book aside. "Speak."

"Yes."

She directed me to drape myself over her, 69-style. Her open legs dangled over the corners of the table. With delicate determination, my tongue danced inside her. She gripped my open thighs and sucked my clit in what felt like slow motion.

"Use your teeth," she instructed.

I raked my teeth over her sacred secret. Her hips jerked and my waves rose with her. Felt like I was floating toward my climax. Back and forth. She raised her hips and I dipped as far inside her as my tongue would reach. Wanted to take her with me. It worked. She clamped her thighs tightly around my neck and I tried to swallow every sweet drop of her. Her tongue tapped wildly inside me, pulling me under. Suddenly I was submerged in orgasm. Suffocating and ejaculating. Pushed to the peak of pleasure, I exploded into a million electric sparks.

That's when she took me to the next level: she bit me. There. Stinging ecstasy shot through me in every direction. My entire body spasmed as she held me entangled. That shocking bite, the soft insistent sucking that followed, and her slick, swollen pussy gyrating in my mouth sent me into sensory overload. Ripples of orgasms drained me until I collapsed. *Game over.*

"Was that my initiation?" I asked later.

"No, silly." She laughed. "That was the erasure of every woman before me and the measure for any after. Still, don't ever disclose the secret of my body. One slip and we're done."

Yeah, I know what's at stake. But I had to give you my side of things.

❧❦

Born and raised in Texas, Raquel Moore is currently a graduate student in Florida. When she is not writing her dissertation, she nurtures her soul with hot sex, the company of friends, or a good book. She thanks the ancestors, especially Audre Lorde and James Baldwin, for showing us how to turn suffering and pleasure into equally powerful weapons of resistance. You continue to move us all toward liberation. She also thanks the S.I. for their very special contributions to this story. It belongs to all of us.

Sensei ni Rei

Tigress Healy

Frankie screeched into the parking lot, jerked the car to a stop, and rushed inside to try to explain her lateness again. At this hour, there were no sparring children to avoid, no sneakers to trip over, and worst of all, no students left but her son.

"Darryl," she called through the one-story building. "Darryl, honey, I'm—"

"I'm right here," he said, exiting the dressing room in his street clothes. His earphones blasted the latest hip-hop song. He didn't look happy to see his mother.

"Where's your instructor? I need to talk to him."

"Ma'am?" Darryl asked, pulling the left speaker out of his ear.

"Turn it down so you can hear me. I asked about your instructor."

Irritably, the boy pointed toward the office.

"Watch your attitude, boy!"

"Ma, why you startin' with me already? I ain't even do nothin' to you. I'm the one been sittin' here two hours."

"Go wait for me in the car. I just wanna go in and apologize."

"Yes, Ma'am," he said, replacing the dangling earphone.

"What's his *name*?" Frankie yelled.

"Sensei Reid," Darryl replied on his way outside. Frankie rapped on the door and waited for permission to enter. A bit taken aback by the instructor, she ignored the frustrated facial expression, surveyed the trophies, photos, and certificates, and finally said, "Listen, I'm sorry for running late. I got caught up at work with—"

The athletically built black woman raised her hand in protest. She then leaned back in her massive black chair and said, "I hear where you're coming from but we don't tolerate excuses from parents or students. The records show you've been late almost every night since Darryl's enrollment. We don't want to punish him for your behavior but we can't continue to stay late to supervise him."

"Well, you don't really have to stay late *or* supervise him. I mean, he's twelve years old. He can look after himself."

"Ms. Greene, it is my responsibility to ensure the building is empty when I leave."

"I know, and again, I apologize for the—"

"Yame!" the sensei exclaimed.

"*Excuse me?* I don't eat sweet potato!"

"Yame means 'stop' in Japanese. I need you to just stop talking."

Frankie crossed her arms and sucked her teeth. Rolled her eyes and neck like oats. "I think it's nice you're teaching the kids respect, concentration, goals, and all that along with the karate but you can't talk to me like that. I ain't one of your goddamn students!"

"Why not?"

"I don't have the time or money to—" Frankie stopped herself. "Why am I explaining myself to you? You ain't nobody!"

"Okay, have a seat. We may have started on the wrong foot. Call me Rita for now, but in public or if I'm ever your instructor, call me Sensei Reid. What's your name?"

"It's Frankie and I'll stand. Darryl's in the car."

Rita looked at Frankie earnestly. "Do you have a second for a quick sistah-to-sistah talk?"

"I don't see what there is to talk about and I don't like you talking to me like I'm a child. I'm late, I apologized, and that's that!"

"Iya!"

"Bless you!"

"Frankie, I didn't sneeze! 'Iya' means 'no'! It's not, 'I apologized and that's that.' Your lateness inconveniences everyone. Besides, how can you help your son with karate if you don't know the commands or the basic principles of respect?"

"That's what I pay ya'll for! I can't be *everything* to the boy. I have work, school, Bible study, housework...and I can forget about having a social life!"

"How about enrolling in lessons and letting that be a part of your social life, like it is for your son? Not only is it good exercise but it'll give you focus and discipline."

"Bitch, I *am focused* and *disciplined*! I don't care if you are a fuckin' Black Belt. You don't know me! You can kiss my black ass!"

"Ms. Greene, I won't tolerate the disrespect!"

"How 'bout if I pull my kid out the school? Then what?" Frankie posed.

"You'd be punishing your child. That's *what*. I'm gonna keep it real with you. I don't own this joint and I'll get paid whether or not your son shows up, but if you want him to benefit from attending, you're gonna have to make some changes."

"Sensei Reid, I mean, Rita, I don't need the lecture, and as far as the lessons, right now I can't afford them. I have enough trouble paying for Darryl's by myself."

"How about if your first three are on me?"

"Why?"

"Out the goodness of my heart. I don't want to see Darryl suffer. He's almost up for his Green Belt promotion but he'll be expelled if you continue to be late. I figure if you're already here that won't happen."

"And, why else?" Frankie asked suspiciously.

"If you enjoy the private lessons and decide to sign up, I'll get a commission. It won't make or break me but it'll be nice. You should be here tomorrow by seven."

"I don't have time for karate. I don't get off 'til seven and I'm supposed to be here to pick Darryl up by eight, which is difficult enough as it is."

"Where do you work, if you don't mind my asking?"

"At home. I work for myself!"

"Then surely you can manipulate your schedule!"

"No, I can't. I have lots of work to do. I have to work ten times as hard as everyone else to make my money 'cause I don't get a nice paycheck like you."

"Do it for your son, Frankie. I expect to see you here tomorrow at seven. Here's a brochure to look over. From now on when you see me, you'll bow. 'Sensei ni rei.' That reminds me, I have to get your Gi. You wear about an eleven, right?"

"Yes."

"The term is, 'hai.' It's in the book."

"Hai," Frankie said sarcastically, bowing to the instructor. She hoped Sensei Reid appreciated her show of "respect."

৪৩৫৪

"Man, come on, Ma," Darryl groaned, when Frankie arrived at the dojo at six forty-five, stating she was there for class. "This was supposed to be a thing I did on my own. It's not unique if you do it too."

"D, it's not like we'll be in the same class. I'm here for private lessons. And it's not like I take this seriously. I don't even have a belt and you already have a Green White Stripe."

"Ma, can I go over Larry's after class so I don't have to watch this? His father won't mind me leaving with them."

"As long as you do your homework I'm cool. And as long as you give me a hug before you go!"

"Alright, Ma," Darryl said, returning for the rest of class.

ഔരു

At seven p.m., Sensei Reid handed Frankie a new Gi. "Here, put this on. Classes are over for today but I'm the only one here so you have to wait 'til the place clears out before we can start."

"That's cool," Frankie said, heading toward the dressing room. As she reached the door, Darryl said, "I'm leaving, Ma."

He gave her a quick hug that seemed to pain him, before trotting off. Later, they'd have to have a serious talk. Even when she wasn't late, he was angry.

ഔരു

When Frankie emerged from the dressing room, the place was quiet. She was amazed that all those parents had been on time. She waited on the bench outside the sensei's office for nearly twenty minutes before knocking on the door.

"I'll be out in a minute," the instructor called.

Frankie looked at her watch in annoyance. Twenty minutes

later, the sensei emerged and announced, "Twenty more minutes!"

"But I've been waiting almost an hour and a half."

"How does it feel?" she asked, shutting the door.

"Feels shitty," Frankie muttered, staring at the Black Belt display case. She had successful grasped the first lesson.

∽∝

"Yoi!" Sensei Reid called, jolting Frankie awake. "Attention! Walk this way."

She led Frankie to the main room containing a rectangular window for people to watch through. The women left their shoes at the door.

Once on the bright red-and-blue mat, she bowed to the instructor—Sensei ni rei— and assessed her reflection in the massive mirrors. She looked good in her white uniform but felt she could always look better.

Sensei Reid frowned. "Frankie, why aren't you wearing a bra?"

"Because—"

"Especially since you don't have a belt on. That's extremely in poor taste."

"My um…titties are independent. I mean, they've always supported themselves! I'm blessed to have them perky and not need a bra."

"I can see that, Rita! Good Lord, that's me! I mean, Frankie, Ms. Greene, it's just that your breasts are somewhat of a distraction."

"Why, do you like them?"

"Wear a bra next time, Deshi. *Deshi* means student. It's an honorable title," Sensei Reid said, walking toward the center of the mat. She gestured for Frankie to join her and went into the history and principles of karate. Eventually, she moved on to preliminary blocks and stances but Frankie was bored out of her mind.

She was ready for chops, punches, and roundhouses. Wanted to be like badass Michelle Yeoh, who starred in almost every action movie alongside actors like Jet Li and Jackie Chan.

"All this is cute but what happens if someone comes up from behind me?"

"First things first. Patience, Deshi."

"Patience is for children but with adults, you have to be practical. I need to know how to *use* this art. There's no man in my home and I'm deathly afraid of being raped or robbed."

"Understandable, but you must first have a foundation."

"I thought the customer was always right."

"Very well. I'll show you what you want to learn. Stand here." She shifted Frankie's body. "Now, let's pretend you're walking down the street and I come up behind you. Look over your shoulder like this," she said, demonstrating. "Now lean forward and pull your knee up."

Frankie tried the form.

"No, like this." Sensei Reid grabbed Frankie's leg and pulled it to the correct position. Held it, then stretched it out, saying, "Flex your toes."

Frankie loved being close to Rita. Loved her feminine masculinity. The moisture on her panties began to feel uncomfortable, making her want to take them off. Her breasts had already maneuvered themselves loose. Nipples were hard enough to break boards. She wondered if the sensei noticed.

"Now, when you kick, you gotta kick hard. If it's a man, kick him in the groin. If it's a woman, do the breasts. Now lean forward, knee up, extend your leg, now kick…that's right…kick… kick…"

Frankie was having fun. She'd be in Kung Fu movies in no time.

"Now, you expressed fear of sexual attack. That's a strong concern for us women. Karate is a military art, which is psychological as well as physical. Some women see an attack coming and try to thwart it immediately, but sometimes they miss the target because the attacker had a chance to plan his defense. Personally, I prefer to let the aggressor get close by pretending to be helpless. Then I maul and disfigure him, breaking every bone in his body. I'll show you that strategy first."

"Cool," Frankie said excitedly.

Sensei Reid taught the moves while Frankie admired her strength. She practiced a few times before the role-play. Coming up behind her, the sensei rested her hands on her student's mid-section, slid them up to her breasts, and squeezed her erect nipples. Grazed her lips across her neck. Frankie stood frozen.

"You're supposed to be fighting me, Deshi."

"I am. God knows, I am."

"Even if it's not karate, you gotta do something. Stomp on my toe, elbow me in the stomach, knee me in the balls, strike me in the throat, poke me in the eye...you can't get caught up in emotion when you're supposed to be fighting."

"I know, Sensei, but, I'm just so...I can't concentrate on this lesson. I think I should go."

"Why?" the sensei asked. Her hot breath tickled Frankie's neck. Hands slipped into her panties, discovering her wetness. "The customer is always right. If you're horny, Deshi, don't fight it."

"Good one but I think I'll go now," Frankie said, holding her Gi closed.

"Matte! Wait! Are you offended by my actions? If so, I apologize. I—"

"It's not that. I enjoyed your actions. It's just, I promised myself I wouldn't be a lesbian once my son got old enough to know, and when you were touching me I felt those familiar feelings. I felt a surge in my body that wouldn't let go and I'm afraid…"

"Afraid of what? Karate teaches us to be centered and not to be afraid. We use the techniques to protect ourselves, whether it's from physical attack, which we work not to engage in, criticism from others, or self-doubt. Here, sit on the mat with me. Let me talk to you as a friend."

Frankie let out a long breath. "I apologize for the way I behaved the other day. Lately, I've been on edge."

"Probably because you've been denying yourself the experience to live. You have anger, frustration, and pent-up emotions because you're living someone else's life."

"If you want to put it like that." Frankie smiled.

"I do. Because I know that to honor yourself is to honor the Creator, regardless of what other people think. When you honor yourself, you feel much better. You give yourself the power."

"Thanks, Sensei. Can I give you a hug?"

"Sure," Rita said, embracing her student. She rubbed Frankie's back as she cried. Gently wiped her tears. "It's okay, Deshi. Just be yourself."

The phrase of encouragement brought on more tears. Rita held Frankie's face in her hands and spoke sternly. "Listen to me. You need an outlet. Even if it's not karate, you need something. Holding things in leads to many illnesses. That, and a poor diet."

Frankie touched Rita's face, then pulled it to hers. The moisture in her pussy thickened as they kissed. Rita reached for Frankie's light-skinned breasts. Fondled them again. Held one in each hand and brought her mouth to them. Sucked each nipple like butter-scotch candy.

"I love your tits," she said breathlessly, as Frankie moaned.

"Thank you. I wish I had your confidence."

"You can, once you let go of arrogance and ego."

Frankie lay back and pulled Rita to her. Fumbled to untie her white pants.

"We're not supposed to have sex in these uniforms," said Rita.

"Then why don't we take them off?"

Frankie looked at the clear window where anyone could see in. Rita assured her the doors were locked. However sexy it might be, no one would be watching.

"You know, my son is with a friend. I really gotta go," said Frankie, straightening her Gi. She dashed out of the room, leaving Rita on the mat, perplexed about what had just happened.

෨෬

"Darryl, I want to talk to you before you go to bed."

"All right," said the impatient preteen.

"What you so mad at, son? Why can't I ever make you happy?"

"Can I be honest with you, Ma? Or do you really want me to just shut up and listen?"

"I want you to be honest. Sit here at the table."

"Ma, I'm angry cuz you're angry. You always got an attitude. You be yellin' at people and being rude for no reason. Then there are times like when you strugglin' with money that you don't even talk to me. Like I'm a pain in the ass. Then at karate you act like everything is all good and you love me so much, but you don't treat me like that at home."

"Oh, honey, I do love you very much and you're not a burden at all. Everything I do, I do for you."

"Plus, Ma, you a little masculine. For real, sometimes I think you like women. In fact, I think that's what happened to Dad."

"No, that bitch, Carla, happened to your cheatin'-ass father."

"See, Ma? You ain't have to go there."

"I was faithful. And yes, I do like women, but I suppressed it for him and I suppress it for you. *That* is the root of my anger."

"Then I guess you need a woman in your life but don't expect me to like it."

"I don't expect you to make it difficult either."

"Ma, I won't."

"Thanks. I will make every effort to be more loving and attentive in and outside the home, and would appreciate it if you did the same."

₧₧

The phone rang the next evening as Frankie was leaving the house.

"Frankie, it's Rita. I was hoping you're gonna be on time for Darryl because I'd hate for him to be penalized."

"I'll be there in a sec."

"Frankie, bring your Gi."

"I will, Sensei Reid. See you shortly."

₧₧

Lessons were going well. Frankie had received her White Belt while Darryl, who was at Larry's house, had received his Green.

"Shower time," the sweaty sensei said, leading Frankie toward the dressing room. Once inside, Frankie marveled at Rita's sturdy brown body—small breasts, muscular legs, abs, and arms. Her dark-brown ass was round and firm. She didn't have an ounce of flab.

Frankie became self-conscious, crossing her arms over her stomach.

"You're stunning," said Rita. "You really are."

She turned on the water, extracted soap from the dispenser, and spread the lather on her student. Frankie did the same, running her hands along the contours of Rita's body. Rita's clitoris was so big it looked like a little dick. Frankie rubbed it before slipping her middle finger in and out of her warm hole as they pressed their bodies together and kissed.

"Yes," Rita said, gyrating slowly. "Hai! Hai, Deshi!"

Her voice echoed in the steamy shower. Frankie got on her knees and buried her face in Rita's womanhood as the water poured down. She made sucking noises on the clit until Rita's legs trembled.

"You taste good," Frankie said, rising.

They kissed intimately under the water.

"Sensei ni rei," Rita directed.

Frankie complied, taking a lick of Rita's pussy while her head was down.

"Mawatte! Turn around."

Frankie did as instructed. Felt two fingers slide into her ass. "Oh shit, Rita, that feels so good!"

Rita reached around and rubbed Frankie's clit while pressing her own against her ass.

"It feels like a dick," Frankie cried. "Fuck me with it."

"The water's running cold. Let's get out," Rita replied.

The dripping women padded to the dressing area. Frankie lay on the narrow bench and put her foot on the lockers while Rita hummed on her clit to create a vibrating sensation.

Frankie cussed and groaned in pleasure as Rita rubbed her own clit, licking the inside of Frankie's thighs, pussy again, then asshole.

"Oh, shit, it's been too long! Oh God!"

Rita kissed Frankie's foot, sucked each toe before sticking her tongue between them, saying, "The foot is the root of wellness and stability."

Rita lay on top of Frankie, easing her clit between her legs. Fucking and bucking wildly, she screamed, "I love this pussy!"

"If you keep fucking me, I'm gonna cum," Frankie said, smacking Rita's ass.

"Karate ni Senta Nashi!"

"What's that?"

"'There's no first attack in karate.' So please don't hit me."

"That Japanese shit is sexy. So is kissing you in the mouth."

"I like kissing you, too," Rita said. They tasted each other's tongues before Rita nibbled on Frankie's neck. She pulled her to a standing position, placing her back against the lockers.

"Lift your leg, Deshi. Rest your foot on my thigh."

With Frankie's leg cocked up, Rita gave her a full body massage. Frankie masturbated herself and touched Rita where she could.

"Rub my pussy, Deshi. Make me cream."

Frankie complied, licking each tit as she did. "My pussy is juicing, too. I want you to eat it."

"You're lucky you're not my uchi-deshi or you would have to serve me all the time. I wish you could come home with me."

Before long, the women were kissing again. They moved into the sixty-nine position on the floor and brought each other to orgasm.

Frankie said, "I know what you said was in the heat of passion, but do you really want me to come home with you?"

৪০৫৪

The next day, Darryl called Frankie's cell phone to ensure she would be on time to pick him up and prompt for her own lesson.

"Honey, I'm already in the building, dressed and ready for class. I can assure you I learned my lesson about lateness. It makes the sensei very mad. And I would never *ever* want to do that."

৪০৫৪

Tigress Healy is one of many pseudonyms for this flourishing writer. Originally from New York, she now resides in Georgia with her family. She is currently working on several erotica and cultural fiction projects. She can be reached at tigresshealy@yahoo.com.

Interfacing

MJ Williamz

I can see her dark eyes watching me, staring at me, studying my every move. She's tall, trim, and mysterious. She likes to watch me. I see her gaze fixed between my spread legs. She likes my legs wide, likes to see my fingers inside my pussy. And I like her to watch. I get even wetter while she stands there, mouth never speaking, eyes never wavering. I can hear my fingers moving in and out. I know she can hear it, too. She likes the suction sound. It gets her hot.

Her eyes flash when they see my bulging clit. I look at her, begging for a signal, a sign that it's okay to rub it. Her tongue flicks briefly between her lips, and I know she wants to see the finale. I move my sticky fingers to my clit and pinch it between two fingers while I press it hard.

Oh, God, that feels good. Oh, Reggie, I need to come. I'm going to come for you. Are you ready? She's ready. I know she is. The rock inside my stomach begins to melt, slowly…slowly…until it erupts, shooting white heat to all my extremities. I arch my back and slip my fingers back inside, fucking myself through the orgasm.

Once it subsides, I relax back onto my bed and close my eyes to savor the moment. It's only later, when my soul returns to my body, that I realize she's not there. Not this time. Maybe someday.

The next morning, I arrived at work at seven-thirty, as usual. A few desks were occupied on the first floor, but most people wouldn't get there for another half hour or so. Clutching my oversized handbag against me, I ducked my head and hoped no one would speak to me. If I could get to the IT department, I could climb into my technical world and forget that people exist. Well, most people.

My workspace is actually the server room. They tried to give me my own office, but I found that people were more intimidated by the machinery in the server room, and if I spent enough time in there, they would leave me alone. Eventually, I made it my office. No one complained. It's as painful for others to talk to me as it is for me to talk to them. Or close.

I turned on my coffeemaker while my computer booted up. My morning routine never varied. Once my computer was on, I checked my company email. The usual messages from Linux telling me about scheduled conference calls to help us with updates. I sneered. I could teach those people a few things. I didn't need them. I could have worked for any programmer, but I chose to work for the number one communications company in the world. I made sure that people from Singapore to Seattle, from Bangkok to Boston had telephones and broadband and any other forms of communication they might need.

I also had an email from another employee. Specifically a project manager in New York who was transferring to our office in Chicago and setting up a new department. She had detailed needs of what she wanted in her department as a whole and her office in particular. I'd heard of her. She was technologically savvy and I looked forward to working with her.

"Hey, Keisha?" A voice intruded on my space. My heart raced, my muscles clenched. I told myself to breathe.

Looking up, I saw *her*. Reggie Campbell. The head of our maintenance department. All five feet ten inches of her leaning casually against my doorframe. Why was she there? *Speak, Keisha. Say something*.

"Did you see the email from Gibbons?"

Gibbons. I know that name. Who is Gibbons?

"Is this a bad time? Look, if it is, I'll come back. I just want to set up a timeframe to get Gibbons's department set up. You'll see the email."

Speak! Say something!

"I'll contact you telephonically."

Her eyes grew wide, then narrowed as she nodded.

"You do that," she said, pushing off from the wall and sauntering down the hall.

I dropped my head into my hands. I don't care that I can't talk to people. Except her. She was so handsome and so nice and I got so tongue-tied around her. My whole system short-circuited. My motherboard shut down. My surge protector malfunctioned. I had just read the freakin' email from Gibbons. As excited as I had been to set up her new department, I hadn't even considered I'd be working with Reggie to do that.

When my heart rate returned to a normal level, I wiped my sweaty palms on my thighs. I immediately wondered what it would be like to run my hands up Reggie's thighs. I was sure they were solid—muscular yet all woman. I felt moisture between my legs. I closed my eyes and imagined Reggie kneeling between my legs, her tongue tasting the milky wetness she caused. I could feel her tongue pressed into my clit, licking the length of me, sucking me into her mouth.

With a start, I realized that my hand was rubbing my pussy. I knew I should stop, but I couldn't. I needed Reggie to get me off. I closed and locked the office door. With one ear on the hallway, I rummaged through my handbag and found my pocket rocket. I slid my hand under my nylons and pressed it into my hardened clit and began to shake immediately as I climaxed hard and fast. For Reggie.

ഇൻരു

I reviewed Gibbons's email again, paying close attention to the details. I knew that if I had a solid grasp on what I needed to get done, it would be easier to communicate with Reggie. The more in control I was, the less stressful it would be. If I could keep it professional and distant, I could talk to her. I believed that. My confidence bolstered somewhat, I took the elevator to the twelfth floor, the east wing of which would be Gibbons's new department.

Walking down the hall that had been empty for three years, I visualized where the workstations would be and kept my eyes open for where the phone jacks and computer plugs would have to go. I scribbled some notes on my pad before continuing to the end of the hall, where an executive suite sat waiting for Gibbons's arrival.

Backtracking, I walked to the open area where I took my tape measure out of my handbag and started measuring and making notes. I got on my hands and knees and made some markings on the wall.

"Great minds think alike, huh?"

The sound of her voice made me jump. I looked over my shoulder and saw her looking at me. And there I was on all fours.

And she was watching me. I felt my clit grow again and wondered if my juices would flow down my nylons. How embarrassing. Unless it aroused her. Maybe she'd peel my nylons off and clean me with her tongue.

She cocked her head to the side. "You're not much for talking, are you?"

Coming to my senses, I made myself stand. I smoothed my skirt and tucked my long black hair behind my ears. I was fidgeting and told myself to stop.

"You know, you don't need to be nervous. I'm not gonna bite. Unless you want me to." She flashed a dimpled smile and my heart skipped a beat. Her brown eyes were laughing, yet warm. Although we were separated by several feet, I felt like she was close enough to touch. To touch and be touched. Her short dark hair beckoned to me, tempting my fingers to run through it. I wanted to run my hand over her cheek, to trace her strong jaw line.

"I was simply ascertaining the extent of linear space available—"

"That's twice now you've spoken to me." Reggie leaned back against the wall with her arms crossed and her eyes gleaming, her mouth a cocky grin.

I froze. I was fine until she interrupted me. I was being pulled into her eyes. They twinkled, hinting at a private joke. I looked out the window, where the view was safer.

"Or maybe I imagined it?"

Great. She was mocking me. I was alone with the woman of my dreams and she was making fun of me. She wouldn't if she knew what I did for her and let her do to me every night. I wanted to rip my dress off and let her have her way with me. I needed her on me and inside of me.

"I'm sorry. You were saying you were measuring?"

My head snapped around to her. She understood me! It had to be a sign. I swallowed hard and willed myself to speak. I opened my mouth, but no sound came out. I tried again.

"I needed an enumeration of potential workstations, so I am able to requisite the appropriate amount of network interface cards."

Reggie pushed her lanky frame away from the wall and closed the distance between us. With her looming over me, any possible thought flew out of my brain. My gaze locked on her mouth. Her lips parted and her tongue slipped out, briefly moistening them.

"Are you trying to intimidate me?" she asked.

Barely able to breathe and completely unable to speak, I simply shook my head.

"Because I understand geekspeak." She stepped back. "I've seen you looking at me. I think you like what you see. But you think I'm just dumb muscle, don't you?"

I started to hyperventilate. I was so embarrassed and so nervous that I thought I'd be sick. I didn't know if she was dumb or not. I didn't care. Not true. If she was smart, it would make her all the hotter. So she was smart, hot, and staring at me. I was feeling light-headed. Dear God, please don't let me faint. Not here. *Breathe, Keisha. Breathe.*

My peripheral vision got fuzzy; my legs turned to rubber.

"Keisha!" I heard from a distance. "Keisha, talk to me. Say something, anything."

I opened my eyes and saw Reggie's staring into mine. I realized with a start that my head was in her lap. I rolled over to get up but felt her strong hands on my shoulders.

"I don't think you need to be getting up just yet," she said quietly, brushing her hand over my hair. "Just relax for a minute…if you can."

Relax? Was she kidding?

"You're tensing again, Keisha. Close your eyes. Let your nerv-ousness go. Take deep breaths."

If I kept my head in her lap much longer, she'd be hearing some heavy breathing. I closed my eyes as instructed, which helped. At first. With my eyes closed, my other senses were heightened. The feel of her fingers lightly combing through my hair made my nipples as hard as my clit. More intense was my sense of smell. My head was inches from her cunt and I could smell her musky scent. It was strong, yet muted. My mouth watered with each breath as her aroma tickled my nose.

"Why are you so uptight? Man, you fainted rather than have a conversation. Much as I'd like that to stroke my ego, I know it's not just me. You're intelligent, successful, and attractive. Do you really not see that?"

I didn't answer. I couldn't. I closed my eyes and reveled in the feeling of her fingers in my hair. Combining that with the heat radiating from her crotch, I wondered if I could come lying there.

"You're starting to relax," she continued. "I can tell you're a special lady, you know. I sure wish we could have a regular conversation."

A regular conversation? Like what? Wanna fuck? Do me? I wished I could talk to her. My mind was racing, searching for a suitable statement.

"You're tensing again. What's wrong? Look, Keisha, I *would* like to talk to you sometime, but it's not worth you fainting again. Settle down."

I knew this was my chance. If I didn't act then, I'd never forgive myself. If I told her how I felt, would I scare her off? There had to be something else to say. To start things off. If I said nothing, she'd think I was an idiot. I was in a veritable quandary.

My whole body tightened. I felt nauseated, frozen with fear. But I knew I had to do it.

"How is it that you understand geekspeak?" I inquired.

She laughed. "See? That wasn't so hard, was it? To answer your question, I'm a closet technofreak. I love computers, electronics, anything like that. I happened to minor in computer science at DePaul."

"You did?" I sat up and turned to look at her, finding her more attractive than ever.

"You wonder why I'm working in maintenance, don't you?"

But I wasn't. I was thinking she was even more perfect than I could have imagined. Every hot fantasy I'd had—every time I'd come for her—at no point had I ever been that turned on. Fuck conversation.

Leaning forward, I placed my hands on her solid, broad shoulders and pressed her to the ground, quickly pressing my lips to hers. She resisted slightly and I panicked. I was about to pull away when I felt her relax and kiss me back. It was better than I'd dreamed. Her lips were soft, yet firm. When her tongue pressed against my lips, begging for entry, my mouth welcomed her gladly. My pussy clenched, and I knew I needed to come and soon.

Our tongues caressed each other, teasing, pleasing. I spread my legs and tried to straddle Reggie, but my skirt was too confining. I started to hike it up, but she stopped me.

"Hey. We're kinda in a public place," she pointed out. "Maybe we should continue this a little later. When we have some privacy."

Was she kidding? I grabbed her hand and put it on my cunt. Even through the nylons, I knew she'd feel how wet I was. I heard her groan and joined her when she pressed the crotch into me.

"Why wait?" I managed to ask.

Her mouth claimed mine again, this time with an intensity beyond my wildest fantasies. Her lips moved against mine possessively while her hand continued to rub my pussy.

Reggie broke the kiss again. "Someone could walk in."

"Who? Nobody's going to walk in. Please, Reggie. *Please*. I've wanted you for so long. Please don't make me wait any longer."

I stood up and quickly undressed, throwing my clothes on the floor.

"Take me, Reggie," I said, lying back on top of her.

She rolled me onto my back, then propped herself on an elbow and just looked at me. Her eyes bore into mine before glancing down to my breasts. Being the object of her attention made my nipples harden painfully. I felt them pucker, begging for her mouth.

"I really like what you say when you finally talk," she teased.

Her free hand lazily traced the path of her gaze. Her mahogany fingertips brushed over my chest—slipping over my right breast, around my areola, making small circles around my taut tawny nipples.

"You're driving me crazy, Reggie."

"Yeah?" She grinned.

"Are you enjoying teasing me?"

"I'm enjoying interfacing with you." Her eyes twinkled.

"But my microprocessor is about to overheat," I panted.

"Don't you want to be sure that our systems are compatible?"

"I'm certain that your hardware will be able to operate my software with ease."

"You're sure about that?"

"I believe the configuration will run flawlessly."

Her fingers closed on my nipple. "You've got some nice hardware goin' on yourself."

"My system responds well to your commands."

"I've noticed."

"You need help finding the insertion point?"

"I think I'll find it. When I'm ready," she whispered before she bent and took a nipple between her teeth, sucking hard while she continued to knead my breast.

I closed my eyes and lost myself in the feeling. I didn't want to miss a thing. Every touch, every nibble had to be recorded in my memory to be enjoyed again later. She knew exactly what she was doing.

Reggie released my breast and slid her hand down my flat belly. I arched my hips, every muscle in my legs taut as I awaited her entry. She ran her fingers along either side of me, teasing. Just when I thought I couldn't get any wetter...

"Reggie. Please."

I felt her teeth close harder on my nipple while her fingers finally entered me. Her tongue flicked my tit while her fingers moved in and out of my slick pussy. I bucked my hips and met every thrust. Her mouth released my nipple and she kissed me hard, her tongue driving into my mouth in time with her fingers. My hands framed her face before sliding over her short curly hair, meeting behind her head to hold her mouth to mine.

She slid her fingers out of my cunt and pressed them into my turgid clit. As she made little circles on me, I felt the pressure building in my very center. I writhed beneath her touch, working with her, searching for the nirvana I knew she was guiding me toward.

"Oh, God, Reggie. You feel so good."

She plunged her fingers deep inside of me again and pressed her palm into my hardness. My breathing became shallow as I let consciousness go and felt the prelude to the explosion.

"Oh, God," she breathed against me, her voice raw. "Let it go, Keisha."

"Oh, yes!" I cried, throwing my head back as I felt the molten core break loose, sending waves of heat throughout my body. I rode wave after wave until the spasms stopped and I floated back to Earth.

I lay there completely sated, eyes closed in orgasmic bliss. When I dared to open them, I saw hers looking into mine. It was real. She was there. She was still inside me and I closed my legs around her. Now that I'd had her, I was never letting go.

ഇൻൽ

MJ Williamz grew up on California's central coast but now calls Portland, Oregon, home. Regardless of where she hangs her hat, she's always traveling to some far-off exotic land and coming home with plenty to write about. She is proud of her dirty baker's dozen—the thirteen short stories she's had published—and is working on more, with a novel currently being considered.

Crave

Rachel Merriweather

I was sitting at home all alone; stressed out and lonely because she had left me. How could I give three years of my heart, body, and soul to someone only for them to leave me in shattered broken pieces? I lay in the middle of my floor, my almond-hazel eyes looking up in the ceiling; my long black curly hair hanging loosely on the gray carpet. I lay in a wifebeater with no bra, and a pair of black booty shorts. My honey-brown skin was so pale from stress and tears. I lay on the floor with a bottle of Lemon Vodka in my hand and the CD player remote in the other. Shareefa's *Point of No Return* CD was on repeat playing "Cry No More" until the tears finally fuckin' stopped.

I love hard and give up easy but I never thought it would have come to this. I finally got up when I heard a knock at my door. For three days I didn't answer but, for some reason, my body told me to get up. When I opened the door, she was standing there with the same expression on her face as mine: a mixture of pain, sorrow, and loneliness.

Five feet two, sexy chocolate-brown skin, light-brown tight eyes, and long dark-black braids that fell to the middle of her back. In a bomber jacket, a white tee, and some jeans, looking so petite but still a sexy stud and the friend of my ex. I let her in.

"How you holding up?" she asked me as she brushed past me.

"Just great. Can't you tell?" I answered as I shut my door.

I sat back on the floor as she got situated on the couch. KC and I had been friends for only a short period of time, but she had needed me when her ex had left her for another man. Damnit, I needed her advice and guidance to get through this tough time. Funny how this was the first time she had come to visit me alone; without all our friends.

"I noticed you weren't answering your phone, so I thought I'd check up on you."

"Yeah, well, I didn't want to be bothered with the questions like, 'What happened?' 'Why?' 'Are you sure it's over?' I didn't need that today." I had been checking my voicemail periodically and there were over twenty messages with those exact questions and concerns.

"I know. I understand." KC looked down at the bottle of Vodka in my hand. "You can't drink all your troubles away, Sweets."

"Well…" I took the last sips. "I can damn sure try."

I burped and we shared a laugh. I hadn't had one of those in a while.

"I know it's hard, Angie, but you have to try to move on from her."

"You know what's so fuckin' funny?" I was in a drunken stupor; that last drop having finally hit me. "She told me that no matter what, she would never hurt me. She said that she wouldn't let the past hurt or harm us at all. And you know what? That's exactly what she did."

I started to cry. I couldn't take the pain. KC held me in her arms. I could smell the cologne she used and it smelled exactly like *her*.

"Angie, you have to look at it like everything happens. Everything happens for a reason. If you don't want her back, then let her go. If it's true love, then try to get her back. I realize with me and Wendy, it wasn't meant to be." Her words somehow made me even angrier.

"I love you, KC, but I don't know what the fuck you saw in her ass. I mean, she was rude, she was immature, and she always brought you down. I don't know what you saw in her anyway."

"I saw what no one else saw and that was the problem. Everyone else saw the truth and all she kept giving me was a lie. I gave up too much for her; it's like I lost a piece of myself, messing with her. I'm glad that I at least get to say that I was good to her."

"Yeah, I made sure that I get to say that shit, too. I was damn good to her. I mean, I deserve an Emmy for the Wifey Performance of the Year."

I got up and stumbled to the kitchen. I went to get her a bottle of water and another bottle of Vodka for me. I took a sip of my drink and I heard KC get up.

"Angie, how many bottles do you have?"

"Enough!"

"I'm not gonna let you drink your pain away, Angie." KC snatched my bottle and broke it on the floor. "You know how I feel about that."

"You know you cleanin' that up, right?" I asked her; shocked and surprised. She had never cared before when I drank.

"I don't want to see you drunk, Sweets. You know I can't stand it."

"Well, damn. Do you have some weed, then? 'Cause if I can't fuck and I can't drink, then I need to smoke."

Of course, she pulled out a blunt, sat back down, and lit it up.

"Who says you can't fuck?" She smiled. "You know you got a couple studs waiting to beat that booty up."

"Shut up, and pass the blunt." I gave a little shy smile as I walked over to the couch to sit next to her. "How are your meetings going?"

"Fine. I've been sober for six months now. I'm doing really well. But I gotta keep my weed tho. I ain't letting dat go." She smiled.

God, I had never noticed how much her smile lit up a room.

We sat there and talked, and smoked. I thought KC only had one blunt but I knew how she rolled. We went through eight blunts all by ourselves. We smoked and listened to different CDs, switching from Ciara, to Keyshia Cole, to Ginuwine. Not that new Ginuwine but the old school: "Pony," "Anxious," and "Tell Me Do You Wanna" that grown and sexy music. I had never noticed how sensuous she was. I mean, she was so much more appealing than my ex. She barely dabbled in any drama, and she had a strong spiritual side. She kept it real.

"Look at me, Sweets." I looked up at her and she held my oval face in the palm of her soft hands. "You are beautiful and no one should be treated like this; not you nor me." She pulled the hair away from my face.

"I just wish it could go back to how it was when we first met. You know, like the freshness of our relationship before it all crumbled. I miss when she made me laugh, when she finished my sentences, and even looking at her when she'd sleep. But all the good times quickly turned into bad ones."

"Yeah, the more you get to know someone and their actions, the more it seems like you're meeting a totally different person than what you expected." She looked over at me and I started crying.

"I just don't feel right without her. We had plans and we were supposed to be together forever, and she just up and leaves like I never meant anything. Like everything was a fucking lie. I can't take this pain and this loneliness."

The more I broke down, the more I realized KC was holding me tight. I felt so wanted and needed that I didn't even realize that my heart was finally feeling whole again.

"I know you miss her but don't drown in the pain, Sweets. You're going to be okay."

She kissed my lips and I pulled back, thinking, *Am I trippin' or did she kiss me?* I looked at her; confused and anxious at the same time.

"I'm sorry, Angie. I shouldn't have crossed…"

"No." I pulled her closer to me. "Don't be." Then, I kissed her.

Her kiss was soft and gentle; like her touch. This time I let the taste of her tongue fill my mouth with hunger and lust. I loved the way her mouth fit mine perfectly. She grabbed my waist and pulled me closer. I wrapped my legs around her and started giving her a sample of what I could do to her.

The hunger of us wanting to fuck was taking over. I started pulling off her jacket, then took off her shirt as she placed soft, gentle kisses on my chest. I pulled my head back as her tongue ran from my chin all the way down to the middle of my chest. KC pulled back and gazed at me. I shared the same expression; guilt.

"Are you sure we should do this?" she asked.

I was hot and bothered and wanted to fuck her, but this was crossing the line. She was my ex's friend. It was wrong but, at the same time, felt so right. I had always thought of her as my friend but I never thought we'd take it to that *Jerry Springer* level.

"You sure you wanna turn back now? And just wonder what if?" I asked her. "I know that's what I'm going to do."

"Yeah, I know that you're drunk and high. You might also regret this later. I don't wanna hurt you, or come between anything."

"I don't wanna pretend like I don't want you right now either."

"But, Angie, if I was ever to make love to you, I'd want you to want me as much as I want you."

Now that surprised me. Had she ever thought about fucking me before that day?

"I do want you. Always have," I said, finally admitting my feelings.

I got up and walked toward the door. Something told me she was about to leave, and I wasn't going to stop her. I didn't even hear her behind me before she started kissing my neck, and massaging my back. I got more anxious and aroused with every touch. She took off my wifebeater and squeezed my breasts. I could feel her breathing on my neck. KC kissed my back all the way down to my ankles. I felt like my entire body was on fire.

I turned around and kissed KC. I let the one ounce that was left of passion and lust take over my body. I could hear Ciara and R. Kelly playing in the background. She kneeled down and pulled off my shorts in the process. I always say the first lick is the best; and it was and it only got better. KC was hungry for my body. She placed my leg over her shoulder and looked at me with those sexy eyes before commencing to lick all my walls.

I started moving to the rhythm of the beat, letting her mouth hit every note in the song. I didn't even notice both of my legs were around her shoulders. I kept moving to our rhythm. I licked my lips and enjoyed the feeling coming over me. I grabbed her head and started fucking her face. I wanted something else to hold on to but she was able to handle all of me as she lifted me up and continued eating.

KC picked me up and laid me on the floor. She looked down at me so seductively. Her eyes had this beautiful glow. I could tell that she had wanted to do this for a long time; the way she touched me and kissed me. I knew that this was something more than a friendship and more than a one-nighter or a quick nut could ever be.

She grabbed my body and caressed it gently; just right. Touched me light like a feather; it actually tickled me and turned me on. KC examined my body and my tattoos. She slowly caressed me and kissed every part of my skin. Made my toes curl. Her pants came off and she rested in between my legs and kissed me. Then I felt her enter me. And I screamed. I loved it, the sweetest touch is a woman inside of me; I just never thought it would be KC. Her hand caressed my face and she whispered in my ear.

"I'm glad I stayed. You look so beautiful when you're about to come."

That made me moan even more. Her playing with my pierced clit was starting to drive me crazy.

"You taste so sweet. I always knew that you would."

I felt it; it was building up and waiting to be released. She was going harder, and going faster. It was making me feel so good. My legs were spread out so I could feel all of her inside me. KC got on top of me and started grinding. She pulled my body closer to her so I could feel all of her. My legs wrapped around her body and I was riding her like earlier. She pulled my hair and my head went back. I put her fingers in my mouth and sucked them while still riding her. My moans were out of control and I knew she was going to cum; like I was. I pulled her even closer to me; just hugged her.

"I've craved your touch for the longest time, baby. I'm not going anywhere," she whispered to me.

"I've wanted you, too." A tear cascaded down my cheek as we both came. I closed my eyes and enjoyed the feeling. "Damn, baby! Shit!"

When I opened my eyes she was staring back at me. I kissed her lips and smiled at her.

"So what's next?"

We both giggled. I kissed her lips again.

"I have this killer craving for chocolate and a jumbo jack." I laughed and she shook her head at me. "What? Like you don't have the munchies?"

We both got up and I put on some sweats while she got dressed. I grabbed my purse as she pulled me in for a kiss. As we were headed out the door, my phone rang.

"Hold up, babe. Hello." I picked up the phone and heard the voice of my ex. She said she was outside my building.

୬୦୯୫

RDM is an upcoming novelist from Palmdale, California, who currently lives in Los Angeles. Some of her favorite books are written by Zane, Nikki Turner, and Eric Jerome Dickey. In her spare time RDM likes to write stories, listen to music, and enjoy life.

Lipstick on Her Collar

Samantha Green

"Hey, Baby." My boyfriend Raymond greeted me as I walked in the house.

"Hey, Boo." We shared a quick kiss. I made the kiss brief so Raymond wouldn't suspect anything.

He gave me a hug. "How was work?"

"Another long, boring evening. I feel like getting in the tub and going to bed." I made a move to get around him and headed to the stairs.

Raymond called, "Hey, Karen?"

"Huh?" I turned around.

"How'd you get red lipstick on your shirt?"

I looked down.

"No, on your collar," Raymond continued. "How'd you get lipstick on your collar?"

My mind reflected on the past couple of hours.

৪৩৫৪

Being editorial director for a weekly magazine was wonderful; except when big stories hit and the magazine had already been designed. I loved the work. I began *Eminence* when I was sixteen.

What had started as a pastime of interviewing the local celebrities and pastors had blown up into a publication the likes of *Vogue*. Simply put, I was huge. I was also organized so when big stories hit, though amusing, they were also annoying because I had to reorganize the entire magazine. It was a welcome challenge every time.

I was sitting at my desk, looking over what would become the finished magazine, but something was wrong. I couldn't put my finger on the problem, and that was aggravating me even more.

There was a knock on my door. "Come in," I said, barely raising my head.

"You still at it?" Sasha, my administrative assistant, asked.

"Yeah, I need to take this to the printer first thing in the morning, and I want to be through with this tonight."

"What's wrong with it?"

"I'm not sure, but something is wrong with it; I guarantee you. I can feel it." I finally looked up. "Oh, you didn't have to bring me anything to drink," I said, referring to the cup of black tea in her hand.

"You definitely needed it."

I took a sip, then set the tea on my desk. "Thank you. It's delicious, as always."

When she didn't make an effort to leave the office, I asked, "Is there something else?"

"No, ma'am. I just wondered if you wanted me to look at it."

"Yes, it would be nice having someone else to look over this, since my eyes aren't working correctly."

She laughed and took a seat across from me.

"You should really be on this side of the desk to get the full effect."

A smile crossed her face as she pulled the chair to my side of my desk and took a seat. She looked over the magazine articles laid out and asked, "Is this the order you have them in now?"

"Yes, and I don't like it."

"I see why. How about if you…" She rearranged two articles completely, looked at her work, and then moved three more. "Do this? How's that?"

I looked down at her work. "I like it better than my original thoughts, but…"

"Something still feels wrong, huh?"

She reached across me again and began shifting articles. As she reached over me, her breasts touched my arm. I tried to ignore it, but as she kept reaching, the breast grazing continued. Either Sasha didn't notice or she didn't care.

"Okay, how about now?"

I looked at her work again. "Wait, I can work with this." I grabbed an article that Sasha had placed at the end of the magazine and set it down. "If this is moved right here…"

"Oh, I see. Then it flows better with this one. And this one can go next."

Sasha and I spent the next fifteen minutes arranging and rearranging articles until the magazine had both of our stamps of approval. I tried not to notice her perfectly shaped breasts, but that was not an easy task. See, I'd never looked at Sasha in a sexual way at all. I'd never looked at any woman like that, but especially Sasha. She was always looked at as my administrative assistant. But it was after hours, and she wasn't as primped as she'd been that morning. Her hair was not as put together as it had been and her clothes were not as straight. She looked different; sexy.

The expression on her face indicated that I hadn't answered a question that she'd apparently asked. "Yes?"

"I asked if we were done."

"Yes." I put the finished magazine in a case for the printer and began straightening up my desk. "Thank you for staying later than usual."

"It was no problem, Ms. Jameson. I enjoyed being on that side of the desk for a change."

"None of that Ms. Jameson stuff. Call me Karen."

"Okay, Karen." She moved her chair back in place and looked at me.

"What is it, Sasha?"

"Nothing. Well, it's just, you are beautiful."

I blushed. "Thank you."

She walked back around my desk and stood in front of me. "No, I mean really beautiful. I know you have a boyfriend but, Karen, are you into women?"

"I've found women attractive for as long as I can remember, but I've never been intimate with a woman, no."

"I'm a blunt woman, Karen. I've watched you since I've worked for you, and I've always found you attractive. You have the most gorgeous lips I've ever seen and I sit at my desk imagining those lips kissing me." She began taking steps toward me. "Just let me know if you don't want me to touch you, and I'll back off."

A small part of me wanted to refuse her, but my mouth would not form the words. Rather than push her away, I let her lips caress mine. She grabbed me around my waist and pulled me toward her. I had my first kiss at the age of fourteen and the kisses that I'd shared with men since then had nothing on the way Sasha's mouth was on mine. Her tongue relentlessly mated with mine. Her mouth left mine and I nearly whimpered until I felt her nibbling behind my right ear and my neck. I was certain she had no idea how much she was arousing me with just her mouth; or maybe she did. She moved one of her arms from around my waist to under my skirt.

"Tell me if you want me to stop," she said as her hand went higher under my skirt.

"I can't. Don't stop."

"Sit down for me, Karen."

I sat down in my chair. Sasha dropped to her knees in front of me. It had been warm that day so I had no stockings on. Sasha reached under my skirt and removed my blue thong. Her fingers worked their way across my mound. She put one, then two, and finally three fingers in me and began moving them back and forth. She boldly stared me straight in my eyes as she worked me to my first orgasm, and then she pulled her fingers out of me and licked them one by one.

"Lift those hips for me, Karen."

I did as she said and she removed my skirt. She then took off my blouse and bra. My jacket had been taken off when I began working hard on the magazine. I sat in front of Sasha, as naked as the day I was born and without a care in the world. She reached out and touched my left breast with one hand while the other one grabbed my right breast. "Your breasts are gorgeous."

"I would say the same, but I can't see yours."

"I can fix that."

Sasha pulled off her black blouse and bra. I reached out and nervously touched her breasts. As she leaned forward, she took her skirt off. I was shocked to see that she didn't have on any panties.

"I don't like them," she said as my eyes widened. "They tend to get in the way."

I gazed at Sasha's bare breasts and licked my lips. I pulled her closer to me and grabbed a nipple with my teeth. Sasha sucked in a deep breath as I licked her left breast. I caressed her right breast with my hand, then put my tongue on that nipple.

"Damn, Karen, are you sure you've never done this before?"

"Yes, I'm sure."

Sasha straddled me. When her pussy grazed my thigh, she left some of her feminine juices. I wiped it off with my hand and licked it. She tasted nothing like peaches or strawberries, but she did taste sweet.

Sasha said, "Here, I want you to penetrate me."

"With what?" I softly laughed.

She placed three fingers inside me and said, "With those."

I slowly placed three fingers inside of her.

"Oooh, like that Karen. Now, just do to me what you, umm, do to yourself."

I began moving my fingers as Sasha did the same. We caught a rhythm quickly. I could tell when Sasha was about to cum because she started moving quickly. I pulled her close to me.

"I've got you," I said.

She came, then brought me to another climax soon after.

She rested her head on my shoulder. She kissed me and caressed my breasts. I rose up and bumped my pussy into hers.

Sasha giggled. "Yeah, we bumped coochies."

I laughed. Sasha stood up.

I rose and stretched. Noticing that at some point we'd knocked over my jar of paper clips, I leaned over my desk to pick them up. I felt a gentle pressure on my back as Sasha pushed me forward. I heard the squeak as she sat in my chair. She scooted up right behind me. I felt her hands run up my thighs. She put her hands around my waist and arched my back. I felt her put a finger in my ass as her tongue found my pussy. The pleasure I had from her tongue action and the rhythm of her finger caused me to cum quickly. I fell forward.

After resting a little more, I stood up. Unfortunately, it was time to leave. I straightened my desk and started putting on my clothes. I glanced over at Sasha, who was staring intently at me.

I was the first to speak. "I wish I could stay with you, but…"

"I know, you have a man." I began buttoning my shirt. "But tell me this." Sasha walked to me and fixed the collar on my blouse. "Has he ever made you cum as hard as you did with me?" She placed a series of small kisses along my neck.

"No, he never has."

Sasha looked me in my eyes. "We could be so good together."

"If it's meant to be, it will be."

We shared a hug and a final kiss before parting ways.

As I drove home, I thought of what I'd told Sasha. My boyfriend had never made me cum as hard or as many times as she had. Shit, many times I found myself handling my own needs long after he went to sleep. If tonight was any indication, I would never have to worry about that with Sasha.

ౚౚఴ

I looked at Raymond. "I went to visit Mom earlier today. That must've happened when she hugged me."

"Oh, okay." He easily accepted my answer.

I made my way to our master bathroom and started the water. I was about to put the gel beads in the water when Raymond walked through the door.

"Baby, I know you're tired, but your assistant Sasha is on the phone. She said you dropped a page out of the magazine you need to take to the printer tomorrow."

"Shit."

"She said she's waiting for you at the office."

"Damn, okay, Raymond. I'm going back to the office. Since it fell out, it might take us a while to put it back in place and make sure we have the perfect order."

"My baby, the workaholic."

I gave Raymond a kiss. "I'll be back as soon as I can."
I practically ran out the door; trying to get back to Sasha.

ഇൗരു

Samantha Green is a nineteen-year-old from Shreveport, Louisiana. She loves reading and writing and currently attends Centenary College of Louisiana. She can be reached at dal8ydestiny@aol.com.

Underneath

Alison Tyler

A bevy of bras dangled becomingly from the silver metal shower bar.

Silk stockings in a rainbow of colors were pinned carefully to the clothesline strung across the bathroom.

And then there were the panties—lace-edged, ruffled, sheer, satin. More choices than you'd find in a Victoria's Secret catalog.

I admired the vision as if a patron at a high-end art gallery. A patron who would look but never, ever buy. Sure, I understood what lingerie was for. I simply didn't have a use for frilly under-garments myself. Pretty panties were for pretty girls, and I hadn't in my entire life felt pretty. I wasn't wallowing. I'd simply grown satisfied with my slightly rough-girl style: jeans, *always* jeans, dark denim Levi's paired with short-sleeved T-shirts when it was warm. Long-sleeved plus a hoodie when it was cold. Lingerie was for the sultry sorority chicks on my dorm floor, the girly-girls who went to ice cream socials, who wore wee little miniskirts, who knew the names of the different fingernail polishes they adored: *Romeo Red, I'm not Really a Waitress, Vamp.*

I observed these twittering chicklets in the communal girls' room getting ready for dances or dates, and I felt more than a bit out of place in my striped cotton boxers and tight-ribbed T-shirts.

What use would I have for their bras, even if I wanted one? I'm as flat-chested as they come. Still, I knew where I fell in the beauty hierarchy, and I knew that those candy-colored confections were not for me.

"Why the *fuck* are you wearing that?"

That is, until Doreen came along.

I stood in the bathroom, brushing my teeth, and I had to rinse and spit before I said, "Excuse me?" My eyes were wide at the tone of her voice.

"What girl in her right mind would wear underpants that look like that? No wonder you don't have a date on a Friday night."

I couldn't think of a response. From the gossip, I knew who this dark-skinned Amazon beauty was: a recent transfer student from Nevada. From the girls, I'd learned that she was thirty-six, and had been working in Las Vegas as some sort of wine steward for the last twenty years. From the boys, I'd learned that she was a bombshell beauty, gorgeous enough to have been approached by *Playboy* magazine, not once, but twice. At eighteen and again at thirty-four.

"Guys can't tell what your panties look like through your clothes," I said, sounding lame even to myself. Had she guessed that I didn't care what guys could or couldn't tell? Boys meant nothing to me at all.

"You walk different when you wear pretty lingerie," she insisted, proving her point by doing an impromptu catwalk across the tiled floor. She had long legs revealed by tiny white denim cut-offs and a perfect stride. I admired her in silence, before she nodded toward me. I'd heard that she was opinionated, strident, and already feared. And yet I had no idea why she was focusing her dark feline eyes on me. "Now you."

"Now me what?" I still had my cobalt-blue toothbrush in my hand.

"You try."

I didn't want to walk across the cold tiled bathroom floor; especially with this stunning she-cat watching my every move. And yet I found myself unable to refuse. Quickly, I rushed across the floor to the far wall and then back again, as if the goal had been speed rather than poise. Doreen doubled up laughing. "*That's* how you walk when you're trying to be sexy?"

"You didn't say—"

"You knew what I wanted. Try it again."

"I'm *not* sexy," I said, feeling heat rush to my cheeks.

"Not like that. Not in those baggy-ass shorts. Not with that piss-poor attitude. But you could be."

Why was she doing this? Was she simply dateless on this Friday night, with nothing to do but harass the dorm-floor loser?

"Try again."

"I don't want to." I was starting to feel my old defenses come up. What had made me do what she'd said at the start? She'd simply caught me off-guard. That was all.

"With a swivel in your hips this time," she added, as if I hadn't spoken.

"*I don't want to*," I repeated, more forcefully this time.

"Better yet," she continued, clearly deaf when she wanted to be. "Take those off."

"I'm not taking my underwear off!"

"And the T-shirt, too."

I stared at her, incredulous. Who the fuck did she think she was?

"I'm waiting." She said this last in a sing-song voice, and she tapped her bare foot for emphasis. Was the woman crazy? Why on Earth would I strip down for a stranger, simply because she'd said she was waiting? We locked eyes for a minute, the gazelle and the lioness, and in that brief span of time I realized that *I* was the crazy one, pulling off my T-shirt and kicking out of my red-and-white striped boxers. And why was I doing that? Because nothing like this had ever happened to me before.

While Doreen watched, I strode across the bathroom floor, and this time, I put a bit of swivel in my walk. She was right. I felt better not to be in the baggy clothes, felt as if I were more animal than human as I strode across the floor.

"That's it!" She sounded truly excited. "I knew you had it in you. You were muffling all that power under those stupid underclothes."

I returned triumphant to the sink, then made the mistake of looking in the mirror, and my confidence evaporated in a heartbeat. All I saw was a pale-skinned girl with a heart-shaped face and untamable curls. What the fuck was I doing? Prancing naked in the girls' room in front of a virtual stranger. Doreen didn't let me wallow for a second.

"Now," she said, "let's get you into some pretty knickers, and we'll see what you can really do. Follow me."

She started out of the bathroom, and I bent to scoop up my T-shirt, but she returned before I could slip it back over my head. "You're done with all that," she commanded, grabbing up the Hanes men's shirt and tossing it into the nearest garbage, along with the boxers.

"Wait," I said, breathless. "I don't have any other clothes in here."

"Then I guess you'll just have to come naked."

I shook my head. There was no way.

Of course, I hadn't realized that with Doreen, there was always a way.

"I'll give you to three," she said, standing there like a queen regarding an insubordinate subject. "And if you aren't out of the bathroom by then, I'm going to spank that lush ass of yours until you promise to behave."

Jesus Christ, lady, I said—in my head—*where did you come from?* I knew the answer to that: Vegas. But my query went deeper than that. How had she known the buzz words to say to me? How had she guessed what I thought about at night, long after my room-mate had dropped off to sleep, when I finally gave in and touched myself. Doreen wasn't a queen. She was an X-rated fairy god-mother. And now I had to decide whether to do what she said, or get what I wanted.

"I'm not walking naked down the hall," I heard myself tell her, taking a stand. It was a test. Would she pass? Would I?

Doreen shook her head. "Here I am, trying to help out a poor girl in need, and all I'm getting is lip."

She was towering over me in seconds, dragging me by the ear to the wooden bench in front of the showers. Then she sat down and hauled me over her lap and her hand came down in a series of supremely stinging slaps, blows that had me squirming and kicking from the start.

I'd been fantasizing about being spanked for longer than I could remember, but I'd had no idea of what the actual pain involved might be. The pain and, of course, the pleasure because both came together. I could hardly wrap my mind around the fact that this gorgeous woman, who I'd never even been formally introduced to, was now heating my curvaceous hind end. But she was, talking darkly as she spanked me.

"Bad girl needs a bit of a tune-up, I'd say. Lose some of that haughty attitude. Next time I'm going to send you out to cut your own switch."

I almost came right then.

Doreen shoved me off her lap.

"Now," she said, "I'd suggest you follow me to my room."

I went meekly, aware that I was sporting blush-red rear cheeks as I followed the stunning minx down the hall. To my complete relief, we ran into none of our fellow dormmates. Perhaps Doreen had known all of the rest of the clan would be out—at parties or on dates. Far more likely was the fact that she simply didn't care.

I sighed as she shut the door to her room, and then I waited, realizing that although I had safely walked unseen down the hall, I was now locked into a small square room with an extremely unpredictable female. I looked around wildly. Doreen had the room to herself—the other girl, beset with homesickness, had dropped out to move back to Chico. There was no chance we'd be interrupted.

Doreen regarded me with those dark, gold-flecked eyes. "Panties," she said, "pretty ones. And a simple camisole. Do you a world of good." She headed to her own dresser drawer and started pulling out different items, until finally she'd spread out a whole array on her bed. "Try them on," she said. "I know we'll find something that suits you."

I hesitated only long enough for her to come to my side and set one firm hand on my still smarting ass. "I wasn't kidding about the switch, sweetheart. You're begging for me to get angry."

I moved quickly after that. Slipping on a white lace camisole and a matching pair of lace bikinis. Doreen admired the view for a moment before shaking her head and offering over another. She had me in scarlet lace, then a swirl of lavender, before ultimately settling finally on a dove-gray chemise. The material felt luxurious against my skin. Why had I robbed myself of this sensual sensation? Why had I always insisted on the no-nonsense menswear fabrics, from plain cotton to scratchy synthetics?

Doreen was beaming at me, and then she turned me so that I could see my reflection in the mirror on the back of her closet door. "Pretty," she said, "right?"

"The slip is," I observed, hesitant. I couldn't agree to anything else. That not only was the nightie pretty, but that *I* was, as well.

"That's not what I meant," she said, spinning me around once more, then pressing her full lips to mine and kissing me. A shudder worked instantly through my body, an intense rush of pleasure that had me breathless when we parted, but desperate not to stop. I reached out to her, and she grinned and swatted my hands away, her dark skin against my light. "Not yet," she said. "You wait."

"For what?" The words escaped before I could stop them. I could tell already that Doreen had to be in charge. But my legs were weak from the kiss and I didn't want to pause. Not even for an instant.

"Sit down."

I perched on the edge of her bed, staring up at her. She came closer to me, stroking my hair off my face, running her fingertips over my cheekbones, resting her thumbs on my bottom lip.

"*You're* pretty," she said again, softly this time. "You're pretty, even in the baggy clothes. Hidden, maybe, but still. I've watched you since I got here. I've seen the way you hide yourself. The problem isn't what's on the outside. It's in here—" She tapped her fingertips against my temples next. "Let me show you."

While I stared, heart racing, she reached for a heavy-handled wooden brush. Then she sat down on the bed, and motioned for me to climb over her lap. I knew what was coming now, and I knew how wet I was. Still, I felt embarrassed. But one look in her eyes let me know not to hesitate.

Over her lap I went once more, and now she lifted the silky

chemise in the back, revealing my naked, blushing rear. This was sexier than in the bathroom. The feel of the sumptuous fabric rustling over my skin, the sensation of her pressing the smooth back of the brush against me once before she started. Started for real.

She didn't go slow. She didn't begin with a pat-a-cake type spanking to warm me up. Doreen punished me with serious strokes, the heavy wood bouncing against my bare skin, and I was crying out by the time she let go of the brush. But this time, she didn't push me off her lap. This time, she dropped one hand between my legs and slowly began to touch my pussy. Wetness immediately enveloped the tips of her fingers as she stroked up and down between my nether lips. I was drenched.

"My bad girl likes that," Doreen crooned, continuing to touch me just right. She made dangerous little circles around my clit as my hips twitched on her lap. I was begging, softly, crooning non-sense words to her, hoping against hope that she wouldn't stop. And this time, she didn't. She teased me with the tips of her strong fingers until I came, shuddering over her lap, my body on fire with the power of the orgasm. It was just what I'd dreamed of. Just what I thought about late at night, my fingers making similar rotations as I tried my best to come quietly in my bed.

Doreen held me after that. Sat me up on her lap, so that we were pressed together, the chemise sticking to my sweat-sheened skin, her arms firm around me. My face was tear-streaked, but I didn't care. My heavy bangs were in my eyes, hair a jumble of midnight curls, when Doreen finally stood me up once more, led me back to the mirror.

I looked different now. I had to admit that.

There was a pleasure beating in my eyes, a glow coloring my

cheeks. She'd transformed me in less than an hour, given me a makeover from the inside out.

"You're pretty," she said softly, clearly pleased with herself. "See now? See the difference?"

I nodded. I did.

But how had *she* known?

How had she known not only what was underneath my clothes, but underneath my skin? The cravings raging within me. The urges I couldn't deny. I looked at Doreen as she settled back against the mattress, one arm folded under her head, regarding me with those mesmerizing eyes.

She answered the question without me having to voice it.

"It's always easy to see what's underneath," she said in that soft growl of a voice. "At least, it is when you know what you're looking for."

೮೦೧೪

Called a "trollop with a laptop" by the East Bay Express *and a "literary siren" by* Good Vibrations, *Alison Tyler is naughty and she knows it. Her sultry short stories have appeared in more than seventy-five anthologies, including* Sex for America *(Harper Collins),* Sex at the Office *(Virgin), and* Best Women's Erotica 2008 *(Cleis). She is the author of more than twenty-five erotic novels, and the editor of more than forty-five explicit anthologies, including* Naked Erotica *(Pretty Things Press). Visit www.alisontyler.com for more information.*

Island Goddess
Yuri

The taxi driver opens the door for me. I step onto the sand-sprayed steps in front of the hotel. The front entrance looks much better than it did in the brochure. The blush-colored building blends into the sky like a compact sunset and the people enjoying their view atop the balconies are like heavenly deities watching as people frolic on the white sand beach. I pay the driver and begin my trek into heaven. Making sure not to mess up my day-old French manicure, I drag my clearance designer suitcase behind me.

While I'm here I will be every girl's wet dream. I am a vixen sweeping through this exotic paradise, only to leave behind broken hearts and longing lovers. For my debut, I chose a wide-brimmed straw hat, cat-eye glasses, and a halter flower-print dress themed in red to match my lipstick. My stiletto sandals click on the expensive marble floor of the hotel lobby. It took me over a year to save up enough money to spend one week in this island paradise. With my free hand, I lift my sunglasses and place them on top of my hat, Audrey Hepburn-style.

The front lobby reminds me of Greek myths, where the pantheon would sit on lavish benches, while drinking ambrosia. Beautiful people in elegant clothes chat about the pleasant weather over afternoon cocktails.

As I walk to the front desk, I make sure to make eye contact with at least three of the classy rich women and a few of their husbands. By the time I reach the front desk, it feels like the entire room is watching me.

"Welcome to Paradise." The desk girl smiles at me. She towers over me like a Nubian goddess and her deep mocha skin and eyes catch my breath. "I am Milani. How may I help you?" she says with a tilt of her head, making the tight ebony ringlets peek around her head from their hiding place in her ponytail. To keep from losing my composure, I dig into my carry-on bag. I turn back to her with my cool façade intact.

"Thank you…Milani, is it?" I carry a pretentious accent that I've been practicing on the plane. "I believe I have a reservation for a suite with a balcony."

I offer the chocolate goddess my passport and printed confirmation. She accepts them with a close-lipped grin and a deep, but brief, glance at my cleavage. As she types on her computer, I allow my eyes to wander. Her navy uniform jacket is left open, revealing a white form-fitting button-down over which a man's thick navy-and-gold striped tie descends below the counter.

"Here you are, Ms. Sanchez," Milani says. Our eyes meet as she returns my paperwork; long enough for my face to burn like a summer day. It's like she can see through my diva exterior to the shy teaching assistant hiding beneath. "I hope that you find everything to your liking." She hands me my key card.

"I have so far," the diva in me says. I turn away from her slowly, giving her a full look at my ass. Every step I take toward the elevator is forced into a slow, steady pace; to give her the opportunity to look as long as possible. I only allow myself to relax when I enter the elevator, alone, and collapse against the mirrored wall. *Somehow*

I've pulled this off, I think, smiling. For a moment, I take in the light elevator music. If I were at home, I wouldn't have been able to make eye contact with a girl like her. *Okay, get it together, Alyssa*, I think, straightening my posture.

The elevator doors ding before opening and I return to diva-mode and walk the hallway like a runway model until I reach my door. I release my suitcase to draw out my keycard. It slides easily into the slot and I open the door, ready to experience what only eating Ramen noodles for months on end can buy.

The suite is even better than the picture I taped on my bathroom mirror. A queen-size that promised to be a heavenly experience, covered with Egyptian cotton sheets and marshmallow pillows. The balcony doors ahead of me offer a clear ocean view that's worthy of a postcard, shrouded by white curtains and lined by thicker drapes. In the right corner, the open bathroom door around the corner, I see a Jacuzzi tub I can't wait to get into.

The real me breaks through as I kick off my heeled sandals, hitch up the tight dress, and jump on the mattress with childish abandon. I'm finally here, finally, at least for a week.

৪৩৫৪

When I head out to the hotel bar, I try for the "corporate lesbian at leisure" look. You know, the kind that makes men give respect and women give everything else. Using the makeup tips from the salesgirl at the mall, I paint my face to look natural. Then I wear a cream linen suit, baby-pink tank, and the open-toed Mary Janes that show off my shiny new pedicure. Not to appear desperate, I bring a novel to pull out while scoping out the scene.

I make it down the stairs just after sunset, thanking the rosy glow for giving me another grand entrance. The usual lounge hogs have taken over most of the seats at the bar and surrounding tables so I make my way toward the glass deck doors and set up camp. Women, who have run past the hill, sit atop the barstools in tight sequin dresses to flirt with the bartenders, while old men and sleaze-bag townies hover in the shadows waiting for their trust-fund meal tickets to arrive and start drinking.

I walk outside the main bar, refusing to make eye contact with any of the regulars and leave through the glass doors. Thankfully, there is an empty two-person table giving me the perfect place to look over the bar and say I'm looking at the fading beach horizon. Drawing the novel out of my jacket, I open it to a random page and scan the possible dating pool. The night is still early, plenty of time.

ஐஓ

Around one-thirty a.m., my hopes start to wane. I've actually read through most of my novel, and turned down three men old enough to be my father. The young movers and shakers are making their way out for the evening, wasting their parents' money on alcohol and only God knows what. By three-thirty a.m., I'm ready to call it a night and hang up my diva exterior.

"Is anyone sitting here?" a familiar female voice calls to me from behind.

I turn in my chair to find Milani holding two purple drinks with umbrella straws. She's turned in her work uniform for a floral-print spaghetti strap tank top and low-cut jeans that fit snugly on her hips. The tank cuts off just above her belly button. I nod to the empty chair. The mocha goddess sets down the drinks, to take a chair, turn it backward and take a seat. The more I think about it, the more she makes me think of one of those fertility statues that ancient people used to worship. She has full breasts, a willowy waist and round hips.

"You are off work now," I say as I recross my legs.

"How observant." She smirks, then takes a sip from one of the umbrella drinks.

"Sorry, mojitos have that effect on me," I say. To cover my nervousness, I finger the rim of my empty glass.

"You look like a fruity-drink kind of girl," she says before sliding the other glass with the umbrella straw in it toward me. The drink is a purple-and-red concoction with a nifty umbrella straw. "It's an Island Goddess." I take the glass apprehensively, swirling the straw around and making the ice clink. "Don't worry, it won't knock you on your ass; just give you a good buzz."

"I'm already there, I think," I reply before setting down the glass and then sliding it back to her.

Milani shrugs, then takes the glass off the table before taking a deep drink from the rim. She leaves her mark with plum lipstick before setting it back on the table. My eyes fall on the glass where her lips had been. A tinge of jealousy pains me for a moment.

"Why aren't you out on the scene?" Milani asks.

"What?" She caught me while I was in my thoughts.

"I would think you would be dancing the night away."

"That's not really my style," I say.

Whether it is the alcohol in my system or merely wanting to touch where her lips had been, I take the glass between my lips and drink deep. The fruity liquid burns going down, leaving me in a fuzzy illusion.

"What is your style?" Milani asks. She brings her own glass to her lips. "Mr. Tall, Dark, and Handsome you were talking to earlier?"

"Maybe," I say coyly.

"You didn't look like the type that kisses girls." She places her drink on the table and begins to rise.

"That's not what my ex-girlfriend said." I don't really know where that came from but it felt like the diva thing to say. It's enough to get her attention because Milani sits back down.

"What else did your ex-girlfriend say?" She leans forward in her chair, rocking on the back legs.

Her anticipation makes me want to giggle but the diva in me reforms it into a smile.

"You remind me of her." I relax in my chair, uncrossing my legs. "You both are so cool, so confident, like you can have any woman in the room." I wave a manicured hand to the wind. Then send out a grateful thought to the manicurist for keeping the nails short.

"So, why aren't you two together?" she asks.

Milani rights her chair and waves over a waiter. She quickly finishes her drink and places it on his tray. They seem to know each because the waiter gives Milani a knowing wink before walking away.

"Would you like another?" Milani points to the purple drink I have yet to finish. As she speaks, I take in her swan-like neck, down to her collarbone.

"No, I'm fine," I say. She snaps me back to reality. Suddenly, she rises from her seat. "Where are you going?"

"Let's go somewhere." Milani extends her hand to me.

"Where?"

"I don't know; just out of here." Milani picks up the purple drink off of the table.

"We, we could go to my room," I say. I would say anything to keep her standing next to me. "I have a great view of the beach from my balcony."

"I know." She smiles, displaying a row of perfectly white teeth. "You're in four-thirty-two, right?"

I nod and reach out to take her hand. When I try to rise, I stumble over my heels. She catches me around the waist with a firm hand. I take it and again realize how small I am; even in stilettos.

Still holding me tight, Milani pushes open the glass doors back into the busy bar. A lesser woman would have fallen to her knees and worshipped the ground Milani's thong sandals tread upon. Not me, not yet. I glance around the bar, taking in the few of the stares, some in shock, some in wonder, and it makes me want to fade away. In my other relationships, I barely held my girlfriend's hands, let alone walked arm in arm in public, so I stand proudly beside her. At least for now, I'm not that shy woman.

We exit the bar and stop in front of the elevator doors. After she presses the button, her arms come full circle around my waist, drawing me into the cushion of her breasts. All I would have to do is turn my head forward and I could bury my face there. My hands fall around her hips and slide up the small of her back, to glide along her tank top. When I reach where her bra closure should be, I find bare space.

"It opens in front." Milani's sultry voice melts like warm caramel from her lips to my ear. The elevator dings open. Milani untangles us before guiding me onto the elevator. As the doors close, Milani takes a drink from my glass.

"Are we allowed to take those away from the bar?" I ask. I hadn't realized she had taken it. She leans against the wall, taking me with her.

"It's okay. They won't miss it." She wraps her arms around me, leaving me in her bosom once again. This time she starts stroking my back and I can't help but relax.

"You don't sound like a native." I hear myself sigh. Milani's free hand rises, catching my chin and lifting my head.

"Don't worry, baby. Momma's got you now," she says in a Caribbean accent. "Is that better?"

I rise to my toes as I lean forward and find her lips. She welcomes me wholly and takes my tongue as an offering. The arms around my waist lock me into my heightened position. Fiercely, I try to savor the fruity alcohol that lines her mouth. Milani overpowers my tongue, slowly winding it into sweet submission. Much to my dismay, the elevator dings and she breaks away. I lean against her breasts to catch my breath and feel her heart racing like mine.

"Excuse us," Milani says as we make our way out. I look up to find an elderly couple staring gape-mouthed at us. Milani guides us out of the elevator past the couple. "Good evening," she says casually as we pass. This time I do giggle. "Where's your card key?" she asks me. I draw the slender card out of my back pocket. She takes it from me and, in return, I gain kisses in my hair. Long-legged, lithe women keep me wet.

"This is your door?" Milani says as we stop in front of my door. I nod and she slides the key into the lock and opens the door. I release myself from her embrace and walk into the suite like a movie star. I kick off my sandals to sink into the plush carpet.

"I told you I have the perfect view," I say as I twirl around in a circle, walk toward my balcony doors, and open them wide.

"Yes, you do," Milani says from behind me.

Again, I'm wrapped in her strong arms. Music from below on

the beachfront from a distant bonfire drifts into my suite, urging me to sway. My ass grinds against her thighs, rocking back and forth to the island beat. She takes hold of my hips, rocking me in her slow, sexy rhythm. My hands slide up her arms to find a place at the base of her neck. As we dance, her hands release my hips and begin grazing across my breasts. Her fingers slide off my cream jacket, then toss it aside. They then work down my tank straps. When the straps fall to my shoulders, revealing my strapless bra, she stops. I can feel her hand drawing my hair to one side and her soft lips brush my neck. She keeps me dizzy by alternating between biting and nibbling on my tender flesh.

So much so, that I don't notice her hands disappear once again and reappear, stroking my lower back, then circling around to the drawstring that ties my pants. With a flick of her wrist, my crisp linen pants drop to the plush carpet. I gasp as the cool air caresses my legs like a lover's fingertips. Milani steps back, removing her hands from my body. She bears a look of concern.

"What's wrong?" she asks. I turn around, stepping out of my pants, to face her. I draw my tank top the remainder of the way down my waist and let it collapse onto the floor with my pants.

"Nothing, I just don't like being cold." I reach behind me, unsnapping my bra. "At least, not by myself."

Milani smiles at me and draws her own tank top over her shoulders. While her arms are in the air I unzip her jeans. As I pull down her jeans, I find a simple, white, high-cut bikini and a tattooed tail descending her leg. Further down her leg, the tail becomes a tiger that wraps around her left thigh, baring its claws to me.

Her tattoo brings me to my knees in dutiful worship. I pause, running my fingers down the tattoo, then my mouth begins kissing its claws and working my way up until my tongue glides up its tail. I can smell her musk coming down and I begin nibbling at the flesh just around her panties as my nails sink into her chocolate skin. I move to her moist center. Even through the thin fabric, I find her clit. I can feel it bud for me as I graze the slick fabric with my teeth. Milani takes hold of my hair in firm handfuls, forcing me deeper and deeper into her sex. Above me, I can hear her moans flow down. I take my pointer fingers to catch the top of the bikini panties and slide them down her legs.

She keeps her muff clean-shaven. I run my fingers along her nether lips. She moans in response. I dive in, drinking deep from her fountain. I hear Milani curse, but I continue. It's when I flick my tongue against her clit that she pulls away.

"You're so eager," Milani says. She kneels down beside me on her knees.

"It's been a while," I reply. Even on my knees before her, she's still taller than I. "You are so beautiful." I begin stroking her face as I spread my knees to sit on her thigh. She takes her left hand and secures it around my waist. With her right hand, she cups my breast, then brings it to her lips.

My fingers leave her face to unsnap the closure of her bra. Beautiful, round mounds fall free and her chocolate drop nipples make me want to lick her even more. But Milani has other plans.

She leans forward, laying me on my back. She easily takes away my panties and dives in without a second thought. A moan wrenches from my throat as she laps me up like a kitten does milk. Suddenly, she rises and takes my hands, drawing me to a standing position.

"Did I scare you?" She laughs in my ear. "We shouldn't do it on the floor. I don't like rug burns."

All I can do is nod.

We fall ungracefully on the bed. The sudden weight of her pressed against me makes me lose my breath for a moment, but I wrap my legs around hers to keep her there.

We lock lips, our tongues fighting for control, and I submit. She sucks on my tongue as our nipples tease each other in their hardened state. I reach for her chocolate drop nipples, rubbing them between my fingertips. Milani's hand glides down my stomach, then between my legs. A shock runs through me when the tips of her fingers brush my nether lips.

"Aww," Milani growls when I pinch her nipples a little too hard as her fingers enter me. I buck against them. My hands release Milani's nipples to find a place around her waist. I need her against me. I need her inside me. She fills me like a vessel that shatters when I climax. Milani takes her time unsheathing. She decides to toy with my G-spot just to see me shudder. When she finally releases me, we stretch out on top of the blankets. The cool night air breezes through my curtains, bringing with it more music from the beach. I turn on my side to face Milani. Already, goose pimples ripple her flesh. I reach out to her to graze my fingernails along her stomach, making her catch her breath.

I definitely think this will be a pleasant vacation.

ഹറ

This is the second anthology that Yuri has been blessed to join. She bides her time cubicle daydreaming and writing what she finds.

Hard to Get

Rachel Kramer Bussel

With some girls, you know the minute you meet them you're going to wind up between their thighs, your tongue coasting along their lower lips, diving deep inside, lapping up their sweet sex juices until they're almost gone, then making more. You can tell from the way they say your name, a certain lilt that makes you picture them calling it out, hoarse and breathless, during sex. You know from the sparkle that bursts from their eyes, from the shiver you get as their fingers oh-so-gently stroke your arm. Gay, straight, bi—it doesn't really matter what these girls call themselves; they give away their fuckability instantly. Once you feel that spark, that surge of heat that plummets deep inside, dropping from the catch in your throat to the pounding of your heart to the somersaults in your stomach before giving way to the heat blasting through your pussy, they're all yours and vice versa. Any obstacles in your way, be they a boyfriend or the fact that you've never even met, are nothing compared to the insistent, urgent way your whole body tingles, propelling you forward, knowing that the minute you make contact, she'll feel that magic dance like you're two magnets drawn together as naturally as the sun shines every day. Getting those girls to succumb to your charms is fun, hot even, but it's hardly a challenge.

With other girls, though, it takes longer for the magic message to work its way between you. It's like you can see it, hear it, taste it, and touch it, but for them, they're tuned to a different frequency, and your task is to make sure they hear yours so loudly it fills their head with nothing else. For me, Nikki was the second type of girl. I think I made my way through all her friends before she so much as deigned to call me by name. It was never "Angie" or even "Angela" or "A," as some of the girls called me. It was just "Hi" or "Hey" or even a nod, her eyes glassy, seeming to look anywhere but at me. She was never rude, but I got the sense that Nikki wanted to get away from me, was just waiting for me to leave so she could cut loose. I hadn't done anything to offend her, except date her friends, and run my eyes up and down her luscious curves. But beneath her hostility I knew there was a heat I had to touch, to conquer, to stroke until she exploded against my touch, melting in my arms. More than once, I called out her name as I touched myself, wishing her fingers were inside me, mine inside her, both of us wet, wailing, willing. But Nikki's the kind of girl who's worth waiting for.

One night I sat on a chair at the bar, with Tracy on my lap, her petite body fitting easily against my sturdier one, making me feel powerful beneath my men's button-down shirt and brand-new jeans, my hair shorn so only the lightest layer graced my head. I was every inch the powerful butch to her femme, one of the few black couples at the club who clung so tightly to roles many thought were over and done with. When her ass pressed backward against my crotch, I almost felt like I had a real cock between my legs, not just the one I'd put on for the night. But even as intoxicating as Tracy was, and Cara, Janet, and Nina before her, something about Nikki made her stay on my mind. Later that night, when Tracy got on her knees before me, wearing only a hot pink push-up bra and tiny day-glo pink thong panties that seemed to light up against her deep brown skin while she smoothly took the silver silicone dick between her lips, I almost called out the familiar word "Nikki," catching myself just in time. "Nice, that's nice, baby," I said.

When Tracy crawled on top of me and sank her sweet body down along the toy, pressing her curves firmly against me and giving me access to those big hard nipples right in front of my face, I gorged on them, stuffing them both into my mouth, flicking my tongue as she moaned loudly, but still wishing it were Nikki in bed with me. I wound up breaking it off with Tracy and moping around at the various gay bars, familiar haunts and newer ones on the edges of town where I could drown my sorrow in whatever the bartenders wanted to throw my way. I felt off my game, my crisp shirts losing some of their sparkle; my sharp haircut morphing into scattered, haphazard fuzz; my neat, shiny black shoes becoming scuffed. When I got home one night, I looked in the mirror. My eyes were bloodshot, and a little sad, my clothes ragged. I was no longer the butch stud I aspired to be. "Forget about her," I told myself, but I couldn't. Nikki haunted my dreams, all the more alluring for her elusiveness, for the fact that I knew almost nothing about her save that she worked for a local fashion designer, liked to dance her ass off…and wouldn't give me the time of day.

But one morning, after waking up with my pussy throbbing so badly I needed a solid thirty minutes of my most powerful vibrator pressed flush against my clit while I fucked myself with my favorite dildo, until my body shattered and shuddered and surrendered to the vibrations, I knew I had to do something. Over the past few weeks, I'd wound up confessing to the other girls what was wrong, how much I just wanted to talk to her. Okay, I wanted to do more than talk, but it was a start. They weren't any wiser than I as to what her problem was, but insisted that I just try one more time to make conversation.

With their encouragement, I felt a renewed sense of energy. I didn't merely want to get Nikki into my bed, a one-shot deal that would make things more painful if we hit it off between the sheets, never to see each other again. I was in this for the long haul, I realized, as I perked myself up, determined to show her how suave and sexy I could be. My friends told me to head over to Glitter, the hot new dyke dance night—and to dress the part. I went all out, buying a whole new wardrobe, including a black hat that I tipped across my head, my shoes shined, tight black jeans that accentuated my curvy ass and pressed against my sex just so, turning me on with every step. For contrast, I slashed some bright red lipstick across my lips, the only sign of femininity save for my breasts, and even those were more solid than curve. I like my size, the way I can stomp around with the guys, the not having to worry when I gain an ounce, the way being a butch allows me to appreciate the femmes I see around me. I can be like a guy, but not one, part boy, part girl, all me. But sometimes I like to mess with the all-macho look, to toss in something unexpected, a diamond earring or a splash of pink or a slash of lipstick, to make sure that those who pass me on the street or check me out at a bar can't be sure what to make of me. I like to keep them guessing and was hoping maybe Nikki did, too.

I didn't see Nikki there when I arrived, but I acted like I didn't mind, and soon, I didn't. You'd be amazed at what a little lipstick on a butch can do for her sex appeal. I sat at the bar and ordered a Bud, and no sooner had I laid down the bills than some sweet young thing (and I do mean young—she had to just be pushing twenty-one) sidled up to me. "Haven't seen you around here before," she observed, puckering her lips and giving me the once-over.

"Maybe you haven't been looking hard enough, sweetheart," I said, laughing the first genuine laugh I'd let myself experience in months.

I was letting myself take in the way her caramel-colored breasts pressed together temptingly, her black lace bra resting against her nipples, giving the illusion that they might pop forth at any moment, when I saw Nikki across the room. She'd gone all out, too, wearing a bright red sparkly top that ran from her left shoulder in a diagonal across her breasts, and a black latex mini-skirt that gleamed from across the room. My first thought after licking my lips, longing for a taste of those tits, was to wonder whether Nikki was wearing panties or not. I had to find out.

"Excuse me," I said before I became a cradle robber, and left the girl checking out my ass. It was time to get what I'd come for.

The more I'd lusted after Nikki, the more I'd realized that if I was going to get her, I had to take her. Well, not truly take her; if she didn't want me, I would make my peace with that. But as I went over every cold aside, every time she'd checked me out, then skittered away, and her dangerous combination of a genuine smile mixed with a "stay away" vibe, I knew what I had to do.

I marched over to her, getting right up in her business. She'd been grinding against another, equally hot, equally scantily clad girl in tall platforms and a skirt so mini I could almost see her panties.

"Nikki, I think you've had enough dancing for the night," I said, putting my hand on her sleek, latex-covered hip. She tried to push me away but I wouldn't let her, instead staring at the gold nameplate resting against her sweaty neck.

"And who are you to tell me what I've had enough of?" she snarled back, trying to push me away. I moved my hand lower, so it rested on her bare thigh, threatening to creep upward.

"Nobody. Except the woman who's gonna give you the fuck of a lifetime. Several lifetimes, actually," I said nonchalantly, as if my heart weren't pounding defiantly in my chest, roaring in my ears and trying to warn me away. "You're going to get off this dance floor and get in my car and come home with me, or else I'm going to lift you up, carry you over to that corner over there, lift that little skirt of yours and spank your ass nice and hard until it stings so good you see stars."

That got her attention. She stopped struggling and looked up at me, her glossy lips parted, as if trying to figure out what to say. Her eyes darted to the corner I'd referenced, and I tried to keep the smile off my face as I realized Nikki was pondering which would be more pleasurable, getting fucked hard in my apartment, or spanked hard in public. I had no intention of getting us kicked out of the club for some kinky PDA, but she didn't need to know that. I stepped closer, closing the gap between us, then reached my hand around to cup one ass cheek in my palm.

She shuddered, and this time didn't try to get away. I squeezed her flesh, watching this ultra-tough chick melt before me. Her surrender bolstered my confidence. I played with the edge of her panties, my fingers darting underneath, teasing the elastic as the rest of the dance floor ceased to exist. Then just when she thought I was going to plunge inside, I pulled my hand out, resting my warm fingers on her arm. "Ready?"

"Damn you," she uttered under her breath, unable to keep the hint of a smile from edging her lips upward. "I've been trying to stay away from you, Angie. I don't want to be just another girl in your stable, someone you hook up with, then discard and move on to the next pretty chick to cross your path. You're too good for all that but you don't even see it, like you need to be some big bad black butch stud to prove yourself." She spit the words out defiantly, her wrist shaking and moving my arm with it, but she wasn't really trying to get away. Her face lit up as she talked, and I wondered again about her panties.

"Nikki, Nikki, Nikki…what is wrong with you, girl? I've been dreaming about you since day one."

"No you haven't," she said, her words bratty and sharp, her face pausing to consider whether I might, just might, be right. I didn't want to argue with her, especially since all this time, it seemed our differences had been imaginary ones.

I leaned close to her. "Okay, have it your way. But I'm ready to make up for lost time, even though I still insist you were the one playing hard to get."

She moved closer still, so her breasts were pressed right up against mine, her chest pounding as she looked directly into my face before snaking her hand down between our bodies to fondle my cock. "We'll see about hard," she said, her voice lilting, a foreign but welcome sound.

She toyed with the dildo until I couldn't stand it anymore, and grabbed both her wrists, grateful for the daily workouts I'd logged in the last year. She whimpered as soon as my fingers closed around her skin, trapping her.

"Turn around, Nikki, and show me that cute little bottom of yours, the one I'm going to take across my lap and spank very soon."

Her shudder was visible, her body undulating like a belly dancer for just a moment before she started marching. The stiff, shiny latex sheathed her ass, hinting at what lay beneath, but still leaving a little to my imagination. I followed, my mouth going dry as I realized I was finally going to have the object of my affection in my bed.

In the back of my mind, as confident as I'd tried to be, part of me had thought Nikki was a lost cause, that whatever I'd done, real or imagined, I couldn't undo. So to have her slip so easily into place before me was surreal, yet so right. She stopped outside the club's door, unsure where to turn, and I tucked my hand under the waistband of her skirt, my knuckles pressing against the small of her back.

"I'll guide you," I said, and felt her melt against me.

That moment, when a woman lets her body sink just so into my arms, lets me lead her, lets me control the dance we're about to do, is the one I live for. It puffs me up more than any cock or shirt or "sir" will ever do. It lets me know she trusts me enough to take care of her, to turn her pleasure into our pleasure.

I steered Nikki toward my car, but as I fumbled for the key, I realized I couldn't wait. Not now, not after so long. I reached around her, unlocked the passenger door, then did the same for the backseat.

"Get in," I said, pushing her in that direction. "You'll be fine," I told her, reading the question in her eyes.

I wasn't about to let anyone catch us. I got in behind her and shut the door, knowing we were far enough away not to draw the bouncer's attention, and if any clubgoers should see us, well, we'd probably make their night.

I settled into the middle of the seat, then spread my precious prize across my lap. Nikki wiggled against me, pressing against the dick and making my nipples hard. "Lift up your skirt for me, Nikki, and ask me to spank you," I told her, trying to keep the trembling out of my voice.

It must have worked, because she reached behind her and pulled up her skirt, the act infinitely more erotic than if I'd done so myself. I needed to see and feel Nikki give herself to me, to freely offer her body, giving it as smoothly as she'd withheld it.

"Please, Angie, I want you to spank me. I *need* you to spank my ass for being such a brat all this time."

I wasn't expecting that last bit, and when Nikki buried her face in my knee, smearing her lipstick against the denim, breathing hot and hard through the fabric, I let loose. My hand crashed down upon the perfect apple curve of her bare brown cheek. Oh, yes, I'd been right—the girl had gone out without any panties to protect her pussy, or her ass. Now, both were exposed to me and I savored the view, raining blow after blow against her sweet curves.

"You like that, don't you, Nikki?" I asked, bringing my voice deep and low for the ending as I punctuated my words with solid smacks as her breath hissed, then stuttered, then seemed to stop altogether as I slammed my palm against her hot skin. I gave her a pinch, already feeling the urgent throbbing of her sex. "You're not going to answer me, Nikki?"

"Yes, yes, I like it," she said, then shuddered as my fingers dove into her sex without preamble. I plunged in as deep as I could, feeling a corresponding spasm from her cunt. "Oh yeah," she mumbled softly as I teased her tender wetness, feeling her walls give against my touch.

My own private parts were starting to ache, and I eased myself off of her to kneel between her legs. I was pretending we weren't in a car in a fairly crowded parking lot; that's how bad I had it for her, I literally couldn't wait. "I'm going to fuck you now, Nikki, so hard you'll forget about every other girl who's come before me. I'm gonna fuck you until you forget everything except my name." The words just flowed from my mouth, with none of the practiced toughness I'd sometimes had to muster with other girls. No, she brought out that side of me that's pure animal, raw and needy and hoarse with want. The part where words don't matter; just actions.

I ripped open the buttons of my jeans and out came my secret weapon, the extra-large dick that I only pack when I plan to fuck a girl until the earth really does move, until I feel like all of me is inside her, until I feel like she is inside me too, our bodies merging so well we trade souls; even if just for a moment. I rubbed the head of the cock against her sex, lubing it with her juices, and she bucked against me.

"Wait for me," I admonished softly as I pushed my way in, and then we didn't speak. We didn't need to. Nikki and I had said all we'd need to say, and now were in some other world, where it was just my cock, her pussy, our hot breath steaming the windows.

I pushed deep into her, resting my weight on her body, my hands slipping beneath her to pinch her hard nipples. I kissed her back, nudging the shirt up with my nose to rest against her bare, sweaty skin, as the toy plunged in and out, seeking out her secrets, offering some of its own. My cock told her how to reach me, how to find that spot where I surrender as well, where it hits my clit and the thrill boomerangs back into me. We seesawed like that, shifting the pleasure, the ache, the bolts of desire as she arched her ass upward, giving and taking equally.

"Oh Angie," she cried out when I twisted her sweet pebbles fiercely, tuning her nipples to my favorite frequency, harder and harder as I slammed in and out, my motions so fast I barely knew where she ended and I began. Hearing her say my name catapulted me out of the car, doing a freefall as I came, bucking in and out of her all the while. I bit her back gently, needing to hold onto her in every way I could, as Nikki too succumbed to her climax, blubbering gibberish as she shook.

We couldn't get up for a while, and when we finally did, it felt surreal to pull my clothes back on, to see the dazed look on her face, like we'd both just awoken from a dream.

"Did that really happen?" she asked, her fingertips tracing my swollen lips, then my cheek.

"I think so. But let's go back to my place and try it again just to be sure."

෨෬

Rachel Kramer Bussel (www.rachelkramerbussel.com) has edited over twenty erotic anthologies, including Glamour Girls: Femme/Femme Erotica, First-Timers: True Stories of Lesbian Awakening, Up All Night: Adventures in Lesbian Sex, Yes, Sir, Yes, Ma'am, He's on Top, She's on Top, Caught Looking, Hide and Seek, Crossdressing, Sex and Candy, Rubber Sex, Spanked: Red-Cheeked Erotica, Naughty Spanking Stories from A to Z 1 *and* 2, *and the non-fiction* Best Sex Writing 2008. *Her work has been published in over 100 anthologies, including* Best American Erotica 2004 *and* 2006, Chocolate Flava 2, Everything You Know About Sex Is Wrong, Single State of the Union *and* Desire: Women Write About Wanting. *She hosts "In The Flesh Erotic Reading Series," is Senior Editor at* Penthouse Variations, *wrote the popular "Lusty Lady" column for* The Village Voice, *and has contributed to* AVN, Bust, Diva, Fresh Yarn, Gothamist, Huffington Post, Mediabistro, Newsday, New York Post, San Francisco Chronicle, Time Out New York, *and* Zink. *In her spare time, she blogs about cupcakes at cupcakestakthecake.blogspot.com.*

The Purple Panty Revue
Claudia Moss

J ay stood in a pool of Atlanta sunshine in the back bedroom on the third floor of her downtown, Chamberlain Street loft. She gazed out across the courtyard below. In silence, she took in what was left of a tranquil Saturday in March and stared at everything and nothing in particular. Her scrutiny skimmed the courtyard's centerpiece of bricked shrubbery. Then it winged the wrought-iron separating her complex from the community's sauntering residents, who promenaded the city in a drug-induced splendor. Whenever they took a notion to dream, they stopped and gazed through iron at high-end vehicles and Jay's '07 Mercedes sports car. Beyond this protected enclave, in the distance, a field, in which some of the sauntering found peace, submitted its peppered face of bottles and debris to the heavens.

She knew there was potential in the scene, despite the poor condition of the existing buildings. In part, she already saw the ones not yet built. A dreamer, she speculated what they might be next month or next year since she'd bowed to her intention to invest in this community. For now, though, what she studied on the right made up Edgewood Avenue, with its string of abandoned shops, small clothing stores, and beauty parlors; on the left, it was Chamberlain Street, home of Chamberlain Apartments, a project some city developers in high-rise offices still hadn't quite figured how to erase.

Jay Morrison was a mover and big-money shaker in her own right, in privy circles. Around the way, she was known simply as "the sistah who had her shit together."

But the sistah was in a blue mood right now. Little had gone as she'd anticipated in a developer's meeting that afternoon: it yet amazed her how nobody of color with any real money desired to invest a tad of it in the community. The revelation accounted for her presence in her loft's back windows.

In truth, in these windows, the longer she stood, the more Jay felt blessed. By her calculations—something she was damn good at, had faith in, particularly when it came to growing dollars and scents from nothing—her mind expanded when she looked out on her block. A magical space, answers to every question she posed floated into her corporate locs when she stood where she was now, pondering…

Hmmmmm. But wait.

Jay cocked her head to one side and raised a rakish brow. That was a first. Did the floral curtains in the third-floor window in the loft directly across from hers really inhale the sweet start of spring and exhale a glimpse of an exquisite ass? She could have sworn the loft had been empty a week ago. As far as she knew, nobody had walked through the place in five months.

A green mini bus on its way up Chamberlain sliced noisily into Jay's thoughts. The sound directed her attention to a man "potty-ing" his rat terrier on a fenced-in lawn. Funny. The image clashed with the sight of two other men, dirty and singing, using one another as crutches, as they stumbled to the corner.

Jay sighed and returned an inquisitive eye to the peek-a-boo window, and it was a good thing she did. This time the curtains pooh-poohed with certainty, causing Jay to press her nose against startled glass. *There it was for sure*. A wide, voluptuous, shapely one. A walnut-hued delight in purple panties, thank you. An ass that didn't appear to favor bouncing or climbing poles or gyrating like island beauties.

No, ma'am. Jay was well acquainted with those other kinds of behinds. "Naw, this one," she calculated, grinning, like the magic room had already spread the delectable woman across her platform bed, those purple panties tossed high on one of its four posts, "no, this one did something else. This one simply strolled." The strange part was, she hadn't seen the woman's face, and a pretty face with pussy lips always lit Jay's auto pilot. Yet, this woman could look like whatever. Jay didn't care. In that instance, she realized why she'd been standing there, dreaming, thinking. Her neighbor's pretty ass had to do what it did, capture her, but the lady's mysterious persona would do what it must, keep her.

Evening fell as supple as silk while Jay stared. When fireflies twinkled and crickets sang, the lady's loft dimmed to candlelight. There was no call for desperation. Jay knew her potential. The last time she'd checked, wherever she appeared, looking as tantalizing as the last treat in a box of Lady Godiva chocolates, women—some gay, some straight, (it didn't matter) declared, word had it, that Jay Morrison was The "She-Can-Get-It" Woman. Thus, armed with such confidence, Jay descended the stairs to her kitchen and leftover Chinese take-out. Her mind savored a new intention: to have her mysterious neighbor in every way she could have a woman.

Two weeks later, Jay posted up against the window in her back room, again, but this time, music drew her there. Big band music. Josephine Baker in a banana skirt and no-bra music. Hypnotic, it was the sort of music that conjured images of glossy stages and rows of leggy, dancing angels in flamboyant feathers and skimpy costumes, kicking up their heels and flashing yards of endless thighs. For once, Jay scanned her usual surroundings and never registered a thing outside of her new neighbor's, her next woman's, third-floor window. All investments were put on the back burner, for Jay hadn't seen a flicker of life in the loft for days.

"A traveler," Jay speculated. "Cool."

Distracted by that beautiful butt, on Monday evening, she lay on the room's bed and snaked one hand into her pants. Damn. She felt good masturbating, releasing. No lady and work dominating her days, she ached for some good loving, every fiber in her hollering for punany: its spice, its flavor, its juice. She closed her eyes and imagined those purple panties strapped to her nose. Breathing in their fragrance, she prayed their owner boasted a face with a pair of the prettiest pussy lips she'd ever seen. Pussy lips that left her on her knees, begging to lick and kiss, suck and nibble, same as she got stuck between a woman's thighs, mesmerized by her other pair of pretty lips.

She dreamed herself straight into Wednesday, the day those curtains waved to her on a gusty evening breeze. In a rush, she lifted the back closet window and filled her lungs with the beginning of April and snapshots of the strolling beauty just beyond the floral curtains. Shoot! Jay had a mind to—fuck it—show up at the woman's door with a housewarming gift, perfume, and a dinner proposition the sistah couldn't refuse. As Jay stood there, strategizing, she heard it again. That music. She listened spellbound, an addict hooked on the next glimpse of mind-altering ass. The compelling melodies transported her back, decades back. By the time the CD changer reached its final cut, Jay had made up her mind. She ripped herself from the glass and headed for the shower. A half-hour and her sports car was dodging Boulevard's craters and traffic-defying teenagers to pull into a parking spot steps away from Best Buy's electronic double doors.

In the CD section, a cute, turbaned woman leaned on the ordered counter. Rajima was stenciled in black on her name tag, a sensuous smile stenciled in pink on her lips.

"May I help you?"

"Hey, baby." Jay mirrored her enthusiasm. "I'm in a hurry. Do you have Ella Fitzgerald and Louis Armstrong's 1957 rendition of *Porgy and Bess*? If not, bring everything you have by them, separate or together. Please."

"Yes, ma'am," Rajima purred, rounding the counter to gracefully take Jay in fully, before walking away, her hips swaying under a long summer skirt.

Jay grinned. Sexy-ass women. They kept her nerve endings racing. She shifted her attention to a basket of discount CDs, but none whet her curiosity. Leaning against the counter, she panned the store's wares and wondered how long her mystery woman would be in town, wondered if she should leave her a love note, candy, an airline ticket.

"This is everything we've got." Rajima spread a handful of CD cases across the counter and rang her total. "Is there anything else you'd like?"

Jay slowly considered her offerings. "Huh, not now. Thank you."

"Whenever," Rajima promised, accepting Jay's three C-notes, her stare fierce, tongue glossing her bottom lip. Jay nodded, advised her to keep the change and departed the store in long, determined strides.

No music. No lights.

Only stillness, when she returned.

Jay felt powerless for a moment, standing in her open garage, a thing she rarely did, gazing up at an obviously empty loft and emptier sky. "Hell, maybe that's her crash pad," she rationalized. "Won't sweat it," she encouraged herself, utilizing her investment savvy. "I am patience personified. She belongs to me."

Miss Purple Panties failed to sashay those jaw-dropping hips past the still fabric of her curtains for what must have been an eternity and one more weekend. In her absence, Jay's faith wavered and cut the absolute fool, filling her mind with doubt. Under it, she almost passed out; her longing and the ache in her pussy heavy, intense. So, until muted lights burned an amber haze in her loft once more, Jay ended up licking the view from across the courtyard's bricked blooms with eyes meant for, at the least, fucking...or prayerfully...if she could hold a joyous image long enough... for making love to a woman who rattled her without one hello.

Jay's dog, Valentino Starr, lay in on her doorbell one Friday night, like a drunk without a bottle. Behind her, Jackson Street joined in with its late-April night music.

In Valentino's pockets were tickets for a different type of Saturday-night entertainment. It was no secret her gyrl had been working serious overtime hours in an effort to bring new horizons and renewed dreams to the strolling disenfranchised under her loft windows. And that alone, Valentino knew, deserved appreciation, being she rarely thought of streetfolk, unless it was to remember to lock her car doors or keep loose bills handy—what with her demanding wife and life.

"Just don't keep a sistah waiting," she'd forewarned Jay just last night. Despite that, here she was, waiting for those second-floor curtains to part so she could cuss.

"Glad I didn't invite Justina," Valentino muttered to herself and doubled-checked her watch. Knowing her wife, she'd have waited five minutes then politely stuck Jay's ticket under the welcome mat.

Just as she decided to execute the thought, Jay drove up to the curb, the Mercedes spotless, and flung open the car's passenger door. "Get in, my niggah!"

She smelled expensive, like she looked.

"Don't play, dude. You still late," Valentino growled, but she had to give it to her—her friend was the cat's meow. "In New York, the N-word is illegal, kinda like the L-word everywhere else." The analogy broke her up.

Jay smirked and gave Valentino the finger, frowning. "Shut up and close that door. Look, man, where we off to anyway?"

Valentino cracked up again, relieved she didn't have to drive herself, or worse, attempt to unload last-minute tickets on a street where most intoxicated night strollers couldn't spell burlesque, had no money, or thought only dresses and ribbons were velvet.

The Velvet Room was upscale, noisy and filled with some of the finest women Jay had ever prayed would be in one location. Alluring, they were everywhere. Even outside the club's Peachtree front, in black tuxedos, valet parking a queue of fabulous cars.

"For whatever this is," Jay whispered to Valentino inside the establishment's lavish, darkened interior, "I'm damn sure down."

Valentino winked. "Something told me you would be." Her eyes sparkled with excitement. "Lately, you've been wrapped tight enough to hurt yourself, fucking with that crew you do business with. Learn to relax and let live."

"Ooh, believe me, I'm life's number one fan, my man." She steepled her fingers and sank low in her seat.

"I'm bringing my baby back next time."

"Better ask first. You know Justina."

The floodlights on, the butch on Valentino's right coughed, cut them a reprimanding stare, and draped one arm around her lady's freckled shoulders.

Valentino nodded, then looked at Jay and rolled her eyes. "Did you consider the program's name?"

"Naw." Jay squinted at the ticket stub and nearly laughed out loud. "A burlesque show? As long as cute women are center stage, I'm good."

After velvet curtains swept the stage at the end of Miss Va Va Voom's first number sans all but brilliant purple pasties covering each of her succulent nipples and a few inches of glittery something or other atop a well-shaved coochie, The Purple Panty Revue commenced with Las Vegas-style pomp and pageantry. Indeed, Jay was more than good; she was mesmerized. She hadn't been surrounded by that many half-naked women since she and some of her dogs had made it rain on the beautiful, wiggling, locking, dropping dancers in Strokers and Magic City.

Of all the attractive women strolling the stage in one exciting burlesque act after another, in skimpy, shimmering costumes and shiny dancing shoes and huge feathery headdresses, none made her grit her teeth and sit ramrod straight like the one with the wide, walnut, wonderful ass that strolled sensually, with a downright provocative sway, similar to the one behind the curtains of the loft across her courtyard. Jay's next breath suddenly lodged somewhere between her chest and throat.

She elbowed Valentino sharply.

"Miss Va Va is my neighbor!"

Valentino smirked. "Stop trippin', man. You might want her to be yo' neighbor, but she isn't. Besides, why you think that's her? You can't see the sistah's face. Damn!" She laughed teasingly, cutting a glance in the direction of the butch on noise patrol. "You hallucinating?"

"Not this time." Undaunted, Jay planted her elbows on her knees and fixed her entire being on the thick sistah in shimmering purple panties, obviously the star, although every woman in the revue wore panties of a similar hue and style each time she graced the stage.

At intermission, Jay had seen enough. She had to move, get up, and do something. Excusing herself, she found the restrooms and stood in line a good ten minutes before entering the crowded, artful space with its colorful sitting area décor and classy, comfortable furnishings. Handling her business, she washed her hands and pulled open the door to confront a pair of lips so kissable, so succulent, and so juicy, it had to be magic. The seat of her boxers moistened. Instantly. Dampened as abruptly as, "O shit!" escaped her lips. They weren't simply pussy lips; no, they were the prettiest perfect pussy lips she'd ever beheld.

What could she do but bow? Holding the door for the manifestation of her wet dreams, she watched the magnificent hips she knew by heart glide into the restroom. Other women gawked, though not long.

Jay emptied the room effortlessly. Her entire body communicated clearly what was on her mind.

Attraction in the star's brown eyes assured Jay that whatever she wanted, surely, she could have. And Jay, consenting, quietly locked the door behind them. The verdict was unanimous: she and life were one.

Jay reached out for the dancer's hand and guided her to a commodious blue sofa, where she placed them on silent mode, mere words useless now. A gentlewoman, she maneuvered the elaborate costume so as not to damage it before sitting down.

Leaning into the beautiful face, Jay discovered she couldn't *not* start with those lips. They magnetized her. And she kissed them so delicately it took her breath. The stunning woman's eyelashes fanned her cheekbones while her hands slipped into Jay's locs, her fingertips inching deep, deeper, the heat they generated causing a jackhammer throb in Jay's clit.

Instinctively, Jay anchored her body by gripping the walnut-colored waist, her touch sending currents of desire through them both. The burlesque star's smoldering stare met Jay's half-lidded gaze and saw it all: the butch's mouth twitch, her passion, her drought, her soul.

Pretty pussy lips pouted. Murmured what could have been Jay's name. The utterance released Jay enough to taste her. The neck. The bejeweled earlobes. Jay's lips sucked lightly, not to leave hickies across the fragrant shoulders. Out of need, her hands followed her lips. Under such masterful kisses, the dancer's tantalizing thighs shook, and then parted. Red Sea wide. Jay's hands floated to them. They were toned. And sculpted. Undulating, the beauty draped one exquisite thigh across Jay's dark slacks, as her tongue sought Jay's right ear and danced a fiery tango there, deadlocking Jay's fingers. Momentarily suspended, they wagered whether to head north or south, every moment essential.

Jay's mouth, though, was more decisive. It slowly kissed around the dancer's purple, pasty-covered nipples. Jay pinched them to see her wince, shudder. The beauty's lids fluttered when Jay's palms cradled her breasts before returning to her silky, naked legs. The woman tasted so deliriously divine. Juicy. Jay had to see, to sample her cunt now, contrary to her usual custom.

She eased the dancer backward on the sofa, pillows at her back, and kissed a string of desire down her body. The burlesque beauty's lips parted. A moan escaped the soft mouth. Her ass hunched forward, thighs agape. Again, her hands entered Jay's locs, directing tender kisses to her inner thighs. Her satiny flesh smelled good, fruity. The dancer melted when Jay mined the fabric between her legs to devour the tangiest, the juiciest cunt she'd relished in a long, dry season. Her lover trembled. Shuddered. Clinched. And sighed.

Jay's right thumb swirled over the dancer's sensitive nubbin, and then skated down nectar-slick labia lips, plump and full, before two fingers plunged into pure honey. The creamy pussy swallowed more fingers, then a hand. Jay lay supine in sticky, grade-A nectar, moaning and pumping and kissing. Right then, Jay longed to awake to the gift of this woman's presence every day of her life.

"Aaaah. Oooo, yes, baby. Kiss me. I love it, darling. I feel you everywhere."

By way of answer, Jay's teeth lightly nipped the now trembling thighs. Her strong fingers slowed, and then took charge of the performer's pussy again, appearing and disappearing, fucking her into paradise. That amazing ass bucked and thrashed against the sofa. Heels draping Jay's shoulders, sometimes daintily, at others flexing high above her head, on pussy-perfumed air.

When her screams finally erupted, Jay slowly withdrew. She rose and dampened several expensive napkins and gingerly wiped the scent of cum from the dancer's body. The burlesque beauty lay still and spent while Jay kissed her mouth and hands. She whispered how beautiful she was before deftly readjusting her costume and memorizing her magnificent climax.

"I knew you'd come. Question was, when?"

Jay stretched her six-foot-one frame atop the dancer's body.

"I knew you'd cum, too. Just not here."

The woman's laughter floated into Jay's back-grazing locs.

Delightfully similar, her pent-up natural hair tickled Jay's nose and cheeks. She loved the girlish joy beckoning her closer behind the grown-woman glamour. Sweet and playful, it clashed with Jay's urgency to experience her again, but Jay ignored it, their verbal exchange captivating.

"Thank you for the CDs. I've wanted them forever. Now my collection's complete."

Jay's chin lifted in that sexy way of hers. "I'm Porgy to your Bess."

The beauty's laughter filled the bathroom air with the tinkle of magic. "Oh now that's original, although I hoped you would be."

A female voice soaked in authority bumped up against Jay's suave, "You're welcome."

"Delilah, your bathroom break is up, darling! You may be the star of this revue, but you've got less than fifteen minutes!"

Delilah's pout and eye rolling sent Jay careening into a slow burn. If the night's promise wasn't so fulfilling, she might have hollered to the voice to get herself another star because this one was hers now. Instead, she got, pulled into the goddess's easy flow.

"Gotta go, sweety. One thing, though. I will tell you how charming you look when you're caught up, studying me from your back windows."

"Oh. You noticed?"

"Of course. I like your style, not too flashy, more businesslike. You're about positive things for the community." She paused. "Was thinking, maybe, possibly, we could, with my creativity and your business acumen, be the change our folks need."

"Sounds foolproof to me."

"Good. I'm Delilah, Jay Morrison."

"I know. You're good. *Damn good*."

"Thanks. So are you. May I come over later, after the show, so we can finish what we started here? I give as well as I receive."

To that boon, Jay bit her bottom lip and flashed her cockiest grin. Grateful for their meeting, she rose, offered Delilah her hand, and pulling her to her feet, softly kissed her before embracing Delilah close enough to synchronize their heartbeats. Blessed, she unlocked the door and watched her woman float backstage.

Jay headed back to Valentino, whom she had to thank for investing in burlesque tickets that had already begun to change her life.

ℰᗝᏻ

Claudia Moss lives and writes in Atlanta, GA. The author of Dolly: the Memoirs of a High School Graduate, *her fiction has been published in* Longing, Lust, and Love: Black Lesbian Stories, the Hoot and Holler of the Owl, Catalyst, Labrys, Black Romance, Jive, Venus, *and* Black Issues Book Review *magazine.*

Uma

Sydney Molaré

The patter of small feet, then, "Uma, thuck."

My body tensed at the sound.

"Thuck, now!" The high-pitched little voice now stressed with need.

"All right." Female.

A chair was pulled out. I knew what came next.

I lifted from lounging on the sofa, moved quietly over the Berber carpet to stand next to the door unseen. My stomach flip-flopped, uterus clenched, palms wet.

A zipper being pulled.

Rustling of clothes as she pulled him onto her lap.

The wet sounds of suckling.

I peeked around the door, already knowing what I would see as this scene had been repeated six or seven times daily for the past two years. Uma sat in the chair, shirt flapping open, one nipple in Thor's mouth, his hand massaging the other breast.

I almost came right there as I stared at the exposed breast—large as a balloon, dark brown saucer-sized nipples with purple veins running across it. Thor's head bobbed, mouth smacked around the aureole. My head spun as a drop of milk leaked from the unfettered nipple. My glands salivated. I gulped.

Uma must have heard the sound. She turned her head slowly toward me, meeting my eyes. A slight grin slid onto her lips. I was rooted to the spot, watching Thor, wanting to trade places with him if only for a moment. My pussy gushed as he unlatched, claimed the other nipple, cheeks sunken as he swallowed the liquid sustenance hungrily. His hand lay across the just milked tit, rubbed and squeezed involuntarily, occasionally pulling the distended center.

The garage door opened. Uma shifted, pulled her shirt over the free breast, turned her eyes away just as my husband, Darryl, walked in.

"I see my boy is still keeping you busy, Uma." I heard him sit his briefcase down before opening the refrigerator.

I moved back to the couch, tried to appear composed but I was anything but. My pussy was slippery; my nipples saluting like two popped eyes on my chest.

"Hey, babe."

Darryl leaned to kiss my cheek. Instead, I turned into the kiss, allowed my lips to clamp onto to his as my tongue dipped between his teeth, plundering, coating his mouth with my copious saliva. He was caught off-guard, even more so when I pushed him against the wall, swirling and twirling my mouth organ in a frenetic dance.

"I want you to fuck me now," I whispered before I nipped his earlobe.

"But Thor and Uma are—"

"—keeping each other occupied." I lifted, stared into his eyes. "Please, fuck me right now. I need you in me," I pleaded.

He led the way to the bedroom. Before the door closed, I'd ripped his shirt open and was making good headway on his pants.

"Damn, you are a tiger today. What's gotten into you?"

Uma.

I felt his eyes on me but said nothing as I pulled his fast-stiffening cock from his BVDs. Panties were dropped to the floor before I turned, flipped the skirt over my ass, leaned over the bed. I pulled my slick pussy lips wide, showing the pink.

Darryl inhaled sharply, then a cock was knocking at the door. I moaned as he slipped inside my lubricated walls, sighed as I felt his bush on my ass. I unhinged; pistoned on his cock like well-oiled machinery in my need. I fingered my clit and in seconds, my entire body locked as tingles zipped up my calves, across my thighs and exploded between my clit and pussy. Darryl hiccupped, and said "Oh, damn," before joining me somewhere over our private rainbow.

ഇരു

Uma.

She was hired almost immediately after Thor's birth. Really. My husband was very old-fashioned about some things and the nourishment of Thor was one of them. No formula for his boy. Titty milk is what he wanted and expected.

Oh, I tried. I had great hope when my 32 AA's swelled to 32 C's with my pregnancy. And after the birth, when I saw the first glistening of colostrums, I was more than prepared to nurse my new son. Didn't happen. He'd gummed me for no longer than a minute, then turned to the ceiling screaming. I shifted him to the other slightly leaking breast. Same result.

"Let's try the breast pump," the kind nurse suggested.

I relaxed as the plastic tube was fitted over my nipple and the plunger pulled backwards. What little breast tissue I had was sucked into the contraption. It was a bit painful, but so what? My baby needed milk. After ten minutes of suctioning, I was sick to see less than a tablespoon of milk had been retrieved and not a drop more followed.

My baby spit out the pacifier and was now screaming to the heavens again. I cried along with him. The nurse slid a warm soy-milk filled bottle into my hands and sat Thor back in my lap. I looked at it in horror.

"My husband…he doesn't like formula," I said through my tears, hoping that she'd somehow understand what *sin* I was committing even holding the bottle.

The nurse nodded and patted my hands. "Might not, but I don't like hungry babies either. Feed."

"He'll be upset."

She leaned down to my eye level. "Then you both need to come up with a solution before this baby starves to death." She pushed the hand holding the bottle toward Thor's squalling mouth. "Feed."

Thor hungrily sucked the milk into his stomach as my stomach swirled waiting for Darryl.

As I imagined, Darryl had foamed at the mouth, accusations on the tip of his tongue as he listened to the nurse explain that I was dry. Agalactia, she called it. After she left, he turned disappointed eyes on me. "I'll fix this," he'd said through clenched teeth, eyes drifting down in disdain to my useless mammary glands, before stomping through the door.

And he did.

Uma was waiting for us as we arrived home from the hospital. I was taken aback at the short, brown woman, wide of hips, with a thick waist, breasts jutting from her chest rivaling the best pro-ducing Jersey's udder, helping us from the car.

My mouth dropped. Where in the hell had Darryl found a nurse-maid? It was 2007, not 1807! Darryl explained that Uma had just delivered a stillborn child, was single, alone, and needed a job. And according to him, Uma had told him it was the easiest money she'd ever earn.

All I know is, at Thor's first squall, she'd opened her shirt, positioned his lips and that was that—the beginning of the unraveling of my well-ordered life.

ഌരു

I stared into the darkness, restless, unable to sleep in the wee hours when I heard Thor's, "Uma, thuck." A flash sweat coated my skin. The covers were slowly shifted from my body and, millimeter by millimeter, I rolled out of the bed, and tiptoed to Uma's bedroom door.

From the nightlight in her room—placed there for Thor—I could see him already nestled in the crook of her arm. Slurps and smacks reached my ears, telling me he was already suckling. My pussy juice factory revved to life; sent backup hormone to my now throbbing clit.

I was jealous and turned on. I'd once asked Uma how she felt when Thor was sucking. "Like breathing. It's as natural as breathing," she'd answered. Watching them, I believed her.

I listened until I couldn't stand it any longer. I tipped back to my bedroom, eased into the bed and ran heated hands over Darryl's belly, licked his neck.

"Quit." He swatted at my hand in his underwear. "I'm tired." And rolled over, pulling the covers tightly to his body.

That's my line.

I stared at his handsome features, sexual tension making me bold. I tried to slide my hand between his waist and elbow and was met with a not so pleasant squeeze of my fingers. "Stop it. I've got a big meeting in the morning and I've got to get my sleep."

Rebuffed, I sat back, continued to stare at the back of his head. No, I tried to will him to fuck me by employing my never-before-used telepathic powers until I heard his snores. I looked down at my chest. It was flat as a pubescent boy's with two stiff points relieving it. I cupped the bullets, pulled at the center, wishing for the thousandth time I'd been the lucky chick whose boob cup had runneth over. Resigned to not getting any cock, I let my fingers slide into my panties, imprinted Uma's orbs on my mind, while I mashed and stroked my clit until my eyeballs rolled inside my head as the powerful orgasm fried my brain cells.

୫୦୧୪

Another day, another episode of hide-and-peek for me. But the solution to my problem had finally come in my post-orgasmic high: Uma had to go.

I'd broached the subject tentatively earlier this morning. I'd suggested to Darryl that we wean Thor from Uma. My thirst for the taboo grew daily and I was valiantly trying to hold onto the tenuous thread, the last remnant of my sanity. Besides, Thor was two and had ten teeth to boot. It was time.

Darryl gave me a lazy, irritated look, continuing to pull his tie around his collar before he spoke. "Why would we do that? Hell, Thor is bigger than any other two-year-old we know, he never gets colds, so what harm can it do?"

"It's time," I repeated again, jaw tight from the effort to not scream the words at him.

"Naw. I could see if he was five and going to pre-K or something and had to be weaned, but otherwise, I say let him continue to nurse and we'll revisit this again when he turns three."

Seven whole months away! Who knew what compartment of Hell I would have secured for my soul in that time?

He gave me the perfunctory marital kiss before heading out the door. The topic was finished as far as he was concerned.

Now, I sat tense as a cornered cat, waiting for Thor's little feet and voice. I didn't have to wait long. It was less than a half hour before he shuffled down the hallway, rubbing sleepy eyes. He glanced my way and I motioned him over for a hug. Baby stink breath floated up my nose as I clutched him to my flat chest, wanting his hands to seek my comfort; need *me*. After a quick tickle session, he wriggled from my lap in search of what he truly wanted.

"Uma, thuck."

I slunk behind the doorway and positioned myself just so. I knew Uma was well aware I watched them, yet I needed to deny this urge, this thirst which had rapidly magnified into a fetish. I slid my eyes around the door jam and stopped. Today, Uma sat facing me; waiting for me. I stood enthralled as Thor patted her hand as she unzipped her shirt slowly, eyes never leaving mine.

There was no bra.

I squeezed my thighs together as the huge globes spilled into view. Uma lifted the mountainous tissue to meet Thor's darting tongue and he dipped his head, mouth covering the center of the dark circle. My womb squeezed and released. Milk pooled and ran rivulets down her breast before dripping onto the floor. My nipples blossomed, chest constricted on my lungs. I felt dizzy, the air too dense to breath.

Uma's cat grin greeted me as I composed myself. Her hand held the free orb, and as I watched, she expressed milk. The beads of white moved me to my soul. My tongue unconsciously flicked out of my mouth, sensing the air; preparing for the offered forbidden feast.

"Ow!" Uma's yelped broke me from my trance. "You bit me!"

She had rescued the injured nipple and I could see the indentations of Thor's teeth from where I stood. I winced for her.

Uma slid him from her lap, half-fed, and said, "Why don't you go watch *Power Rangers*?"

Thor's little head nodded. Uma patted him on the bottom and he trotted away, legs churning as he headed toward the den on the other side of the house. I followed in his wake, wanting to make sure his television experience was all it should be. Once I'd slid the DVD in and modulated the volume, I retraced my steps back to the kitchen.

Uma stood by the sink, water running, band aids and triple antibiotic ointment on the counter beside her. She turned as I entered. My eyes immediately fell to the objects of my obsession—one slightly deflated, the other appeared swollen enough to burst if so much as pricked with a pin.

"That must hurt," I managed to eke out.

"Yes, it does." She nodded. "Since your little man got teeth, it's happening more and more often. Soon, I'll have to wean him. Ouch!" Uma cried out as she pressed the wet paper towel over her injured flesh.

I was by her side in a moment. "Let me see."

Suddenly, I was up-close-and-personal with her right nipple. I stared at the landscape of puckered flesh, engorged purple-green veins with the hint of red arteries beside them running across her chest, making the breast throb, lift less than a foot from my face... and mouth. I heard nothing but my heart thudding, pussy weeping, as I pressed shaking fingertips around the mini-craters created by Thor. No blood was evident, but from Uma's reaction, I'd expected some.

"Would you rub some of that ointment on that area where he bit me?" Uma said, voice low and, in my mind, seductive.

I should have straightened up, left her to tend to her own injury, sat my ass back on the couch and returned to the Land of Boredom. Instead, I watched as my arm extended itself, hands grabbed the tube of triple antibiotic and squeezed an inch or two of the thick ointment onto my index finger. Tentatively, oh so tentatively, I dabbed at the offended nipple. Uma moaned a bit in the back of her throat. I rubbed around and around the unfamiliar skin, memorizing each bump, ridge, smooth expanse beneath my fingers.

Our eyes met. Uma's were glazed but the message was direct: suck, now. She lifted the unsucked globe, held it outward, egging me on. I took a deep, ragged breath as the denizen from Hell cut the string holding my willpower intact, and moved my opened mouth forward. Milk spurted as I sucked inward—nectar from the gods.

All bets were off! My hands cupped, held the poundage, mouth unhinged as I tried to stuff as much of her tit as possible into my mouth. My head rotated, teeth nipped lightly on the nipple as the watery manna warmed my stomach. I was further energized when Uma squeezed, caused the milk to spray the back of my throat.

"Wait." Uma pushed me backward, grabbed my hand and pulled me behind her. We entered her bedroom. "Thor might walk in on us in the kitchen." She turned back to me, shed her shirt from her body; allowed me the opportunity to appraise her entire chest unclothed. I left my tube top on since I felt I had nothing in comparison to offer.

She sat on the bed, breasts bouncing, legs splayed wide. Her hand covered mine and tugged downward. I seated myself between those healthy thighs, wasted no time melding my lips to her dripping nipples. In the privacy, I allowed my other hand to fondle, squirt milk from the unattended breast. Uma pressed on the back of my head, urging me on. I felt my pussy release a load of juice, which slowly crawled from the side of my wet panties and trailed down my inner thighs.

A hand slid between us, fingers pinched my alert nipples. I leaned into it, allowed the feelings to wash over me as I undulated my hot pussy in the air. The tube top was pulled over my head. Uma stood and I stood with her, hands wrapping around her back, keeping my lips fused to her nipple, as I was not yet ready to stop this secret tryst.

Hands tugged at my panties. I assisted, shimmying the cotton scrap down my legs and stepping out of them. Uma kissed me then. Her tongue, sweeter than confectionary sugar, stabbed and intertwined with mine. I clasped her cheeks, met her swirl for swirl, twist for twist. I'd never felt this hot, this fevered in my entire sexual life. My skin flushed with excitement, nerves hummed in joy, endorphins swished through arteries.

My body heated further as her lips left my mouth, trailed past my neck and pulled my bud between her lips. I couldn't stop my pelvis from rotating as her tongue lapped, teeth nipped the sensitized berries. My head lolled backward, giving her more room to pleasure me.

Her tongue trailed lower still; I knew the destination. My body, unused to cunnilingus but a willing participant nevertheless, rocked in anticipation. When her lips arrived, it was sweet indeed. Fingers parted my manicured bush, exposing my clit. I felt cool air before a hot mouth covered my stiff clit and sucked. I moaned deep as Uma's tongue whirled and spun up and down between my labial lips.

She lifted, positioned one of my legs up on the bed before opening me slowly. Her head dipped, licked the trail of juice all the way back up from my knees to my pussy. I panted as her tongue eased inside me. My hands twisted in her hair, holding her in place. I slid up and down that luxurious tongue as Uma inserted her fingers; pumped as she lapped. Arms wrapped around my thighs, head rotated and bobbed as she feasted on my pussy.

I pushed her backward onto the bed. I turned, straddled her face. She eased me down slowly to her waiting tongue. I leaned forward, lifted the titty to my mouth. I couldn't understand the words she spoke around my pussy as I sucked her deep into my mouth and honestly, I didn't care. All I knew was she didn't push me off her so it was all good.

I ventured further into pristine sexual territory when I allowed my fingers to slide into her snatch, pinch her clit. Uma ignited! She stabbed my pussy, bucked against my fingers as I diddled her clit. The staccato of her tongue slung me over the edge. I felt the sizzle radiating from my feet, past my knees and explode at my clit. We both cried out as the orgasm shook between us, made us complicit co-conspirators in this illicit affair, created intangible soul ties that would be difficult to unravel…dammit, I was in lust!

Poor Darryl. I informed him that I'd done some "research," found that some children nursed until they were five, so we could let Thor breast feed as long as he thought necessary.

Darryl gave me a smug smile, secure in the knowledge that once again he'd have his way and said, "Good girl. Like I told you, titty milk ain't hurt nobody."

I couldn't agree with him more.

෨෮

Sydney Molaré is one of the latest crop of Southern authors to watch. Her novels' messages cross genres, ethnicities and locales. Her goal is to always have "little messages for everyone." Her books are garnering her awards from book clubs and reviewers across the country. Sydney was recently named, "Mississippi Hometown Hero, Most Likely to Succeed" and the 2006 Mississippi's BEST Author. Her novels include—Somewhere In America; Small Packages; Changing Faces, Changing Places; Grandmama's Mojo Still Working; *and* Devil's Orchestra. *Her website is: www.sydneymolare.com.*

Miss Julidene's Sexy Items
Joy Bringas

Most people loathe their job but I love mine. After graduating college, I envisioned myself working at an office until I realized that in Atherton, the town where I lived, there were no sex stores.

There was a preconceived notion in Atherton that sex stores were bad. When I started my business, I wanted to prove that my sex store, Miss Julidene's Sexy Items, would defy the stereotypes. After having my store open for over a year, I was able to encourage the people of Atherton to embrace their sexual desires.

"Should I get the seven-inch dildo or the eight-inch dildo?" Mrs. Thompson asked.

At seventy years old, Mrs. Thompson was a widow who still loved to get her freak on. She was a frequent customer of mine who enjoyed buying toys for herself.

"Mrs. Thompson, take this nine-inch dildo," I said.

"Are you sure it won't be too big?" she questioned.

"Have I ever been wrong about my recommendations for you?" I asked.

"Never."

I completed her purchase and before I could hand her the dildo, she grabbed it and hurried out of the store. I smiled at her excitement to go home and use it.

Just as Mrs. Thompson left, I saw Calena Parker enter. She was an Atlanta native with a heavy Southern accent. She was here yesterday to find some items for her and her new wife, Allie, to use on their honeymoon.

"Miss Julidene! Glad to see ya here!" Calena exclaimed in her twang.

"Hello, Calena."

"I wasn't expectin' to return so soon but Allie has been buggin' me to come here again."

"Oh? Why?"

"We went crazy last night! While she was using the spanking paddle, she used it too hard and it broke. I need another one."

"Excuse me then," I said going to the aisle where the spanking paddles were.

Yesterday, I sold Calena a wooden spanking paddle. I discovered she had a spanking fetish. This time I decided to get her a leather paddle so she could experience a different feeling on her big black ass.

"Try this leather paddle and please come back to tell me if you prefer this one or the wooden one," I instructed.

"Ooooh, my pussy is gettin' wet just thinkin' about the leather hittin' me."

"Save the wetness for your wife," I joked.

After handing Calena her purchase, my eyes scanned the store to see if there was a customer I could assist. My eyes landed on an attractive female customer who I didn't recognize. She was a dark-haired woman dressed sharply in a red business suit. Her skin looked smooth like chocolate milk.

"Hello, ma'am, I'm Miss Julidene. Do you need any help?" I politely asked.

"No," she replied and quickly walked away.

New customers were usually shy so it was no surprise that she wanted to avoid me. I followed her as she walked to the porno film section.

"You don't need to be shy, ma'am. I saw you looking at the strap-on dildos. You're not the only customer I've seen purchasing one," I said.

She gulped and walked away again. This time, instead of walking into another section, she headed straight for the exit.

"Ma'am, I'm sure you didn't come all this way just to look and not purchase anything. You'd be amazed at how many women buy strap-on dildos. I'm sure your pussy is itching for one," I said.

The young woman stopped in her steps and looked at me.

"I wonder what it would feel like to have a cock in my ass," she quietly confessed.

"Do you finger your ass while you masturbate?" I asked.

She blushed. "Yes, I do."

"Follow me."

I walked to where the anal beads were and thought about which set of beads would be compatible for her. The vibrating anal beads looked perfect so I pulled them off the shelf and handed them to her. She looked at them in amazement. I could see the lust forming in her eyes.

"Before you have a dildo in your ass, you should start with those anal beads so that when you have a dildo in there, it won't hurt. Are you married or single?" I asked.

"I have a girlfriend," she replied.

"Have you discussed your desire to be fucked in your ass to her?"

"Yes."

"Then let's look at the strap-on dildos," I said.

I recommended a simple latex strap-on that she and her girlfriend could test out. When her purchase was completed, I smiled and felt proud. I wished that I could watch her be penetrated in the ass.

"Thank you for your assistance, Miss Julidene," she said happily.

"It surely is my pleasure. I never got your name."

"I'm Jayda Brown."

"It's very nice to meet you, Jayda. Please come again."

After closing my store, I went home and soaked in my bathtub. With my waterproof vibrator in my hand, I fucked myself senseless as my thoughts drifted to Jayda. Images of her shoving the anal beads up her ass and getting fucked by the strap-on dildo floated in my mind. I imagined it was me, instead of her girlfriend, jamming that fake cock into her.

"Oh, Jayda," I moaned out loud as my pussy vigorously exploded.

As I came down from my orgasm, I wondered when I would see Jayda again. I was anxious to see her and hear her feedback on the toys.

80C3

"I enjoyed the leather paddle a lot! It feels much better on my ass!" Calena exclaimed.

"I'm glad," I said.

"I was watchin' this porno with Allie and it had a bondage theme. We decided we wanna try bondage."

"Bondage can be very pleasurable with the right items. How extreme was the bondage in the film?"

"There was one scene where the female was blindfolded and tied to a pole. The dominatrix whipped her and teased her."

"Unfortunately, I don't sell poles here but I do have rope. Allie can tie you to a chair or your bedposts. Here's a leather whip that you'll also enjoy. A gag and nipple clamps will also be useful."

"I feel like I'm gonna come, just holdin' these items."

"Down, girl," I teased as I walked over to the erotic clothing section.

"Fuck, I wanna see Allie in that!" Calena exclaimed as she pointed at the nurse uniform.

"It's yours," I said while taking it off the rack.

While I was ringing up Calena's purchase, I noticed a new customer had entered. My heart skipped a beat when I recognized it was Jayda dressed in a skirt and blouse. Her eyes locked with mine and she approached me. I quickly finished Calena's purchase and then focused my attention on Jayda.

"Hello, Jayda, it's good to see you back. Did you use your toys?" I asked.

"I did," she said shyly.

"How did it go?"

"The anal beads were wonderful. I've never come so hard before."

"That's good to know."

Jayda blushed. "It was intense."

My pussy tingled while I imagined Jayda with the anal beads up her ass. I just wanted to grab her and cram my fingers into her asshole as I licked her pussy.

"Did you and your girlfriend enjoy the strap-on dildo?" I asked her as I shook my head to rid the dirty thoughts in my mind.

"We didn't use it. She refused to put it on," she said sadly.

That surprised me. I wondered why her girlfriend changed her mind.

"I thought you two discussed using the strap-on," I said.

"We did but when I showed it to her, she told me she wasn't

serious about actually using one. She laughed at me for wanting a fake cock up my ass," she said.

Stepping toward Jayda, I gave her a hug. I was disappointed that her girlfriend was not up to exploring her sexual desire. My body melted as it pressed against hers and my nipples started to tingle as they smashed against her breasts.

"Miss Julidene! I need another dildo!" Mrs. Thompson exclaimed as she barged into my store.

Pulling away from Jayda, I looked at her apologetically. I walked over to Mrs. Thompson and saw she seemed jittery. As I got closer to her, I could smell the scent of wet pussy.

"Another one?" I asked her.

"I want something thicker and longer!"

I brought Mrs. Thompson a twelve-inch dildo and handed it to her. She gazed at the cock hungrily and I could see the drool leaking out of her mouth.

"Will twelve inches be enough?" I asked.

"Yes!" she shouted.

When I finished completing her purchase, she ran out of the store. I looked around for Jayda and spotted her in the vibrator section. I walked over there and stopped when I noticed her hand was between her legs. She was gently rubbing herself while looking at the vibrators.

My pussy twitched as I watched her masturbate. I wanted to go to her and be the one rubbing her instead.

I checked to see if there were any customers around and, unfortunately, there was a couple looking at the erotic clothing. I would have loved to approach Jayda and assist her.

I watched as she quietly masturbated in front of me. I wondered if she knew I was watching. Her hand began to rub faster and, within seconds, she let out a soft sigh.

"See anything you like?" I asked her.

"Oh, no," she said and quickly removed her hand from between her legs.

"Are you sure?"

"Yes. I have to go now," she said.

Before I could stop Jayda from leaving, she was already out the door. I did my best to resume working while trying to rid what I had seen out of my head.

ഇൽ

The hours slowly went by as I anxiously waited for closing time. I wanted to leave and relieve the tension that had been building up in my clit ever since I saw Jayda masturbating. When it was nine p.m., I closed up and headed toward my car.

"You're closed already?"

I turned my head toward the direction of the voice and smiled when I saw Jayda.

"The store closes at nine."

"I'm sorry but I was wondering if I could make a purchase?"

I usually refuse but, for Jayda, I made an exception. Going back into the store, I followed her as she walked over to the vibrator section.

"I thought you didn't want a vibrator," I said.

"I couldn't stop thinking about one. What do you recommend?" she asked.

Looking at all the different types of vibrators, I decided that Jayda should start with a seven-inch vibrator. After she paid, we went our separate ways. Once I got home, I undressed and shoved my own vibrator up my pussy. I wondered if she was fucking herself with her vibrator at this moment. Images of her with the vibrator going in and out of her asshole began to swirl in my mind. My orgasm came fast as my pussy walls convulsed around my toy.

As the days passed, I kept an eye out for Jayda. Each time a customer would walk in my heart would jump. It seemed like forever since I had seen her face and I craved to see her again.

I hoped it wasn't Jayda's girlfriend preventing her from coming back to my store. It was unfair to me that she wasn't single. There was no denying the chemistry between us.

While I was rearranging some blow-up doll boxes, I felt a tap on my shoulder. Looking up, my eyes widened when I saw Jayda. I resisted the urge to jump with joy.

"Hello, Jayda. I haven't seen you in a while."

"I've been busy with my vibrator. I think I've overused it though and need another one."

I led Jayda into the vibrator section and selected a nine-inch vibrator.

"This vibrator comes with a remote that you can set to any speed you desire. It also has a rotating feature that will make you come harder than before."

"It sounds wonderful." She smiled.

"I'm sure you and your girlfriend will enjoy this," I said.

"Girlfriend? We broke up about a week ago. She caught me with my vibrator and was disgusted."

"That's too bad."

"It's all right. I'm having more fun with my vibrator than I ever had with her."

I secretly smiled, knowing that she was single now. I finally had a chance to be with her. As she left, I stared at her wide ass, hoping I could fuck it soon.

The next day, Calena and Allie came to the store together. This was the first time I had seen Allie and was surprised. They looked like extreme opposites. Calena was a fashionable woman who wore designer clothing. I didn't expect Allie to be the gothic-looking woman standing before me wearing a Renaissance-inspired dress.

"Miss Julidene, this is my wife, Allie," Calena said.

"Nice to meet you, Allie," I said as I shook her hand.

"You really have helped us out with your items. I had to come here and see what else we could buy," Allie said.

"Is there anything you two are interested in trying?" I asked.

"It would be fun to try using a strap-on dildo on her," Allie said.

"I have plenty of those," I said and led them over to the strap-on section.

"I want that one!" Allie exclaimed as she pointed to the eleven-inch purple strap-on.

"Many customers enjoy this one," I said as I pulled it off the shelf and handed it to Allie.

"It's perfect for us," Allie said as she caressed it.

After admiring the strap-on, Allie slipped into it. Lifting up her dress, she admired the way the purple cock stood up at attention.

"You look so fuckin' hot, baby," Calena purred.

The couple began to kiss passionately, forgetting I was there. It touched my heart to see my product bring a couple closer together. While they kissed, I noticed Jayda walking toward us.

"Good afternoon, Miss Julidene," Jayda said.

Once the couple heard her voice, they broke apart and blushed.

"Hello, Jayda," I said.

"We'll take this," Calena said as she handed me her credit card.

We all walked to the register and I completed their purchase. When the couple walked away, Jayda stepped in front of the counter.

"The vibrator I bought is great. The rotating feature is fabulous," she said happily.

I was about to speak when a loud moan echoed through the store. I excused myself and followed the sounds. As I got closer, the moans grew louder. When I reached the back of the store, I saw Calena and Allie in a corner. Calena's body was smashed against the wall with Allie behind her slowly thrusting the strap-on into her.

I was about to stop their fucking when I noticed Jayda standing beside me watching them. She licked her plump lips and appeared to be fascinated with what was occurring before her.

"Do you like what you're watching?" I asked.

"Yes," she said softly.

I decided this was my chance to have Jayda. Getting down on my knees, I reached out and began to massage her thighs. Her fingers quickly undid her pants, allowing them to fall down. My mouth salivated when I saw her shaved pussy.

Spreading Jayda's pussy lips apart, I slid my tongue inside and licked all around her wetness. I looked up and saw her eyes still transfixed on the couple fucking before us. I moved my hands to her juicy black ass and inserted a finger into her asshole. Her hands gripped my hair as she grinded her pussy onto my tongue.

"I'm gonna come," she groaned as her thighs tightened around my head.

Moving my tongue to her clit, I rapidly flicked my tongue against it and felt Jayda shake with pleasure. She let out a long moan and rode my face as she came vigorously around my mouth.

Standing up, I kissed Jayda and let our tongues move together. Her hands squeezed my ass cheeks, which brought our bodies closer. Without breaking the kiss, I took off my blouse and removed my bra. My breasts pressed up against hers, causing my nipples to harden.

I moaned when Jayda slipped a hand between my thighs. Her fingers found my throbbing clit and she began to fiddle it like a fine instrument. I broke away from the kiss and attempted to catch my breath.

Jayda was still looking at Calena and Allie. This time I noticed she was smirking at them. Turning my head, I realized we were the ones being watched now and a rush of excitement went through me. It wasn't just Calena and Allie though; other customers of mine had huddled around us.

Before I could come, I pushed Jayda's hand away from my wet pussy. She looked disappointed but I assured her with a smile before jogging away. I grabbed the strap-on dildo I had envisioned fucking her with and snapped it on.

Gripping the collar of her shirt, I yanked her down toward the fake purple cock. Without hesitation, she slipped it into her mouth and suckled it like a delicious popsicle. It was empowering to watch her suck my cock and I finally understood how men felt while getting a blow job.

"Please put it in my ass, Miss Julidene. I need it so bad," Jayda whimpered as she stroked the dildo.

"Then bend over and stick your pretty ass up," I instructed.

I admired Jayda's abundant ass for a moment. I loved the way it jiggled before me. Holding the dildo in my hand, I guided it inside her until all nine inches were stuffed in. She moaned and began to back her ass up toward me. Digging my fingers into her thick hips, I started to thrust.

Jayda groaned and grunted underneath me as I fucked her like a jackhammer. Every time I would thrust forward, she would slam her ass backward. This caused my clit to rub against the special knob in the strap-on designed for clitoral stimulation.

"Feels so good," Jayda whispered.

I looked at the audience we had and noticed some of my customers were rubbing themselves as they watched. I could not fight the sweet friction that had been building inside me and I started to fuck her harder. With each thrust I made, her ass jiggled like jelly.

"Yes! I'm coming! I'm coming!" Jayda chanted as she began to play with her clit.

A sudden wave of pleasure crashed over me when I heard Jayda announce she was coming. My body let go as my clit exploded into a blissful orgasm. The intense feelings surged through my body as I came fiercely with the dildo lodged deeply into her ass.

Our spent bodies collapsed onto the floor and the two of us laid there with our limbs intertwined. As I attempted to catch my breath, I thought about what had just happened right there in my store. I couldn't believe I'd just fucked Jayda in the ass with an audience.

"You two really stole the spotlight from me and Allie," I heard Calena remark.

"They are absolutely hot together. I wish I had my video camera," Allie said.

Once I regained my breath, I stood up and smiled at Calena and Allie. I noticed a ruckus happening at the strap-on section. Not even bothering to adjust my appearance, I walked over and saw my customers scrambling to get a strap-on dildo.

"Miss Julidene, I never thought a strap-on dildo would turn me on. The way you demonstrated it was off the chain," a female customer said.

"I'm glad I could give you a new idea," I said proudly.

When I was on my way back to where Jayda was standing, I noticed a long line had formed. Each customer in line had a strap-on dildo in their hands.

"That was amazing," Jayda complimented.

"It sure was. I think we helped create a strap-on dildo trend."

All the strap-on dildos I had in my store were sold. I constantly had customers coming in and asking for one. It gave me a wonderful feeling to know that people were very interested in them. Fucking Jayda with one really boosted my sales and the popularity of my store.

Jayda and I now hold special sessions once a month where we demonstrate a new sex toy for customers. We hope to encourage customers to enhance their sexual desires. Due to my new sales tactic and new partner, I love my job even more. Who knew a strap-on dildo could help my business and get me the woman I love?

80Q3

Joy Bringas lives in Northern California. Her stories and poems have been featured in anthologies such as Zane's Caramel Flava *and Alison Tyler's* Got a Minute. *When she's not writing a story, she's either listening to Backstreet Boys music or updating her website: http://www.flirtingwithobscene.com*

Wet

Dylynn DeSaint

The bedroom is softly lit by the candles she's placed around the outside of the bed. Taking my hand, she guides me to the big king-sized bed with red satin sheets. I watch her in silence, gazing into her eyes as she unbuttons my blouse and tosses it onto the chair nearby. Her face is intense as she strips me bare. Stopping momentarily, she feasts on my nudity and flashes a wicked grin.

I move to touch her shirt and she brushes my hand aside. Standing naked like that and, she with all her clothes on, leaves me feeling vulnerable, yet I shudder inwardly in anticipation.

The wetness pooling between my thighs betrays any attempt at hiding my excitement. Instinctively, I part my legs and let the night air cool the slick juices. She notices this and runs her hand agonizingly slow near the wet entrance and on the inside of my thigh, but makes no attempt to penetrate me with her fingers.

As she moves her body closer to me, I brace myself. I am her prey and she is the sinewy, feminine creature of my dreams. She surrounds me with her burning hot sensual energy, wickedly calculating each move to drive my senses wherever she damn well pleases. Every muscle in my body is tensed.

When her hands make contact with my breasts, I flinch involuntarily and suck in my breath from the heat of her touch. I watch them travel up and around each one and down to my stomach. The darkness of her ebony skin contrasts beautifully against the milky paleness of my flesh. I cover her hands with mine and together we travel the smooth terrain of my body. Her touch, both gentle and warm, creates a sensual image in my head of how beautiful our bodies look intertwined.

My nipples ache to be touched, sucked and teased. She obliges my desire by tonguing each one, coaxing them to become beautifully hard.

Holding my hips, she turns me around and grinds her crotch against my bare ass. The rough fabric of her jeans accentuates my nudity but it also excites me. I feel the hardness in her groin and my heart jumps. I can barely contain myself, knowing what this means. Moving sensuously against her, I arch my back so that my ass is rubbing against the strap-on dildo in her pants. I moan softly and whimper impatiently, letting her know that my desire for her is rising.

She gently pushes me down on the bed. Lying there, face down, I hear her removing her clothes behind me.

"Don't turn around."

I do as she says, waiting anxiously, closing my eyes and taking in the softness of the satiny sheets underneath my naked body.

Soon she joins me. Crawling from behind, she lies on top of me, her breasts and stomach resting on my back. Her skin feels wonderfully warm and inviting. I close my eyes and take in the luxurious feeling of being enveloped by her silky body.

"Take me, fuck me; please do anything to me!" I tell her as she kisses my neck and shoulders.

She responds by pushing herself up on her hands and straddling me. I feel the dildo moving in the crevice between my ass cheeks.

Her soft caresses on my back are driving me wild. Satiny lips trace a path along my shoulders where her hands have been and a chill runs up and down my spine each time her breasts lightly brush against the skin on my back. Soon she moves over me and positions herself behind me.

Both of her hands are now on my thighs, opening my legs and spreading my pussy open to meet her tongue. The wetness between my legs finds its way onto her lips as she laps at me in long, slow strokes. I move against her mouth, pushing my pussy onto the tongue that is bringing me such exquisite pleasure.

I want her to fuck me with the dildo that she has strapped on. I beg her to give me the release that I need. She ignores my pleas. Instead, I now feel her tongue on the opening of my ass. I try to squirm away from her but she holds me in place and begins to dip her tongue into the tight bud. Soon the sensation and wetness begins to take on a shockingly pleasurable feeling. I allow her to continue and soon feel the sensation of being prodded and filled. She has inserted a finger into my ass and is fucking me gently with it. When I realize what she is doing and is about to do with the dildo, I plead with her to not take me in that way, but she holds me tightly and continues to fuck me with her finger.

"Relax; hold still, baby-girl," she coos.

Soon she withdraws it and I feel the dildo pressing against the tight opening of my ass. I try desperately to resist but she grips my hips tightly and plunges forth until the dildo is buried deep inside.

"Ugh!" I gasp, unaccustomed to being fucked like this.

Brushing her lips against my neck, she lies on me, giving me time to adjust to the thick silicone cock inside of me.

"After I'm done with you, you're going to come begging me for more," she whispers in my ear with sultry confidence.

"Yesss…," I say, uttering in a low groan, moving my hips against her.

She starts to pump the dildo in my ass slowly, grinding it deeper and deeper each time. Soon though, she becomes an animal, biting my neck and shoulders as she pumps roughly into me, using her weight to keep my body pinned to the bed. The pain I initially felt now turns to pleasure as I welcome each delicious bite and thrust. I know that I will find marks on my skin in the morning but don't care. I love being engulfed by her passion.

In one smooth motion, she pulls me up on my knees while still inside and wastes no time fucking me harder. I can feel her pussy grinding into my ass in an attempt to push the dildo even deeper. Trying desperately to keep from collapsing onto my belly, I writhe under her body as my own is pushed forward from the force of her thrusts. My face thrashes against the pillow she has laid out for me. Soft moans escape my lips and my fingers clutch at the sheets beneath me. She is relentless, pounding herself into my body.

"Beg me to fuck you harder," she demands.

"Please…oh gawd, yesssss," I moan in a hoarse and jagged whisper. Completely delirious with pleasure, I'm experiencing sensations that I've never encountered before.

I am keenly aware that I have raised my ass up higher to receive each and every wicked stroke of the dildo as it glides smoothly in and out of me. It is if I am in another world. My body is reacting to the fire, the electricity of her touch until I soon become no longer aware of the sounds that I make.

My soul is lost in the heat emanating from our bodies. I have completely surrendered to her at this moment. There is nothing that I will not do for her. I wanted her to take possession of me completely and she has.

I scream out in both pain and pleasure as she pulls me upwards, with my back resting against her breasts. She is kneeling, leaning back on her legs as I sit impaled on the dildo, my legs spread wide apart on each side of her thighs.

She reaches her arms around me and cups my breasts. She has dipped her fingers into my pussy and is now using that wetness to stroke my nipples. Slowly, she traces each one, lingering until I think that I cannot endure her touch any longer. I sigh out loud and watch her leave a glistening trail on each one. Her hands, wet and scented from my sex, edge their way up my neck and to my chin. She puts her pussy-moistened fingers to my lips and I lick and suck each one languorously as she holds them out to me.

I feel her breath on my neck and then the softness of her lips burning on my skin. Just when I think that my body can no longer take it anymore, she thrusts the dildo upward and bites softly into my shoulder. At that moment, I shudder and my body trembles with the most exquisite orgasm I've ever felt. I reach up and pull her arms against my breasts as my body shakes with each wave of pleasure that overtakes my soul. She holds me close, supporting my body with hers as I collapse against her, my head resting against her neck.

She kisses my temple as my breathing returns to normal. I can feel wetness on my cheek as she kisses the side of my face and holds me even closer. Warm tears fall from her eyes onto my face and begin to flow down my neck. I can feel her body shake as she cries softly, unable to control her emotions, each sob muffled by my hair as she buries her face in it.

Beep...Beep...Beep...Beep...BEEEEP!...BEEEEEEEP!...BE EEEEP!

The alarm clock shrieks loudly and abruptly wakes me. I'm

stunned and discombobulated. My fingers fumble clumsily in an attempt to find the snooze button. Hitting it, I'm finally able to turn the damned thing off.

Wow, what a dream. That was so freaking hot! I wipe the sweat from my forehead and stretch languorously.

Yawning and with half-open eyes, I look across the bed and see the still slumbering form of my best friend, Shaundrice, snoring on the other side.

We had both been at a party, drank way too heavily and somehow ended up at my apartment and in my bed. But why wasn't she sleeping on the couch? *Shit!*

Wait…it was *her* in my dream! *She* was fucking me.

A moment of panic hits me as I attempt to recall the events of the last few hours.

I turn away from her and lay on my side squeezing my eyes closed in attempt to get my mind to wake up and process my thoughts. In doing so, I roll over onto a wet spot on the bed. Wincing, I feel between my legs…I'm *wet*.

Can it be true? Did I have sex with her? I'm on the verge of hyperventilating. I can't even begin to fathom that after all these years we'd do anything so stupid. I've always fantasized about what it would be like if we made love and had even been attracted to her in the past, but had never crossed the boundaries of our friendship, *ever*.

I lay there, afraid to look down on the floor for fear of finding leftover remnants of the dirty deed. I dread finding any evidence of a heated tryst.

Slowly I peer over the side of the bed…nothing. I sit up quietly and look over the foot of the bed…still nothing. Lying back down, I let out a big sigh of relief.

I hold my breath as she rustles about, getting into a more comfortable position and then returns back to a peaceful sleep. When she stops moving I allow my body to relax. I lay there, still looking around the bed and the nightstands, checking for tale-tell signs that might have been left behind. Out of the corner of my eye I spot what looks like a small flat bottle of lubricant peeking out of the underside of her pillow. I want to get a closer look but I'm afraid to wake her. Sucking in my breath, I slowly edge closer and closer toward her to get a better look. I still can't make out what it is. My cheek is now lying flat against the bed and only one foot away from her face. With two fingers, I carefully latch onto it, ready to pull it out from under the pillow when a long stretchy drop of drool from her mouth lands on my hand. I cringe but hold perfectly still, watching the clear fluid as it leaves a shiny path on my skin and makes its way toward the bed. Shaking off my squeamishness, I proceed to tug at the object.

She stirs again. I pull my hand away quickly, in a panic. I watch her as she grabs the corner of the pillow and tugs it under her head, effectively burying the plastic bottle out of my sight. Argh! To make matters worse, her forearm is now completely blocking any path I might have to the pillow.

I give up!

Staring up at the ceiling, I rationalize that it was probably one of those little bottles of hand disinfectant. I knew she always carried one in her pocket. Maybe in her sleep, she pulled it out. That had to be it. I stopped worrying about it any further, convinced that I was letting my imagination get out of control.

So it *was* a dream!

Damn, what a relief!

Now that I felt safe, I tried to recollect everything I could remember about it all in my head. I guess subconsciously I really would like to be fucked by her but was very satisfied with an occasional fantasy. She frequently confided in her sexual escapades in high school and even up until now, so I knew almost everything about her and the one-night stands or occasional girlfriend. I definitely got the impression she was a fantastic lover. I even teased her about it, calling her "King Daddy Stud Muffin." She'd laugh and wink, cockily admitting that it was true.

"Once you go black, sistah, you never go back," she'd brag.

"Yeah, well, once you go blonde, you…you…oh hell…quit bragging, Shaundrice!" I'd always reply, never able to come up with a good enough retort to top her.

It was a miracle that we became friends. I grew up in a typical middle class neighborhood on Long Island. She lived in Queens. Our worlds collided back in high school when our two basketball teams met during a heated championship game.

Brenda, a girl, from the opposing team, was playing and I had a huge crush on her. The sight of that basketball jersey clinging to her sweaty, voluptuous body always made me instantly wet and hot. I couldn't take my eyes off of her.

Instead of keeping my eyes on the ball and who had it, I threw a quick glance Brenda's way. What I didn't see was Shaundrice barreling down the court headed in my direction. When I turned around, it was too late.

"Owww!" I screamed as her elbow made contact with my nose, making a sickening cracking sound, as she flew up to make a shot. Pain shot through my face and jaw instantly. Instinctively I brought my hands to my face when I felt the wetness. Blood flowed every-where, like a river onto my jersey.

"Damn, that looks bad." Shaundrice smirked as she looked at my face from a short distance away.

"You freakin' broke my nose!" I yelled at her, holding my jersey to my nose to try to stem the flow. I couldn't believe her indifference.

"If you hadn't been staring at Brenda's tits, you would've' seen me coming, girlfriend!" she countered. "That…" She pointed to my nose as she walked away. "…is why you got to keep your eyes on the damn ball, boo!"

I had to leave the court for the rest of the game. Incredibly, the next day, the phone rang and it was Shaundrice. She said she felt bad about what happened and wanted to make it up to me. We went out for coffee and the rest is history. She liked my spunk and said that I wasn't a bad basketball player for a skinny white girl from Long Island. We've been friends ever since, each one still trying to top the other.

As I lie in bed, I try to pick up where we left off in the dream. My pussy is throbbing and in a state of urgent need. I turn on my stomach and reach down between my legs. Finding my clit, I rub it gently and then dip my fingers into my pussy. Returning my wet fingers back to the center of wicked pleasure, I slide them over and over my clit again, roughly feeling the heat build in my groin. Soon my mind and feverish body are entering the ecstatic point of no return. I feel a climax coming on and groan quietly as a deliciously strong orgasm begins to roll through my body like a huge tidal wave, rendering me helpless and painfully struggling to be quiet so as not to wake her.

"Ahhhhhhhh!" I hoarsely whisper, waiting for my orgasm to subside.

Fortunately, she is a hard sleeper and doesn't move. I'm relieved.

Almost immediately, I fall blissfully back asleep once I've come.

While in a deep sleep, I stir slightly when I feel the sensation of something brushing against my neck. *Mmmmm…*

Soon, I feel weight on my body. I open my eyes.

Straddling over my hips, I feel the heat from Shaundrice's hot crotch searing through the sheet onto my back.

She purrs in my ear. "Pretty white girl from Long Island, you ready for round two?"

It wasn't a dream after all!

Holy freakin' mother of God, I am screwed...*literally*!

I'm glad she can't see my face because I'm holding it between my hands with my mouth open in a silent scream, like that blonde kid in the movies.

"Your body is so hot, baby. I want to fuck you again."

She's kissing my neck, nipping at my shoulders and licking my skin.

I grimace and grit my teeth as I flinch and yelp with each nip, twisting my body and writhing with her still on top. She interprets this as me getting turned on.

"Wooohooo!" she hoots. "You go, girl! Baby likes it rough!"

She's laughing gleefully as she slaps my ass every time I squirm.

If it were someone else, this would be comical situation. The more I buck and fidget, the more she scolds and delivers a slap to my butt. Soon the slaps are getting harder and harder, to the point of stinging. She's not laughing anymore either.

Whack! This blow is much harder than the rest. The skin on my ass is getting hot, yet I find myself inexplicably wanting more. The pain is transforming itself into a delicious, sultry burning pleasure.

"Oh!" I yelp as she delivers yet another slap.

I involuntarily tighten my ass cheeks and grind my hips into the bed in violent reaction. Moisture is seeping between my legs as I slide my thighs together with each thrash of her hand. Whether

I want it to or not, my body is surrendering to her, despite my apprehension about what this will do to our friendship.

Suddenly she shifts and pulls the sheet away from my body. Her hand tugs at my panties while she uses her upper body to hold me down now. I feel her tongue as it darts around the outside of my ear, sliding up and down until she finds my earlobe and sucks on it. Chills run down both my arms and legs. Soft moans escape my mouth and my pussy aches with unrelenting tension.

I feel the familiar warmth of her breasts as they press into my back.

"Wait!" I exclaim, pushing her gently off of my body and away from me.

She looks surprised and stares blankly at me.

"We made love last night because we were drunk! What's this going to do to *us?* What about our friendship?"

"Nothing is going to change," she says, totally in denial.

Of course everything will change; how could it not? I think to myself as I stare back at her for a few minutes in silence. But what's done is done. My body doesn't want to stop and I'm going to ignore my heart.

"What does your king daddy stud muffin want to hear, baby?" she asks in a low, taunting voice as she crawls on her knees and back over my body.

"So much for our friendship…this is much better. Fuck me harder this time, *lover*," I reply, raising my ass for whatever she has to deliver.

"Thas' my girl."

৪৫৪

Dylynn DeSaint lives in the Southwest with her partner. Disguised as a librarian by day, Dylynn finds pleasure in letting her mind wander to the naughtiest of places at every free moment. By night, she is a freelance writer. She finds her inspiration for stories while people-watching in all worlds, both physical and virtual. Her works are included in the following anthologies: Best Date Ever: True Stories That Celebrate Lesbian Relationships *and* Iridescence: Sensuous Shades of Erotica. *Contact her at DylynnDesaint@gmail.com*

Mom's Night Out
Regina Jamison

I had originally joined Mission Mommies as an outlet for my children. It was a way for them to meet and make friends with other children. It was also an outlet for me. It allowed me to make connections with other African-American women who were stay-at-home moms. The activities that were arranged for the children were always great. But the moms' night outs were even better.

Tammy was not the leader of Mission Mommies but she had a tendency to take over. High of spirit and behind, both her mouth and her ass were always in motion. Some of the moms silently disapproved of Tammy's buoyancy, but I found it and her exciting. Needless to say, we became fast friends.

We would meet, outside of the group, at each other's homes. While our children played blissfully together upstairs, Tammy and I conversed downstairs. We would talk from one thing to the other, moving in and out of each topic with ease. Then one day we got into a discussion about lesbians. Who was; who wasn't. Which movie stars had come out publicly and those, whom we suspected, who were still hiding.

"Well, there's Rosie O'Donnell and Melissa Etheridge," Tammy said. We had walked into the kitchen where she was getting us some lemonade.

"Yeah, I know," I said, watching her ass as she moved from the refrigerator to the counter. "But where are all the African-American lesbians? There's only Jennifer Beale who pretends at being a lesbian on *The L Word*."

"Oh, my God. You watch that show, too?"

"Yes."

"Why do you watch it?" Tammy asked. She walked over to the table and set our glasses down. Sweat rolled down the front of mine. I wiped my hand and my brow. I watched her breasts jiggle as she moved around in the kitchen chair, trying to make herself comfortable.

"Well, the sex is hot for one. Two, the sex is hot and three, the characters are believable."

"I agree," Tammy said. Then she took a long gulp of her drink.

Her eyes were on me the whole time. It was as if she were studying me. Weighing the words she wanted to say. I kept my eyes on her—not shying away from the challenge. But, for some reason, I was nervous. I disguised my trepidation by holding onto my glass tightly and sucking down my drink. Tammy lowered her glass slightly from her lips. She spoke over the top of her cup.

"Have you ever had a lesbian encounter?"

"Me?" I said almost immediately. "Umm…why do you ask?" It was an avoidance strategy I'd picked up years before. Answer a question with a question. It took the focus off of me.

"I'm curious, is all. When I was in college I had a tumultuous affair with my roommate. The sex was great and I loved her dearly, but I didn't know what to do with us at the time. So, I inadvertently treated her badly and jeopardized the relationship. Years later, I realized that she was the first person I, truly, ever loved."

"You never saw her again?" I asked.

"No. Sadly, I haven't. But I think about her often."

"Have you been with any other women since then?"

"No. Shortly after my breakup with her, I got married and had kids."

I took a long pull from my drink before I said, "Would you like to make love to a woman again?"

Tammy looked at me for a moment. She sat her glass down on the table. "I would. My husband is an excellent lover but...I mean, really, it has nothing to do with him. I just miss the feel of a woman. The softness. The sexiness. Maybe even the whole taboo aspect of it. So, I'd have to say, yes, I would like to make love to a woman again. What about you?"

"Me? What?" I asked. I was playing the avoidance game again.

"Oh, come on, Gail. I just spilled my guts to you about something very personal and you keep avoiding the issue. Now, why is that?" Her words held suspicion.

I got up and walked over to the counter to pour myself some more lemonade. I thought it would be easier to respond to Tammy's questions if I didn't have to face her. With my back to her, I said, "Yes."

I heard Tammy turn around in her chair. I kept my face to the wall.

"Yes, what?"

"Yes, I have had lesbian encounters and, yes, I'd like to continue to do so."

"I *thought* you had done some dabbling."

"Why did you think that?"

"Because of the way you look at me sometimes. I've seen the way you've looked at some of the other moms in the group. It's like you're touching us with your eyes. Soft and tiny caresses."

"Oh." That was all I managed to say.

Tammy's chair rubbed against the floor. I heard her coming toward me but I remained as I was; my back to her, my face to the wall. Then I felt her breath on my neck and her pussy on my ass. Her hands were wrapped around my waist. My heart pounded. I couldn't breathe.

"You know, Gail," Tammy said softly in my right ear. "I was thinking, it could be you. You could be my next lesbian experience. Would you like that?" Her right hand slipped down toward my crotch.

"Yes," I said.

I rolled my head back and closed my eyes. Slowly, she stroked the lips between my thighs. I gasped, leaned into her and parted my legs. Tammy reached in further. She fondled my pussy deeply and gently. It felt good. I moved to her rhythm. My vaginal lips swelled and filled with moisture. She pressed her fingers into my wet pussy and pressed her cunt into my wanton ass. Her stroke hastened. I pumped faster. I was in a frenzy. I'd dreamed of this moment since the first time we'd met. Now, my wish was being fulfilled. Our movements quickened still. Tammy rode my ass like a rodeo cowboy and I fucked her hand steadily. She lifted my halter top at the waist and squeezed my breasts and nipples. My nipples hardened to her touch. My pussy and panties were drenched. I was so close to coming.

"Ahh, yes, Gail. Yes," Tammy said. "I'm finally fucking you."

Apparently, it was a shared dream. Her words resonated right through me and I came with a fury immediately after they were spoken. I collapsed onto the countertop. Tammy continued to pump her pussy into my further protruded ass.

"Yes, I'm fucking you, Gail," she said. "I… am…fucking…you!" She accentuated each word with firm, forward thrusts. Her hand still worked on my pussy and I continued to spasm. Tammy's humping quickened still.

"Gail. Oh, Gail. I'm coming," she said. "I'm coming. Oh, I'm coming. Yes! Oh, yes."

Tammy came, nearly lifting me off the floor with every thrust. Then she fell over on top of me. We stood this way for awhile. We caught our breath and listened to the children playing upstairs. Finally, we stood up. I turned around to face Tammy. I looked at her. She looked at me. We grabbed and embraced each other. Our mouths clamped together, like magnets, in a deep, lingering kiss. When we pulled apart, Tammy said, "We must do that again… soon."

I smiled. I kissed her gently on the lips, this time savoring the taste of her.

"Yes. I agree. But when? Where? I mean, I'd like to make love to you. All of you."

"Yes, I'd like that, too." Tammy thought for a moment. "Hey, what about Saturday? Are you free?"

"I'm free, but our husbands will be home."

"We'll tell them it's moms' night out. We'll get a hotel room and indulge ourselves fully," Tammy said.

"That sounds like a plan," I said. "I can't wait."

"Neither can I," she said. A long, lingering kiss was our handshake.

෩ଊ

Saturday finally arrived. The morning and afternoon proved busy for me with errands, art classes for the kids, and fencing practice. But all the while my thoughts were on that night and Tammy. The experience we had shared in her kitchen was exhilarating. When my husband made love to me two days after my tryst, I had thought of Tammy. His tongue was her tongue. His hands were her hands. His dick, her pussy. Thank God, it was Saturday because I wanted more!

As the evening approached, I was uncertain about what to wear. It was a June night; around eighty degrees and a slight breeze blew. I wanted to look sexy for Tammy but not too sexy so as to be questioned by my husband. I decided to wear a plain, softly pleated, blue skirt and a white sleeveless top. Underneath, I wore a frilly black satin bra and thong with garters and stockings. I felt sexually ripe. I wondered what Tammy would wear. I pictured her in a candy apple red, laced teddy. The color, a beautiful contrast against her deep, dark skin. I saw her lying back on the bed, legs spread, her pussy glinting in the light. I had to stop imagining and focus. Time would bring us together soon.

When I got to the hotel, Tammy had checked in already. The desk clerk gave me the key to room 413. I went upstairs. I let myself in. I was taken aback by the sight before me. Tammy and two other women were seated on an ostensibly large bed. They were kissing and groping one another. Finally, Tammy saw me.

"Gail." She got up and walked toward me.

I looked at her. I raised my eyebrows a bit. This slight gesture evoked all I wanted to say. Tammy took my hand and kissed me. Her breath, lips, were warm and laced with wine. Pinot.

Or was it Chardonnay?

"Don't worry," Tammy whispered in my ear. "I know them very well. We'll have fun. I promise."

I didn't doubt that fun was to be had. I wanted fun. Fun, I could do. But I wanted Tammy for myself. Who were these women? Why did Tammy opt for the bigger experience? Were she and I, together, not enough?

Tammy pulled me further into the room, toward the bed where the other women waited.

"This is Gail," she said as she pointed to me.

"Hello, Gail," said a pecan-colored woman. She had naturally red hair that hung down to her waist. It was locked. Her breasts billowed out over the top of her shirt. A blatant invitation.

"That's Sierra," Tammy said.

"Hello, Sierra."

Then Tammy pointed to the other woman. She was brown-skinned. Her hair was cut in what we used to call a "Caesar." African designed earrings hung from each ear. She seemed average to me. But then she smiled and said, "Hello, Gail." They were the same words uttered by the other woman, but this time, they were sexually infused. There was a heat to them and her smile lit up the room.

"This is Bronique." Tammy massaged the woman's shoulder.

"Bronique, you have a lovely voice," I said.

"Thank you." She smiled that sexy smile again. I decided to sit down next to her. *This could be fun after all*, I thought.

Tammy handed me a large glass of wine, then took center stage. "Now that we're all acquainted, I'd like to propose a toast."

We lifted our glasses and waited. Our suite had a balcony. The doors of which were thrown open. Warm air and faint city noises rushed in. The sky was several shades lighter than our wine. The view from where I sat was breathtaking.

"Here's to love, lasciviousness, and lesbians," Tammy said. "Cheers."

"Cheers," we said.

I drained my glass. Bronique got up to get me another drink. I watched Sierra as she got up and walked to the small bedside table. She put a Sade CD into the CD player. Tammy sat down beside me.

"Good-looking women," I whispered to Tammy as I checked out the other women's bodies. "But who are they? I thought this was going to be just you and me?"

"I know. But Bronique and Sierra are old friends and they wanted to try something new. All of us, together, here, is something new. Don't you want to try something new? I thought I'd surprise you."

"I'm very surprised," I said.

"I thought you'd be pleased. I think you are...especially with Bronique. I saw the way you looked at her. I think she's into you, too. Did you see that ass? Girl!! Shhh, here she comes."

"I thought you'd like more wine," Bronique said. She bent slightly to hand me the glass.

Our hands touched and a warmth spread through me.

"Come. Sit," I said. I patted the space beside me. Tammy got up and walked toward Sierra. Bronique sat down.

"So, what is it that you do, Bronique?"

"I do voice-overs," she said. The sound of her voice thrilled me.

"Your voice is so sexy."

"Thank you. You sound pretty sexy yourself."

I looked into her eyes. They were big and brown with long, flipped up lashes. "No, you don't understand. Simply hearing you speak is making me hot."

"Well, let me say more. Maybe I can talk you out of those clothes."

"I'd like that a lot," Bronique said.

I emptied my wine glass and put it aside. I turned to Bronique. Our lips met. Hers were hot, soft and full. Soon, my tongue found hers and our kisses deepened. I touched her face. I felt her head. I pulled her closer. We fell back on the bed. Our lips remained locked. I pulled away, looked at her, and said, "Say something."

"Fuck me," she said. I moaned, laid on top of her, and, again, I kissed her deeply. She felt my ass through my skirt. She traced the divide of my ass with her fingertips. My pussy watered. I rubbed it against hers. I wanted more. Bronique wanted more. I could tell.

She pushed my skirt down over my ass and hips. Someone, not Bronique, pulled my skirt down the rest of the way. I straddled Bronique and removed my shirt. She felt my breasts through the black satin bra. She ran her hands down the front of my thong, tracing the "V" that made its way between my thighs. She felt my heat. My wetness. I kissed her and pulled off her shirt. I unlatched her bra. Her breasts spilled out and begged to be kissed, sucked, nibbled. I fulfilled every request.

I looked around. I noticed that everyone else had stripped. I got up and removed my thong and bra, but I left my heels on. I felt lustful in them. We were all on the bed naked. Bronique and I were side by side. She pulled me into her arms. I kissed her. Beside me, I heard Sierra and Tammy kissing. Hearing them pleasuring each other filled me with pleasure. A feeling I wanted to share.

I slide my fingers down toward Bronique's clit. It was hard and she was wet. I slipped three fingers into her pussy. She moaned, rotated her hips and spread her legs wider. I thrust my fingers in and out of her wet pussy and kissed her again. She arched her back to meet each blow. Tammy and Sierra moved closer. I stopped kissing Bronique. I looked over at Tammy. She lay next to Bronique with her legs wide open. I could smell her sex. I was brought back to our encounter on her kitchen counter.

"Fuck me, too, Gail," Tammy said. "I want you and Sierra to fuck me."

I reached over and rubbed Tammy's mound. It was hot, hairy and horny. She wiggled when I entered her. Then Sierra pushed her fingers into Tammy along with mine. Tammy moaned and gyrated.

Bronique moved faster. My other hand was deep inside of her. It dripped with her juices. I stroked her faster to match her rhythm. I could tell she was about to climax. I pulled my hand out of Tammy and focused on Bronique.

"Oh, yes," she said in that sexy voice of hers. "Faster! Faster! Give it to me! Don't stop! I'm…I'm…coming!"

Warm liquid washed over and down my hand. She called out and gyrated her hips. Her toes curled. She reached for my hand and pulled it further into her pussy. I slipped another finger into her wetness. She moaned loudly and tossed her head from side to side. I pushed my fingers in further. She spread her legs wider in acceptance. I pumped and I prodded. Bronique gyrated and moaned. Her vaginal walls clenched and released, clenched and released around my hand. Her movements slowed. Then she collapsed deeper into the bed.

Tammy fingered me now. "Wait," I said. I could barely get the words out. "I know a way we can all be satisfied at once."

I turned Bronique over onto her stomach. I told Sierra to get on top of Bronique. I told Tammy to lie on top of Sierra. I got on top of Tammy. The ultimate sandwich—pussy to ass, pussy to ass. We fucked like a well-oiled train. Tammy's ass was plump and sweet. I broke a sweat giving it to her from behind. I felt like such a stud. This time, I was the cowboy. Tammy bucked and swayed beneath me. I held on to her waist and rode her ass. The juice from my pussy spread across it. Up and down. Up and down. We moved in unison. As if choreographed, Bronique came first, then Sierra, then Tammy, then me.

Well into the night, we found new ways to satisfy each other until we were spent. We showered, exchanged phone numbers, promised to get together again and kissed each other good-bye.

When I got home it was one o'clock. I put on my pajamas and eased into bed. My husband was asleep. I didn't want to wake him. Besides, I was dead tired. My husband turned on his side.

"How was moms' night out?" His voice was groggy.

"It was great," I said. "We're going to do it again next month."

"That's nice, honey." I heard him snoring before he finished the sentence. I smiled and fell asleep.

ഇൻ൚

Regina Jamison has been writing since she was twelve years old. She has always dreamed of becoming a writer. Her love of language led her on the path to speech therapy. She is now a speech therapist by day and a writer by night. She is finally finishing her first novel.

Woman of the Year
Charlotte Dare

Outside the luxurious Bay Side Inn, morning fog hovers over San Francisco Bay as a haze of sun tries nudging through. The conference room overlooking the city's famous Fisherman's Wharf bustles with an eclectic array of business-women gathered for the annual event honoring the achievements we sisters have long struggled to attain in this man's world. Ladies of all shapes and sizes, creeds, colors and zip codes descend upon the spread of tofu omelets, bagels, croissants, fruit salad and yogurt dip like squirrels stockpiling food supplies for a New England winter. Who could blame them?

The National Association of Female Small Business Owners spared no expense in making guests feel they're getting every penny's worth of the registration fee for the weekend celebration. More than just a schmooze-fest, the convention offers a plethora of networking possibilities, support services and plenty of female bonding, all culminating in the awards brunch late Sunday morn-ing in which one highly accomplished, trailblazing American businesswoman is honored for her stellar contributions.

A female small business owner myself, I'm always game for a weekend hailing the successes of my overachieving, go-getter colleagues provided the buffet is long, the speeches short, and I can get a plane out by two p.m. Sunday. I'd gorged myself on the vegetarian welcoming dinner the night before, yet this morning, oddly enough, I'm famished. As I inch along the line at the refreshment table, I grumble to myself about how these shindigs always feature the Queen's ransom in breakfast but set tiny little plates onto which guests must either pile a precarious tower of food or make four separate trips for refills.

"We havin' fun yet?" she drawls, leaning into my arm as she pours a stream of hot coffee from a towering percolator. I laugh before I even glance over at the face producing the quip. It's a relief to learn I'm not the only female who finds the annual festival of upwardly mobile sisterhood somewhat of a bore.

"A blast." I grin, turn away from the fruit salad ladle and feast my eyes on the most exotic beauty I've ever seen roaming earth among mortals.

"Girl, they should hold this event in Vegas each year. At least we can jaunt down to a crap table when it gets really hard to stay awake." She stirs half a packet of Equal into her coffee and reveals a shiny row of impossibly perfect teeth. "I'm Poetess Andrews," she says, extending long, brown fingers with French-manicured nails. "Of Andrews Travel in D.C., specializing in business, pleasure, and any exotic locale near or far, recently voted the Beltway's number one travel planner."

"After a pitch like that I would've guessed you're in advertising. I'm ready to book." I shake her hand gently, snapping myself out of an awkward gaze.

Her smooth, rich caramel skin frames a set of piercing amber eyes and full, raspberry-glossed lips wrap gingerly around the rim of her steaming cup of coffee. For the first time in months, I praise Aphrodite for keeping me single for so long.

"So what brings you here?" she asks, eyeing the mixed fruit I piled high atop a wheat bagel. "Business woman or did you just hear there'd be a bunch of party girls crammed into one big-ass convention room for the weekend?"

"Gee, and I thought I was so good at passing," I joke, stuffing a square of honeydew melon in my mouth.

"Gee, I didn't know twenty-first century white girls had reason to try," she fires back, her wit nearly upstaging a radiant smile.

"I run an online catalogue company," I reply, trying to mimic Poetess' cool. "I sell action figures, T-shirts, calendars. Whatever unnecessary item you need, just go to Tammy's Trinkets dot com, your one-stop, shop-at-home crap superstore."

She swallows and snorts a laugh simultaneously, covering her mouth to avoid showering me with coffee. I wouldn't have minded. It would make a wildly authentic excuse to prolong the dialogue.

"I'll have to check it out some time," she says, moving down to grab a smear of cream cheese for her blueberry bagel.

"That's an interesting name…Poetess. Is one of your parents a writer?"

"My father's a professor at Georgetown. He teaches the Harlem Renaissance. Huge fan of Langston Hughes but never did have a son he could name Langston. Guess the Man upstairs was looking out for me on that one."

I smile as she nibbles the tip of a strawberry impaled on a plastic fork.

"You here with anyone?" she asks, examining the unbitten portion.

Small talk or reconnaissance? I can't tell, but I guess I can hope anyway. "No, I'm here alone. Just needed a little tax-deductible weekend away from everything."

She sucks the rest of the strawberry off her fork with narrowed eyes. I think I just got my answer. "Well come on then," she commands with a tilt of her head. "Let's go grab us a table near the exit." Her tailored Donna Karan pantsuit hugs every inch of her tall, slender frame. I trail a few steps behind, deciding the best sight San Francisco has to offer is wiggling right in front of me.

ഇൻൽ

By four p.m., I'm squirming in my seat. The speeches are running long and out of the ten thousand glances at Poetess I've stolen since lunch, she was nodding off during at least two of them.

"Hey, Poetess," I whisper as guest speaker, Lois Rothchild, senior editor of *Women in Business*, drones on about the insidiousness of the glass ceiling in corporate America. "Wake up. Gloria Steinem is gonna lead the group in stoning a corrupt male corporate executive."

Stifling a yawn, she discreetly clasps her fingers and stretches stiff arms toward the floor. "Tammy, what in the hell are we doing growing moldy in here? I mean we're in 'Frisco, girl."

Next thing I know we're slipping out the side exit, Poetess leading the way with an impromptu plan to take over the city. We stop off at her room first so she can change into something outrageous for the evening.

"I'm a travel agent. I know where enough five-star restaurants and dyke bars are to keep us living large for a year," she brags, turning to unbutton her silky blouse after tossing the suit jacket on the bed.

She absently faces the mirror as she pulls the blouse out from her pants. I catch a glimpse of her candy-apple bra displaying tight, magnificent cleavage above firm, chocolaty abs. A tingle ripples between my legs. She smiles back at me from her reflection. I whip myself around toward the door to hide my complexion, which by now is more crimson than her bra, erasing any doubt as to whether I'd enjoyed the view.

"Uh, Poetess, I think I'll go press the elevator button," I mumble, eyes tracing sage and purple rectangles in the carpet.

"Tam, pull up a chair if you want. I used to model underwear for catalogues. It doesn't bother me a bit." She grins as she slips off her dress pants.

Who needs Vegas? I've hit the jackpot right there in 'Frisco. I smile at her free spiritedness. "Sorry for leering," I confess, "but you do have an amazing body."

"Thanks." She winks as though she'd heard that one a million times. She then draws up a clingy black Vera Wang, jumps into a pair of sparkly silver Manolo Blahniks and runs her fingers through wild jet curls. "Outrageous enough?"

"For both of us, which is good because charcoal gray and pink are as wild as I get," I reply, feeling more like Poetess' bodyguard than her dinner companion.

"We'll see about that," she drawls, grabbing my hand and nearly tugging my arm from its socket.

ಬಿ⧓ೞ

The Café is the Castro neighborhood's premier gay/lesbian dance club featuring three bars of top-shelf booze, a jam-packed dance floor, an outdoor patio, and of course, a line snaking out to the curb on weekends. In that outfit, all Poetess needed was her faux supermodel attitude, and we sashayed from the back of the crowd right through the front doors. Heads collided as we entered, and I knew they weren't gaping at me, or were they? Throughout dinner at Charanga, which consisted of a multitude of unpronounceable *tapas* or appetizers, I sipped sangria and drove myself to distraction wondering why she was wasting her weekend with me, Clammy Tammy, as I was known in high school. Here she is, this vibrant, exotic woman and she sticks herself with a bland, self-conscious gal from Paramus bent on kicking her own ass for letting her tanning membership lapse.

"I love how that v-neck contours your body. Why don't you lose this jacket," Poetess insists. In the middle of the dance floor, she peels it off my shoulders, wraps it around me and uses the sleeves to draw me against her.

"Are you sure you wouldn't rather dance with a woman with some rhythm? There's a nice pick over there," I suggest, pointing to a chic African-American lovely undulating in a cheetah print spandex one-piece and a spectacular afro like Link's from *The Mod Squad*.

"Are you generalizing all white folks as bottom-lip-biting, vanilla robots on the dance floor?"

"Not all white folks, just this one. See?" I bite my bottom lip and twist stiffly, knowing it will elicit from her that sexy, throaty laugh I'd discovered she had during dinner.

She starts grinding against me as Aretha's "Pride (A Deeper Love)" pounds from the speakers. Her hot, fruity Cosmopolitan breath steams up the front of my neck as her fingers creep up the back and twirl tresses of hair bobbing at my t-shirt collar. Sweaty air, pulsating rhythm, and flashing strobe lights fade like clouds of dry ice vapors. All I can smell is Poetess's enticing musk perfume, feel her soft, tight body pushing against mine, her hypnotic amber eyes boring holes through my inhibition.

"How much longer are you going to tease me," she breathes in my ear, sliding her hands down my back, halting them just short of my ass.

"My mistake," I joke, dying for them to keep sliding. "From where I'm standing, I'm the one being teased."

"Well, I know only one way we can resolve this debate." She locks her thigh between mine and we sway to the beat.

"What's that? Allow six inches of interpersonal space while we dance?"

"Uh, no," she sings, loosening the jacket sleeves knotted around my waist. "Go back to my room."

&

She has my jacket off again before the door to her room slams shut. Her plump lips lunge for mine as she tears at my belt buckle and swerves me toward the bed. I caress her soft brown arms and shoulders before falling to the cushy designer bedspread.

"Get out of those pants," she demands. She then lurches upright, crosses her arms and rips off her slinky black Vera Wang, revealing a candy-apple bra and matching thong.

I'm ashamed of myself, drooling over her all evening like a horny high school boy. Then suddenly I feel sympathy for the little creeps. This evening I'd learned how frustrating it is to want someone so badly. I obey her by squirming out of my dress pants and shirt in time to feel her warm, lanky body push mine back down. As she nibbles my ear and neck, her fingers sneak in through the side of my low-rise bikinis and stroke my aching clit.

"That feels nice," I exhale in her ear and bite a sumptuous shoulder that had tempted me all night from spaghetti straps.

Her long fingers penetrate, jolting me with pleasure. I gasp and grab her head as the fingers move slowly in and out. I'm so hot for her, I feel like I'll cum at any second.

"Not yet, baby," she says, pulling her hand out and divesting herself of her thong and bra. She sits up and stretches her long, naked body back, rubbing herself all over. She then begins slowly caressing her clit with one hand and fondling a maroon nipple with the other as I lie tortured, permitted to touch only the tops of her thighs.

"Let me, 'Tess," I beg, trying to pull her pelvis toward me. She slides up my body and offers my mouth her shaved treasure. I clutch at her firm cheeks and swirl my tongue around her ready clit. She lowers herself fully onto my face and throws her head back as I lick and tease her.

"Aw, yeah, Tammy, do it, do it," she moans.

I slip my tongue inside her and she shrieks with delight. Her breasts reach toward the ceiling and she claws at the bedspread as her climax begins. I rivet her clit as fast as I can while her groans fill the finely appointed room. She slowly thrusts against my tongue as an orgasm gathers force in the distance. I'm working her firm and steady, and suddenly feel fingers slide down over my clit, then up, then down again. This woman must be a gymnast. My own climax begins rumbling through, reverberating out to every limb, every organ. I struggle to hold my tongue in place on Poetess as a fierce climax roars in, giving way to an orgasm perfectly-timed with hers. We shudder together in an erotic heap reminiscent of an experimental live art exhibit I saw at some dive gallery in Newark last year.

Poetess then slithers down on top of me and gently kisses my lips, face and neck, all the tenderness skipped in our frantic foreplay. I wrap my arms around her silky torso and one of her long black tendrils falls across my face.

"I'm glad you hit on me this morning," I joke, running the tips of my fingernails down her sides.

"Yeah, right. You were all over my shit the second I snatched my bagel."

She then gazes at me with sweet eyes, and I sigh, knowing I'll never get that face out of my head no matter how many times I bang it against the wall.

"Listen," she whispers. "I know you're in Jersey and I'm in Alexandria, but I am a travel agent. I can get deals."

"I was hoping you'd say that." Just as I'm about to fall asleep in her arms, her lips begin a trip at my collar bone and glide all the way down until I'm once again, shuddering with ecstasy. I think the sun was rising by the time we finally stopped touching each other.

෧෬

The clang from the Powell and Hyde line trolley screeching by stirs me awake. Or maybe it was the fingers dancing across my stomach. "Time to get up," the voice of their owner whispers in my ear.

I pry open sleepy eyes to Poetess's satisfied grin and jumble of wild curls. After a sensual kiss, she flips the covers off her gleaming nakedness and tries to climb out of bed. One stealth attack from my arm and she's on her back again, her head bouncing on the pillow.

"We're gonna be late," she giggles, playfully struggling free.

"I don't care. Let's blow off that lame brunch and stay in bed.

Who needs another long-winded speech from some stuck-up, got-it-all-together overachiever, anyway?"

"Normally, I'd agree, but since all the other stuck up, got-it-all-together overachievers are sort of expecting me…" She grins with adorably humble eyes.

"You're kidding," I shout, roused from sleepiness. "You mean to tell me I spent the entire night banging NAFSBO's Woman of the Year?"

"Sure did. And might I say, damn good for a girl with no rhythm."

"I guess this means I have to stay awake for the closing speech," I tease. She swats me with her pillow before padding off to the shower.

&oc&

After I stuff my carry-on in the overhead compartment and strap myself into seat D, row twenty-nine of Delta flight 1377, I recall Poetess's elegance as she stood at the podium before a sea of professional women enrapt by the weekend's guest of honor. She was eloquent and charismatic as she spoke of the *inconveniences* encountered by black women venturing out on their own in the business world. My eyes welled at the thought of her voice quivering when she shared how her late artist mother told her in childhood that colors are for canvases, not people; that she should think of herself as a blank canvas and paint whatever future she imagines for herself. I stare at her picture stored in my camera phone once more before I'm instructed to turn off all electronic devices. I close my eyes as roaring jet engines drown out the world. After this weekend, I'm going to be a blank canvas, too.

Woman of the Year

ഏറ

Charlotte Dare explores the titillating world of lesbian erotica from her laptop at coffee houses in southern Connecticut. Her fiction has appeared in Tales of Travelrotica for Lesbians, Vol. 2, Ultimate Lesbian Erotica 2008, *and* Wetter: More True Lesbian Sex Stories *as well as in various online erotica journals.*

The Next Girl
Tawanna Sullivan

Raina is my best friend—and I hate her. We've known each other for over ten years. If there was anyone who would have my back, it would be her.

Everything was fine until Raina started dating my next girl. The next girl is the woman you have your eye on while you're trying to break up with your current girl. Jelisa Friday is a goddess. I'm not just talking about her smooth velvet voice or her delicious chocolate curves. She's the kind of woman who can smile at you and all of your worries just fall away. She's smart, sexy, and should have been mine.

I had been laying the groundwork with Jelisa for a few weeks. I still had love for Stephanie, but things hadn't been working out for a while. Going home to her was like going into a war zone. I had timed it so that the transition from Steph to Jelisa would be seamless.

Now, let me set the scene for you. Stephanie and I are at the Allegro to cheer on one of her coworkers in the Mr. Gay USA competition. The house lights are down low and a dude in a thong is on stage flexing his muscles. Suddenly, Jelisa walks into the room and it's like the whole world stops. Yes, even the men all paused. I didn't hug her as usual—I'm not going to disrespect

Steph to her face—but I made space for her at our table. That's when I turned around and saw Raina beside her.

Neither announced they were on a date, but their actions proved it. Throughout the whole evening, there were sly touches on the arm and whispers. Jelisa loved the attention. They barely acknowledged our presence at all. After Mr. Gay USA had been crowned, Raina took her to some dark corner to do God knows what.

I couldn't believe it. My best girl had stolen my next girl and there was nothing I could say about it.

Raina is a notorious playa; no woman can hold her attention for long. So, it didn't surprise me when cracks started appearing in their relationship. We were back at the Allegro playing pool. I had just finished a new version of my Stephanie-is-getting-on-my-last-nerve rant, when Raina finally dropped the bombshell. "Jelisa is starting to move a little too fast for me." Then she leaned over and ever so gently tapped the three ball into the right corner pocket.

I stepped back, took a sip of my whiskey sour, and nodded for her to continue. "She gave me a set of house keys," Raina complained. "She's expecting me to give her a key, too. My mother doesn't even have the key to my place." She tossed down a few peanuts and with a bank shot sunk the seven into a side pocket. "Narcia, this girl is talking domestic partnership. I'm just trying to make it to a six month anniversary."

It was clear that Jelisa was about to get her feelings trampled on and I, Narcia, didn't care. Served her ass right for not being patient and waiting for me.

Since I didn't say anything—hey, I'm not Dr. Phil—Raina kept "processing" her feelings. Shot after shot, she whined about how she was nervous about settling down. "Honestly, I'm not trying to run away this time."

At the end of the game, all Raina had to do was hit the eight ball into the right back pocket. Anyway, that's the pocket any normal person would have chosen. A few other women had gathered around to cheer her on and she wasn't about to disappoint her fans. She pointed her cue at the front left pocket. "Eight ball in the corner," she announced and everyone "oohed" and "aahed" on cue.

When she slid the stick behind her back and winked at me, I looked away in disgust. Next thing I knew, everyone was clapping and Raina had a mini entourage escorting her to the bar.

That's when I started thinking about how Raina never missed an opportunity to humiliate me. She's a better pool player than me, so why the fancy shots? Just because she could. Raina knew how I felt about Jelisa and had no business stepping to her like that. She could have had any girl she wanted, but she had to take my next girl.

As you can see, that shit started eating me up on the inside. The idea hit me on the cab ride home. Why should Raina always have it her way? What if she was the one who got dumped? Even better, what if I stole Jelisa back…

This time was going to be different. I could do it all: get my next girl, make Steph my ex-girl, and burn my trifling best friend. The best part? Raina was going to help me do it.

Every woman, gay or straight, secretly suspects that her lover has or will cheat. It was easy to plant seeds of doubt. When Raina and I went to a football game, I would sneak out of the stands and make a call. "Jelisa, where's your girl? She was supposed to meet me in front of the stadium a half-hour ago. Oh wait, here she comes." Before I got back to my seat, Raina's cell was going off.

During the next round of the pool tournament, I pretended to have a low battery and asked to borrow Raina's phone. I put it in my pocket and conveniently "forgot" about it. Ms. Hustler was too busy performing tricks to realize it was missing. Jelisa had called five times during the night. When confronted, Raina simply told the truth and got chewed out for it.

I didn't see Raina again until Steph decided to have a 70s throwback party. Her vision was to turn the basement into a disco and the first floor into a lounge. I recruited Raina to be the bartender and Jelisa volunteered to help Stephanie with the food. When Raina walked in I almost didn't recognize her. She used to greet everyone with a smile and a hug. This time she didn't even look us in the eyes. She just nodded her head and stood off to the side. You would have thought she was sick or something.

Steph had prepared lunch for us, but Raina wanted to get started. It was like she couldn't wait to get up from under Jelisa. We'd just finished putting up the speakers, when the cooking crew announced they were making a grocery run. The door slammed shut behind them and it was like a weight fell off of Raina's shoulders. "Jelisa acts like I'm fucking somebody if I'm out of her sight for two minutes." She popped the caps off of two wine coolers and passed one to me. "Get this, I'm not doing anything. I go from work to Jelisa's house. If I go home to my apartment, she either calls twenty times for nothing or shows up at my doorstep because she misses me. How do I have time to cheat?"

While my best friend was fighting back tears, I had to take a quick sip to stop myself from breaking into nervous laughter. Honestly, I felt guilty. I thought Jelisa would dump her and Raina would feel the sting but bounce back. I offered her some practical advice. "Why don't you just leave her? You've gotten so wrapped up in this chick that you are losing yourself."

"I love her. She wasn't this person when I met her. I want to get the real Jelisa back."

True to form, once the party started Jelisa was right at the bar monitoring Raina's interactions. She was like a guard dog, ready to accidentally bump or shove aside any woman who was being too friendly. Everyone knew something was wrong and Steph was two seconds from going off on Jelisa herself.

As usual, it was up to me to save the day. I put on Donna Summer's "Bad Girls," grabbed Jelisa's hand, and forced her to dance. It's like the entire crowd sighed in relief. The whole room was shaking its groove thing.

My boy Carlos took over the turntables for me so I could go outside for a minute. My little polyester suit was drenched with sweat. I was holding a cold bottle of water to my forehead when I heard the screen door open and close behind me. It was a slightly tipsy Jelisa.

"What are you doing out here by yourself?" she asked.

I thought it was obvious, but I played along. "Trying to keep cool."

"That's not how you do it." She took the water out of my hand, opened it, and took a good, healthy drink. She pushed herself against me; we were so close I could feel her heart beating. Her cool lips grazed my cheek and lingered there before kissing my neck. A cold chill went through my arms and legs but that triangle between my nipples and my pussy was on fire. The different sensations jangled my nerves and I had to grab the rail to steady myself. Jelisa smirked and went back inside.

Damn, I thought to myself, *she's looking for the next girl*.

There was a change after the party. Jelisa began calling me on my cell just to shoot the breeze. The longer I thought about it, the more my sympathy for Raina's situation faded. If she didn't have enough sense to leave a woman who was treating her bad, it's not my fault. Besides, it was time that the scales of fate tip back in my favor.

Turns out I didn't have the upper hand at all. I was going to the Chambres Shopping Center and cut through the Franklin Square Condo development. It's an exclusive community that has its own security to keep undesirables out, but I knew all of the guards. When Raina was dating Trina, we hung out there all the time.

I had almost made it to the underpass when I ran into Officer Blabbermouth. She knows everybody's business and has no problem broadcasting it. Soon as she saw me, she started grinning from ear to ear. "Narcia, how you been? It's about time you showed up."

"I'm okay. What do you mean?"

"Your buddy is already at Trina's place. Is there a party going on tonight?"

"Yeah, I guess so."

When I finally managed to get away from her, I took a detour to Trina's townhouse. I'll be damned if Raina wasn't walking out of the house. Trina was standing in the doorway pulling her bathrobe closed. They exchanged a few words and then kissed like she was going off to war or something. I looked over at the clock tower. It was 5:30. Raina was working overtime alright.

Stephanie didn't have dinner ready when I got home, but I was too agitated to eat. Raina was acting like she was one argument away from a nervous breakdown, but she had been phasing Jelisa out. How long had she been talking to Trina? What really fucked with me is that I didn't know anything about it. We were supposed to be closer than sisters and she hadn't said shit to me.

It was really time to knock Raina down off of her high horse, and I wanted her to know it was me who threw the punch. When Jelisa got home from work the next day, she found me sitting on her front steps.

"Narcia? What's up? Did something happen to Raina?"

I took a deep breath. "Something has been weighing heavy on my heart and I've got to come clean about it." Hers eyes welled up as I continued. "You should know what's going on."

A few minutes later we were sitting in her den and the tears were flowing freely. All I did was tell the truth. "I caught them in the act. They were nearly fucking in the doorway. Raina's hands were all up under that robe. I knew you suspected something, but I didn't want to say anything until I knew for sure."

Jelisa started wailing. "I hate that bitch."

I got a tissue and started wiping her cheeks. "Nah, girl. Don't scrunch up your face like that. You are too beautiful to go into hysterics over anyone." I started stroking her chin and she moved closer to me and put her head on my shoulder.

"I tried so hard," she said. "What's wrong with me?"

"You're a good woman and you deserve better." Now, I had rehearsed this all night, but something unexpected came out of my mouth next. "I should have just gotten rid of Stephanie instead of asking you to wait. None of this shit would have happened if I had treated you with the respect you deserve. I'm sorry."

I meant it, too. There was just something about seeing Jelisa weak and vulnerable. I wanted to put my arms around her and protect her from the entire world. Raina had done her dirty, but I was the one who had made her cry.

I raised her chin to kiss her forehead. Then, I was kissing the tears from her eyes. Her lips touched mine… In that moment, it wasn't about Raina, Stephanie or anybody else. Both of us had an emptiness that needed to be filled.

Her bold move at the party should have been a clue that she wasn't a pillow queen, but I was caught off guard when she pulled me on top of her. I continued kissing her tears away and she gently raked her nails across my stomach. I was trying to work the buttons on her blouse, but she got my shirt off first and began sucking my nipples.

I tried to pull away, but Jelisa had a damn good grip on my khakis. She was fighting to pull my zipper down. "Let me touch you in all the places your girl won't." Next thing I knew, her hand had slipped inside of my boxers and was massaging my pussy.

When she parted my lips, the hot, sticky pool that had welled up inside of me flooded her fingers and my clit. Jelisa was gently stroking my outer walls, trying to find the way inside. I jerked myself away just as she was about to enter. I felt like I was going to fucking collapse.

I could barely catch my breath. "Nah, babygirl, this is about you."

Slipping down to the floor, I nudged her legs apart. There is nothing sexier than a woman in stockings. When her body is trembling and that nylon is roughly sliding against your tongue, it feels damn good. I swung her right leg over my left shoulder and rubbed my cheek against her thigh. Her essence was intoxicating.

I nibbled my way down to her garter and stopped as she lifted herself to meet me. Jelisa never wore underwear—she made that quite apparent when we first met. My nose nuzzled against her clit and she jumped. "Come on, baby," she begged. "Don't tease it."

We settled into an easy rocking rhythm as I tasted and teased her lips. My tongue had just curled around her clit, when the front door opened.

Bam! I was on the floor. Jelisa pushed her skirt back down, buttoned up her blouse, and went out to meet Raina.

I just sat there; stunned. It was the one night Raina decided not to work late. A minute hadn't passed before the shouting began. "I'm tired of you accusing me of shit I haven't done!"

I got dressed, went into the kitchen and tried to wash the scent of Jelisa from my face. Instead of hiding, I decided to stroll into the living room as innocently as possible. Of course, I picked the worst fucking possible moment. Jelisa was crying again and waving her arms frantically. "You spent the entire afternoon with her."

Raina's voice had returned to normal, but the way her jaw was clenched you knew she could fly off again any second. "I told you I needed to stop by her house to drop off some paperwork. I got there around four and didn't stay for more than five minutes."

"You left her house at five-thirty! Somebody saw you."

"Who?"

"It doesn't make a difference who. You are busted!"

That's when my size nines walked into the living room and they both turned to look at me. Jelisa was still screaming, but my eyes were locked with Raina's. "You're my girl and everything," I said, "but wrong is wrong. I saw you kissing Trina and I didn't think Jelisa should be kept in the dark."

Raina didn't even blink. "You had to tell her in person, so that you could be here to comfort her?"

Jelisa didn't appreciate being ignored and stepped right up in Raina's face. "If you had been where you were supposed to be, none of this would have happened."

"Okay, fine." Raina pulled out her cell phone and stepped out on the porch.

I walked over to Jelisa, but she wouldn't even look at me. "You have soap on your chin," she said.

When Raina came back inside, she put a key on the bookcase. "I don't need this any more." Jelisa started to say something, but Raina wasn't having it. "You could have at least waited to ask me about it first, but you've been looking for any excuse to fuck my so-called friend, right?"

The tissue Jelisa had been using had disintegrated and she was wiping her running makeup with the back of her hand. "Why are you always blaming other people for your mistakes?"

"Let's go for a ride." A smirk slowly spread across Raina's face and she issued a challenge to me. "Come on, Narcia. Why don't you show us exactly what you saw?"

Before I could say anything, Jelisa was back to yelling. "I don't want to talk to Trina. That bitch would say anything for you."

Raina never took her eyes off of me. "No, she wouldn't. Besides, I'm not about to drag her into this mess. I just want to show you that Narcia couldn't possibly have seen what she told you."

This seemed too good to be true. Raina wasn't even fighting to keep her girl, but I didn't appreciate her trying to throw the spotlight back on me. I figured she was bluffing, so I decided to take her up on it. "Jelisa, I know what I saw. Your ex-girl is just trying to save face." Then, I nodded to Raina. "Let's go."

I thought Raina was going to punk out at the last minute, but we were zooming down I-83 before I could button my jacket. She made both of us sit in the back. There were no more tears, but Jelisa alternated between staring at the back of Raina's head and glaring at me.

At night, the Franklin Square area was deserted. We parked on the street and walked to the same corner I had seen them from. I pointed out Trina's townhouse. "See, I have a perfect view. You can see the whole courtyard from this spot."

The fire came back into Jelisa's eyes. "This ain't nothing but some bullshit. Don't waste my time. All the crap you have left at my house will be sitting outside in the morning. It's trash day, so you better get it early."

Raina smiled at me and then turned to Jelisa. "Why don't you ask your new girl what time it is?"

Jelisa was confused. "What? It's seven-thirty. What does that have to do with anything?"

I looked up at the clock tower. It was still five-thirty. I made this gargling sound; words were caught in my throat. That's when Jelisa started screaming at me. She had seen it, too.

Raina started laughing. "That clock hasn't worked in months, so it's always five-thirty in Franklin Square."

Jelisa was bawling her eyes out and punching me in the chest. Then, Stephanie's car pulled up. It clicked—that's who Raina had called.

As my best friend drove away, I could feel the gates of hell closing in on me.

ഌരു

Tawanna Sullivan is the webmaster for Kuma (www.kuma2.net), a website which encourages black lesbians to write and share erotica. Her work has appeared in Longing, Lust, and Love: Black Lesbian Stories, Iridescence: Sensuous Shades of Lesbian Erotica, *and* Spirited: Affirming The Soul and Black Gay/Lesbian Identity. *She lives in New Jersey with her civil union partner, Martina.*

Pleasures

Elissa Gabrielle

Here she comes again, hips swaying to the beat of an African drummer, full and satisfying, as her tits bounce in beat to the drums; look at her, pure perfection. I see her crossing the street, working her way toward my day spa, Pleasures, with the strut of a goddess. She's been coming in here for two weeks now, invading my mental for most nights since her inception. My eyes follow Toni's every move as she approaches me, which seems to be in slow motion, unless of course, she is so fly that viewing her in real time may be just too much for a sistah. The confidence in her stride, coupled with golden brown skin, on a five-foot-nine-inch voluptuous frame, laced with sweet, full honey-coated lips, light brown eyes, and soft jet black ringlet curls cascading down her neck, and off her shoulders, sends a chill through my spine that works its way through my entire being, finally landing on my clitoris, which bulges, throbs, pulsates in anticipation of her.

I wonder if she tastes as good as she looks.

Miss Toni was just in here over the weekend, for a manicure, pedicure and facial. I hadn't had the pleasure of touching her exquisite face, nor to hold her petite hand or massage her thick calves; my employees had the honor. However, my eyes followed her every move, from a lick of her luscious lips to her tiptoeing to the ladies room. I couldn't keep my eyes off of her on that day, just like I can't stop right now.

"Good afternoon, Toni. Back so soon?"

"Hi, Laila! Yes, I was hoping to get a quick massage. I've had a grueling day at the office, and I need one so bad."

"Well, Toni, you know it's just about closing time here at Pleasures, so my masseuse is gone for the evening."

"Oh, I'm so sorry I missed her! I could really use some relaxation."

Giving me a look that makes me want to fall to my knees upon her command, makes me reconsider her dilemma, and just when I try to extend a solution to her problem, Toni beats me to the punch.

"Laila, can you give me a quick massage? I know you've trained all of your employees. I'd pay double right about now."

"You know, Toni, I was just thinking the same thing. Sure, I can do it, but, girl, you have to get here earlier next time. It's past seven in the evening, and getting dark out."

Taking Toni by the hand, I lead her into the room dedicated for body massages, remove her purse and take her scarf, place them into the chair. Reaching into the closet, I pull out a full-length, soft, white cotton towel, and hand it to her. While striking a match, I walk to each of the strategically placed aromatherapy candles and light them one by one. While doing so, my pussy walls are set on fire by the sight I behold, as I turn to instruct Toni to remove her clothes, once I leave the room, to give her privacy.

"Toni. I was going to tell you to take your clothes off once I stepped out of the room." I try not to stare at this vision of love-liness; fresh-smelling, butter soft skin with Tootsie-Roll nipples that stand at attention right before me. *Damn*.

Keeping me in her gaze, Toni's smile had a spark of eroticism.

"Well, you handed me the towel, Laila, so I thought you wanted me to remove my clothes. I'm sorry if I've made you uncomfortable." Either she knows that I am really digging her, or she is the ultimate tease.

While adjusting the heat setting, on the massage table, to low, I can't help but to look, get another quick glance at sexiness in its most deep and seductive form. "Toni, you can lie down on the table, face down, and place your head…" I smiled, pointing to the face slot. "…into this opening here."

Mmmmm, looking at her climb onto the table, her golden skin blends perfectly with the aqua-colored tabletop, as the silkiness of her hair flows uncontrolled over her shoulders, into her face as she lies down. The visual of her smooth back, which leads to the most delectable set of ass cheeks I've ever seen, sends chills throughout my entire being, shooting orgasmic waves through me, reaching my nipples, which harden with ease, as well as my clit, which is throbbing like a rapid heartbeat. A red, strawberry tattoo rests comfortably on the bottom of her left cheek, near the divine crack of her sweet ass, and I'm dying to get a taste.

The things I could do to her.

As I cover her full and bountiful bottom with the towel, the sweet smell of Estee Lauder's Beautiful penetrates all my senses, clinging to my nostrils. "Are you comfortable, Toni?"

"Yes, Laila. Thanks a million for this. I have to find a way to repay you," she said, while burying her face further into the face hole, as she prepares to enjoy a full body massage.

Standing directly in front of where Toni is laying, her face now aligned with my thighs, I fantasize about being nestled erotically between her thighs, smack dab in the middle of her goodness, as I pour lavender oil into the palm of my hands, lean in and begin to massage her back. Her skin glistens and makes for even more eye candy. *She's a sin and a damn shame.*

"Mmm, Laila, that is just what I needed."

"No problem, Toni. I'm glad I was able to help you out."

"Laila, if you don't mind me asking, what do you bathe in?"

"Well, this morning, I bathed in something by Carol's Daughter, but I can't remember exactly what. Why do you ask?"

"Well, you smell good, Laila."

"Thanks, but how can you smell me? You're all the way down there."

"All the way down here is where it matters, doesn't it?"

Okay, breathe easy. I need to tread lightly or else she is going to get it in the worst kind of way. "I guess so," I respond nonchalantly since I'm not sure what she's talking about.

While working my way down her back, I reach the top of her ass and begin stroking deeply and with intensity as she is very tight and needs to be loosened up. Maybe she's stressed.

"Come on, Laila. You know if the kitty doesn't smell right, then it ain't right!" Toni tells me with a slight giggle. Shit, I ain't laughing. She's got my full, undivided attention.

"You're right, Toni," I say as I massage her thighs and calves. "You're almost done. How do you feel?"

"Done, so soon? I thought I had to flip over."

"Oh, sure you can. I'll give you a few minutes and you can lie on your back. Be right back."

"Thanks, Laila."

As I softly close the door behind me, I can feel the rain between my thighs, so I proceed to get a glass of water, down it in a matter of seconds, and return to the room. The aroma from the candles, along with the dimly lit atmosphere makes for a tantalizing moment, as Toni lies there, in the flesh.

"Girl, you are too funny! You have to put this towel over you! Laying here butt naked!" I laugh to ease the obvious sensual tension.

So, with the boldness and grace of a lioness, Toni tells me, "Massage me, Laila."

You ain't got to tell me twice, damnit.

As the oil floats from mid-air and lands into the palm of my hand, Toni follows my every move as I make my way to her, placing my oil-filled hands on her abdomen and begin to massage. Her nipples rise, become perky and persistently invite me to kiss them, but I can't.

"Mmmm, you don't know how bad I needed this, Laila."

"I'm glad you're enjoying yourself, Toni. I aim to please," I say, all the while trying not to succumb to the desire that now insists on swallowing me whole.

Gliding my hands down her thighs, I rub them slowly and watch them begin to shine, when Toni gently grabs my hand. "My inner thighs, too, Laila."

"Sure."

As she slowly parts her voluptuous thighs, I see the fine hairs of her love have started to become slick, and wet, parting ways, like Moses and the Red Sea; and what remains are the loveliness of two juicy, swollen pussy lips, dying to be sucked, licked and loved. Eating her pussy now can cost me my spa. But eating is what this pretty pussy needs.

Toni takes her fingers and delicately begins to massage a beautiful and bulbous clit for me, as she spreads her legs far, and wide. Her sweet vagina shines from her nectar.

"Toni, umm, I think we're done."

"Why, Laila? Suck my pussy a little. I know you want to. And I want you to, so fucking bad, Laila."

Reaching out to me, she pulls me head first into the sweetest pussy I've ever seen in my life, as I devour her righteousness with my tongue, sucking this pussy with so much passion.

"Mmm, that's it. Oh, God, you're so good!" Toni squeals as she pushes my head further into all that is good, precious and dear. "Kiss me, Laila. Let me taste that pussy on your lips."

Toni leans up to prepare for my kiss as I begin to undress, slowly moving into all of her space. I grab her face into my hands, and slowly kiss her, allowing her to taste her sweet nectar on me. Luring me with a combination of her vernacular and confidence, I'm slowly losing my mind as her hands find their way to my breasts, which are now completely exposed, in full bloom, nipples erect and in desperate need of attention. Toni softly tweaks my nipples with her fingertips, bends down slowly and tastes them, alternately placing my breasts into her mouth.

"Shit, Toni, this is not right."

"But you look so good, Laila. I've been wanting to fuck you from the first time I laid eyes on you, baby. You have to let me taste your pussy. I want to eat it, smell it, taste it on my fingers, let my tongue play in it. I need for you to cum on my lips, my face. Can I, Laila, please?" Toni pleads as she places her hands between my legs, roaming to the center of my warmth, which quickly turns to heat as she nears. "Lie on the table, Laila. I need to taste you. But lie on your stomach, let me eat this sweet pussy from the back."

I oblige and lay facedown onto the massage table as Laila guides me with her fingers, feeling on the sides of my breasts, rubbing and smacking my ass, finger fucking me and tasting my juices. "Damn, Toni, you're going to make me cum so hard. You gotta ease up a bit."

"Shit, I been waiting too long for this. Spread your legs. Spread that sweet pussy real good for me, Laila."

The sensation Toni's lips leaves is indescribable, it's so good. "Uh, uh, uh, mmmm, Toni, damn, slow down. Shit! I'm there. Oh God!"

"Flip over, Laila."

As I prepare to turn over, I think about what I am doing, and try to resist once more, only to have Toni interrupt me with more sweet kisses, more caressing to my breasts, as she lies on top of me, rubbing her clit against mine. My nectar flows uncontrollably onto her sweet clit, and I feel the rain pouring out of her sweet hole.

"Ooooh, Laila, damn, you feel so fucking good. I'm coming now. Gotdamn… Mmm."

Several more minutes pass of serious lovemaking, heavy breathing, slow kisses, and lots of licking until we both reach our maximum. A slick display of flesh on flesh, with bated breath, and carnal pleasure, removes all reason from me and leaves me in a state of disbelief. Indeed at a lost for words.

"I don't know what to say, Laila."

"You don't have to say anything, Toni. We both wanted this."

৪০০৪

Fire and brimstone settles into my soul, as my earth shatters and shakes me in a way where I become momentarily paralyzed. You've got to be kidding me? With the "no she didn't" neck roll, I flame at the sight making its way across the street, headed toward my place of business, but this time it is not a vision of perfection, rather one that makes my nostrils flair and that green-eyed monster, better known as jealously, consumes me.

"Hey, Laila, how are you this evening?"

"I'm good, Toni," I respond, not at all interested in what will come out of her mouth next. Pretty young thing has obviously found a new girl toy, which is right beside her. She has good taste, I must admit, reluctantly, of course, but the new Pam Grier has entered the building, seeing pretty in the spot that should be reserved for moi.

"Lay, can I get a quick massage?"

Oh, see, she has lost her damn mind. "Oh, I'm sorry, Toni. I can't tonight."

Glaring at me with puppy dog eyes, melting my insides, but no way is this happening tonight

"Oh, Lay, this is Paris, my coworker."

"Nice to meet you, Paris. I'm Laila."

"I know Laila," Paris responds. "Toni has said so many wonderful things about you."

Well, that warmed my heart. I'm ready to fuck all the good sense out of her. "Do you mind waiting while I give Toni a quick massage? It won't be long, as I'm closing in about fifteen minutes."

"Sure, Laila, you and Toni go ahead. I'll wait here. Hey, maybe we can go out to dinner afterward?"

"Maybe so," Toni responds as she walks hurriedly into the massage room, better known as the den of pleasure.

I close the door behind us, and Toni has already begun to take her clothes off, when she reaches for me, pushes my back to the wall and pulls me into one of the most sensational kisses of my life. With an overconfident, yet sexy grin, Toni says to me, "I saw you getting jealous out there. I like that shit."

I play it off, all the while ashamed that she could actually see through me so. "Naw, girl, I'm good. She's a pretty girl, you have good taste."

"Yeah, she's pretty…"

"I know, Toni, I just said that."

"But she ain't you, Lay."

Okay, that's it. She didn't come here for a damn massage. She must be in search of a good lay, because talking like that is going to get her in serious trouble.

Kissing down her neck, while my hands find the place I want to call home, she moans, and quivers at my every touch, which turns me on like crazy. As delicious as she looks, she smells equally as good, and from the looks of the juices flowing through my fingers from her moisture, she finds me equally as appetizing. I'm ready.

"Get up on that table, girl. We don't have that much time."

She flips the script. "No, Laila. You lie on the table, and let me serve you properly this time. It's on me, baby."

I quickly hop up on the table, in my birthday suit only, and spread my legs, as my sugar walls invite her to come in and have a good time.

"Damn, Laila. Just as gorgeous as I remember."

The delicate and delectable dessert tastes good to Toni, and feels even better to me as I close my eyes, while in the midst of pure ecstasy, only to open them with a serious fuck face.

Shock overwhelms me as I glance to my left, and find Paris standing there, watching Toni dig me out. She stares in amazement. I back up and Toni grabs a hold of my thighs and pulls my righteousness further into her face as she enjoys the feast even more now that there is a voyeur present. I try to speak, and the words form, but don't come out of my mouth.

"Don't worry, Laila. Toni is your woman. I just have to watch," Paris says to me as she approaches, removing her blouse, exposing her breasts to me. Toni continues to suck with purpose while Paris places her tongue into my mouth, licks my lips softly, kisses my neck, and rubs my breasts. An orgasm unbeknownst to mankind just came over me.

"That's right, baby, come hard," Toni says as she kisses my inner thighs. She pulls up and walks toward me, smiling from ear to ear. "You like this, baby?"

"Yes, Toni, I do, but…"

A single finger covers my lips. "Shhh," Toni says to me as she and Paris switch gears.

"Toni, what are you doing?"

"Nothing, Laila, just let me love you."

My eyes wander and find focus on several key pieces in my massage room, like my candles, and my oils, and, well, something new I had planned to share with Toni when I saw her again, but she beat me to it.

"Is this for me, baby?"

"Yes," I respond, red as a beet, I'm sure.

A pretty in pink vibrator fills Toni's hand as she hands it to Paris. Throwing caution to the wind, Paris dives in, gently bites my clitoris, which makes me come instantly and proceeds to long, determined licks against my walls. The sweet smell of hot, sticky, wet vagina consumes me as Toni parts my mouth with her lips, and I smell my pussy on her breath once more. Moving downward, she pushes my breasts together, sucks and kisses my nipples, while Paris inserts the vibrator into me, turns it on and now, I'm psycho.

"Oh God… too much, please, Toni, I can't take this," I yell in ecstasy, while Toni fingers my clit, rubs my juices throughout and Paris wiggles the pleasurable weapon of my satisfaction in and out of me vigorously. Multiple orgasms take control of me and all I can do is give in to the pleasure.

"Toni, baby, uh, uh, uh, uh... aaaahhh! Shit, this is so good!"

Erotic explosions go on for what seem like days, and when it's all said and done, Toni reaches over me, and says, "I'll be in tomorrow for my massage, baby."

ଛଠଓଷ

Dubbed the "Queen of Hip Hop Romance Erotica" by Disilgold Soul Magazine, Elissa Gabrielle is the author of two poetry books, Stand and Be Counted *and* Peace in the Storm, *the highly acclaimed novel,* Good to the Last Drop, *and the sequel,* Point of No Return, *as well as the much anticipated novel,* A Whisper to a Scream. *Gabrielle's literary contributions can be found in* Erogenous Zone: A Sexual Voyage, Mocha Chocolate: A Taste of Ecstasy, The Triumph of My Soul *and multiple poetry anthologies. She is the founder of the greeting card line,* Greetings from the Soul: The Elissa Gabrielle Collection. *Gabrielle has graced the covers of* Conversations *magazine,* Big Time Publishing *magazine, and* Disilgold Soul *magazine. Visit the author at www.elissagabrielle.com and email the author at BooksByGabrielle@aim.com.*

The Finest Man
Wanda D. Hudson

This all began the night I made a mistake. The target was unnerved by my stupidity and continued as if I hadn't spoken a word. My job as a night security officer at a women's homeless shelter was more boring that I expected, and my inaccuracy happened during one of my attempts to catch a spell of much needed shuteye.

Chairs are not allowed during the twelve-to-eight shift, so my bottom side rested atop a garbage can. A can that I wanted to crawl into once I realized what I did.

Knowing I'd be relieved of my shift in less than two hours, I tried not to drift any deeper into sleep. My partner, Simpson, defied the powers that be and confiscated a chair from another part of the building. While we tried to sneak sleep in plain sight, we also tried to stay alert to our surroundings. This was an action that wouldn't be accomplished. My mistaken words came out slow and groggy at first, and then reached their full momentum before I could take them back.

Deirdra, although I didn't know her name at the time, came around the corner and did a double take to see me sitting propped up against the wall. I had startled her, as she me, but her mouth remained closed as she made her way to the ladies room. The first time I opened my eyes I caught a glimpse of her face; the second time, her backside. Shouting was my way of alerting the clients of its presence.

"Man on the floor!" came from me in a weary boasting voice. I pushed these words out of my lungs hard. The ladies bathroom was at the other end of the hall and I wanted no one to get a free peep show due to not doing my job. Feeling I had done my duty, I leaned my head back and closed my eyes to try and recapture the thoughts that danced in my mind in its peaceful state. That's when I had a slight epiphany.

"Wait a minute...no men come on the floor at this hour. And what man would wear flip-flops and shorts up here?"

My eyes opened wide and I sat up when my partner informed me of the slipup I created.

"Wilson, that's a woman."

Horror engulfed me momentarily as I hopped up off of the can and paced the small area. Simpson sat up also, and looked at me as if I were a hilarious crazy woman about to lose her mind.

I wasn't convinced. "A woman? You gotta be kidding me. That was a man...wasn't it?"

Once we both realized I was serious and had genuinely made a mistake, we giggled in delight. Our snickers weren't for the embarrassment of the client, but for my stupidity. My job was to work as a security officer, not to belittle women who were going through God knows what and somehow managed to end up in a less than pleasurable predicament.

I continued to pace and turn in circles. Raising my hands over my head and bringing them down to cover my face was the action that I repeated over and over again, as if I were trying to wipe my features away. Simpson signaled to me that the client was walking back in our direction. We didn't want to look like we were laughing at her manly female exterior, so we became silent.

The client's steps were quick. When she was close enough to hear my voice I said the only thing that might soothe the situation. The words to change it, or take it back didn't come to mind, so I mustered up what little dignity I had, and offered up the first words in winning a friend back.

"Hey, look, I'm sorry. I didn't mean to say that." My words came out sincere with pleading hand movements attached to every consonant and vowel.

"Naw, that's cool. Don't worry about it," was the callous, hurried, brush-off of a reply I received. My target kept walking, but my heart was still heavy. I wanted to shout, "Wait, we need to talk about this," but before one syllable could reach my lips, she was out of my sight.

Simpson came and stood next to me. "Damn, I can't believe I said that shit." We burst out into hysterics.

"Well, believe it," were the only words she got out as she hunched over and continued laughing.

"Anybody could have made that mistake, right? Doesn't she look like a dude to you?" I needed to feel like everyone else was on my side.

"There are a lot of them that look like men in here. It's hard to tell sometimes."

Simpson eased my mind momentarily, but as we continued to talk and wait for our relief, I couldn't get my words, or Deirdra's face, out of my mind.

શ્ર૦લ્સ

The next night really freaked me out. I began to wonder during my silent time if, in fact, I was a lesbian. I rationalized that I wasn't because, technically, Deirdra wasn't a woman. She carried herself like a man. Her walk, her talk, her aroma, her baggy style of dress, all of those characteristics belonged to a man. A rather sexy man with a special connection to the female species—a man that was stuck somewhere between panties and boxers.

I arrived at work at my regular time and pulled up next to a car to easily maneuver parallel parking. A man stood at the back of the car in front of me and turned to see exactly what I was doing, and why was my vehicle so close to his. Looking away from my site of the curb, I noticed his face full on. My thoughts were, "Now that's a nice-looking brotha. He's well-groomed, has a nice car, and is smooth and handsome." When I turned my car off, the man closed his trunk and walked past me. He went under a street-light and I received a much clearer view of him. Deirdra. The man I married in my mind for a few seconds was Deirdra.

∞∞

During my lunch break that night I went and sat in my car to try and clear my head. The first person I thought of was Deirdra. What the hell was going on with me? I actually wanted to step to her and say anything. Anything that would let me into her world. Anything that would give me insight into why I was suddenly feeling her. Was it because she looked like the man that I've always desired, or because I've secretly wanted a woman for my mate all along?

"Shit, I have to stop thinking about her dyke ass." I had to believe those thoughts and be strong in them. Still, I wondered what kind of lover would she be? Would she be hardcore like a thug brotha, or sensitive because she knows how to handle what a woman has?

I found out Deirdra's name by pretending to do a bed check and asked the woman that slept next to her what was dykie's name. It hurt to conceal my emotions, but some things are better left undiscovered.

ൟൟ

The next night as two other guards and I congregated at one post, she walked past. She approached us from behind, so I didn't get a chance to see her lovely face, just her luscious physique from the rear. It was okay for me to look then, because I could blow it off as seeing something like a space creature, and I had to describe its appearance.

My eyes followed Deirdra's frame from top to bottom. I wanted to go into the shower room with her to soap and massage her body. Instead, I hid my feelings by saying, "That's some freaky shit right there. Will you look at that?"

"I know. A woman eating pussy is nasty. Most of the bitches in here do it." Mrs. Portland was a bit older and had been married and divorced twice. She was the one person I could never let see me looking at my forbidden lover.

Foolishly, I replied, "Yeah, I agree," and we went back to discussing the events of the day. My mind stayed on what was behind the shower door, though.

ൟൟ

One night we made eye contact as soon as I reported to my assigned post. It was as if we were looking for each other on some sort of scavenger hunt. Our brief glance held the contents of what we both were searching for. My heart raced when I saw her, and I walked over to try and fish out her feelings for me.

I smiled sheepishly and began to sweat. "Hey, uh, hi." This was the first time I had been in her face without hiding. I took a step closer to her to appear friendlier and she reciprocated.

"How are you?"

Not knowing if I should revisit our awkward moment, I asked, "Are you okay?"

"As fine as I can be in this place."

"Yes, you are fine." My words spilled out the same as a boiling black covered kettle about to blow, and in an instant, she knew.

"Do you know what dorm I'm in?"

"Yes." My words were wet and easy—just like I would be for her.

"Well, why don't you come see me when you get time?"

Another guard calling me on my radio interrupted us. Instead of having a chance to continue behaving like an obsession that needed to be conquered, Deirdra walked away and left me standing, wishing we could exchange wedding vows right then.

At three-thirty one guard went on her lunch break and the other one was asleep. It was then that I walked into the dorm and found her bed. I stepped lightly toward Deirdra's cot, found it, and stood over her viewing her as if she were my prized possession. She slept peacefully on her back and I bent down closer to her face, wanting desperately to kiss her full lips with my moist ones.

What the fuck is wrong with me? Regardless of how she looks or who she is, she's a woman. You can't bring pussy to get pussy. I can't do this shit. But damn she's fine. How can I explain that the finest man I know is a woman?

Trying to suppress my urges didn't happen. We both ended up in the bathroom together, and alone, at four twenty-two in the morning. I didn't try to stop myself. I wanted her. I wanted to taste her. I wanted her to be the one I left in the morning and came home to every night. I wanted to feel her soft, masculine hands all over my body. In return, I'd caress her with my supple ones and soothe away any confusion that might still be between us.

Deirdra, feeling the same as me, lifted her hand and summoned me closer. She pulled me near with her finger and we stepped into a cramped bathroom stall. Her smell of sweet brut musk dazed me as we shared a great kiss of lust. Our bodies meshed together as our hands roamed each other's prohibited territory. I became weak in her touch. I took on the role of the less aggressive one, choosing to let her lead me through a maze that I never wanted to end.

"What's your name, security guard?" is what she asked as our tongues licked each other in perfect sensations.

"Syreeta."

"Ah, my Syreeta."

Our experience came to a halt when someone stepped into the stall next to us. We promised with our eyes that the next day would be the one. The day she would come to my place and we'd be together as woman and woman, man and wife, or lovers in lust.

Before I left work that day I slid my phone number in the crack of Deirdra's driver's side door. She called me that afternoon at two, and my questions splattered out like a hot fool on speed.

"What are you?"

Laughing, she replied, "Whatever I am, you like it, right?"

"Yeah, but I don't understand this. I can't stop thinking about you. I'm, I'm...confused."

She spoke in a soft, mannish tone. "I have a thing for you as well.

When I walked back down the hall and looked into your eyes, I wanted to kiss you. You were so sincere. I felt so bad for you."

My heart quickened as I asked, "Are we going to be together? And if we are, what are we? Or, are you just going to fuck me so I can have an experience and never talk to me again?"

"Look, I'm digging you hard. You made me nervous the first time I saw you. Initially, yes, I just wanted to fuck you, but now, I don't know."

My neck tingled. "Should I take that as a compliment?"

"What? The fact that another woman wants to fuck you harder than a man does?"

Surprised, I asked, "You want me that bad?"

"Yes. And yes, it's a compliment."

I was still confused. "You talk like a man. You look like a man. I don't get it."

"I know you don't. If this helps any, I'm a woman. I was born a woman and I have all the physical attributes a woman has. I just *love* women. I love the way they smell, walk and talk. I love to make love to them. It gives me ecstasy to pleasure them. The way I look is the way I was born to look. I didn't wake up one day and decide to be a man. This is the way I was made."

The line was silent for a moment as I took in what Deirdra said.

Curiously, I asked, "How did you know I was digging on you?"

"Ha, ha... it's the same way a man and a woman dig each other. You just know."

"Do you wish you had a dick?" After I asked that question I felt it was a mistake, but she answered with ease.

"Sometimes."

I wanted her in the best way. She was so damn sexy. "Why am I attracted to you?"

Boldly, she replied, "Because I'm an attractive person."

"I think about you constantly."

"Ah, that means so much. Syreeta, we were meant to find each other. One day you won't be ashamed of me or your feelings."

"I'm not ashamed of you, Deirdra. This is just so foreign, and I don't understand my feelings."

"I know. Until your ready, we can keep us a secret."

Meekly, I answered, "I'm sorry about that, but I need to figure this out."

"That's cool. Many women go through the same thing as you. Women don't fuck women. Women aren't supposed to look like men. But it's a different world than what your mama told you about."

"Yes, it is. So, am I a lesbian now?" *How would I ever explain this?*

"You have to search yourself and answer that. I know I am. You could be someone who simply loves people. You love what's attractive to you."

"Well, right now I want to love you. Will you come over?"

"For you, of course. I'm on my way."

ଈୠ

In the private confines of my home I can release all of my inhibitions and make love to her like she belongs to me. I can look at her outright clothed and in the nude. No more stolen glances at her wide shoulders, her well-buffed statuesque silhouette, or admiring the slight bow in her legs, which gives her the walk that makes me wet when I see her. Tonight we'd become one and worry about the story for the press tomorrow.

Deirdra buzzed my intercom approximately forty minutes after we finished our telephone conversation. I lay my sweaty finger on the door entrance button firm and long, afraid that she'd pull the door handle and it wouldn't open to let her in. Breathing hard and near a fainting spell, I stood in my doorway with a pair of booty shorts on and a sports bra top. When her foot touched the top step I smiled like a second day newlywed. At that moment it didn't matter if she carried herself like a man or a woman, she belonged to me.

"Hey, beautiful," is what my lover said to me. Her words were hauntingly calming and filled with passion. Deirdra wore a pair of knee-length blue jean shorts, a throwback jersey, some Timbs, and a beaming smile that I owned.

"Hi. Come on in."

As she entered with a gift bag in one hand we brushed our arms together.

"You came bearing gifts, huh? Pray tell, what's in the bag?" I held my hand out for her and led her to the couch. We sat close, so close that I could smell the mint on her breath as she spoke.

"A few things for you. A bottle of peach Chardonnay, some candles, bath salts, and a lace thong panty. This will accentuate your booty well...very well."

We sat mesmerized in the moment. Then, at the same time, without a director's cue, we began to kiss and undress each other. She handled me gently and moved about my body seductively.

As she pulled her top over her head, I said, "I don't want to sound like an idiot but I need to ask you this. I always took sneak peeks at you. Will you stand up and take your clothes off so I can look at you without interruption?"

"Ah, anything for my Syreeta."

Standing up, she dropped her jersey on the floor. She then undid her belt and let her shorts fall. She wore a pair of white boxers and bent to take them off. When she stood back up, she was naked.

She was beautiful. Her skin was smooth and held no blemishes. Her six-pack was drinkable. Her breasts weren't like mine. They were more like a young man's who had just begun to work out. Not too big, but firm and tight, just right for gripping.

"Do I pass inspection, Syreeta?"

"Oh, yes, baby. Yes, you do."

My eyes continued to roam her manly yet hard feminine body. Her vaginal area was a neat, hairy mound. A dick wasn't supposed to be there, but if one were, it wouldn't feel out of place.

I lay back on the couch topless and extended my hand for my lover to accept. She placed her hand in mine and lay on top of me comfortably. Music had been playing and eased us into a lovers' daze. My arms and legs were wrapped tightly around her perfect frame as she began to show my bewildered mind why I wanted her. She slid down my body, removed my shorts and slid back up to my vagina. My legs were spread wide at that point and Deirdra dove in softly, making me submit to her every command.

While her tongue was on my clit, she slid her fingers inside of me.

"How does my Syreeta like this?"

Not being able to speak audible words, I said, "Uh-huh. Ah, uh-huh."

My body trembled and released a liquid that quenched Deirdra's thirst.

"Uhm, my Syreeta tastes good."

Her finger remained in me as she slid back up my body and kissed me around my neck. Deirdra pulsated her fingers in and out of me deeper and faster. I spread my legs wider and pumped my pelvis into hers as if we should join. My hands moved about her body, loose and free, not having to worry about being stopped for trespassing on illegal property.

I grabbed and squeezed her breasts and continued to lose control of my senses. By the way I worked my body with hers, no one could ever tell me, Syreeta Hall, that I had never been with a woman.

My hands made their way down to Deirdra's tight, perfect ass. I rolled my fingers in and about her crack, wondering if she would react the same as a hetero male not wanting anything to enter him.

Panting, she said, "Do with me whatever you please. I want to be with you."

And then our lips met. Pressed hard together with tongues intertwined, twisting, turning, grinding, and grooving. I was in my comfort zone with my man, my woman, my boy, my girl. Simply put, my world. We were making love. I'd never been touched this way before. We kissed, licked, nibbled and sucked each other into a passion so strong, a passion that had to be told. Whether it would be accepted didn't matter to either of us. What the coming days would bring would be someone else's worry. All that mattered in that moment was that the finest man and I crossed the first obstacle of our journey.

ഇരു

Wanda D. Hudson is the author of Wait for Love: A Black Girl's Story, *and is the fabulous comedian known as Miss WandaLuv. Please visit this sexy dynamic writer on the web at http://www.wandadhudson.com.*

Hailey's Orgasmic Splendor
Michelle Robinson

"Keep on telling yourself that bullshit, Hailey. You and I both know that you've been in love before. You got everybody walkin' around believin' that you you've got this heart of steel, but I was there. I saw that armor penetrated. All I can say is if I knew where the hell to find Sam Hertz, I would; just to be able to watch that steel veneer of yours melt like fuckin' ice," said Hailey's best friend Sierra.

Sierra remembered it as if it were yesterday. She had come back to their dorm room earlier than expected and had shamefully listened at the door. It was the first time in her young life she had heard such passion. She was so turned on by hearing her best friend cry out in the throes of her incredible orgasm that she had stood outside the door wrapped in a blanket and masturbated, finger fucking her own pussy, playing with her own clit, wishing it was her that was being made love to with such zeal, wishing it was her tongue being washed over with those sweet juices, wishing the pair might invite her to join them. Hailey's relationship with Sam had gone on for at least a year, but Sierra knew her friend well enough to know that it wouldn't last.

"You're makin' me sound like some sort of ice princess. I'm not saying I'm incapable of love. I just don't get this end-of-the-world kind of love that people profess to be in. All I'm sayin' is that that kind of love is nothing more than a chemical reaction; a combination of hormones and pheromones; similar to the reaction you might get to being thirsty. I mean really, have you ever seen a person who hasn't had anything to drink for an extended period of time. There's no difference between that and what some people swear is love. Now, Melvin and me, we love each other, but we're sensible about our love. That's why we're such a good combination. We want the same things, we have the same goals, we're sexually compatible, and we're realistic about our relationship. After witnessing the things my mother did for love, I have no intention of going off 'half-cocked' so to speak, because of some chemical imbalance brought about by lustful urges."

"What you keep forgetting, Hailey, is that you can still fall head over heels in love and not make the same bad choices your mother made. Being in love doesn't necessarily translate to being a victim. That was your mother's choice. It doesn't have to be yours."

"Damn right, it doesn't have to be. That's why I'm being logical in my approach to love."

"Speaking of lustful urges, do you and the Ice Prince have any lustful urges? He reminds me of one of those 'missionary, half-quarter turn of the nipple, three times for the right and three times for the left, with a quarter-turn swerve of the pelvis' kind of guys. I mean, really, Hailey. I know you don't believe in romance and all, but did you have to pick the most boring brother in all of New York to marry?" Sierra asked.

"Melvin is not boring. We go to museums and we've traveled everywhere together. We've gone white water rafting and mountain climbing. We even jumped out of an airplane together and, for the umpteenth time, our lives are compatible," Hailey assured her friend.

"Yeah, yeah, yeah, but can he fuck?"

"Sierra, you are by far the most vulgar person I have ever known."

"Yeah, but you still love me. Now, back to the point. Stop dodging my question. Can Mr. Man lay the pipe; not that I'm sure that's what you're really into anyway? I offered to make the supreme sacrifice when we were in college and make that pussy of yours shake, but you turned me down."

Through the years many of Hailey's and Sierra's friends and family alike just assumed that they were lovers, since Sierra was so open about the fact that she was a lesbian, but nothing could be further from the truth. Hailey and Sierra had never had even the slightest sexual contact with one another throughout four years as roommates in college and another five years sharing an apartment after graduating. Hailey had had her fair share of sexual encounters with both men and women while she was away at college. However, all of that changed when she graduated. Hailey considered her sexual exploration just that—exploration, nothing more, nothing less. She considered herself straight and, as far as she was concerned, everything she did in college was part of her "discovering herself." Her best friend Sierra, on the other hand, disagreed.

"Sex with Melvin is good. We fit. And, that is all I'm going to say about my sex life; thank you very much."

"You fit. What the fuck does that mean? You complete me?" Sierra joked, using her hands to mime a scene from an Austin Powers flick.

"You are one crazy bitch, you know that, Sierra. You are really, really crazy." Hailey laughed. "I know you hate this kind of shit, but as my maid of honor, you better be at my rehearsal dinner tonight, and I expect you to be on time. None of that two hours late shit, okay? Okay, Sierra?" Hailey asked again.

"Okay, okay. I wouldn't miss it for the world. I'll be there with bells on. Besides, this is fun for me. Every gathering of the bride and groom is an opportunity for you to once and for all come to your damn senses and put an end to this travesty; and for me to witness it."

"I hate to disappoint you, but no one is calling off anything. Melvin and I are getting married and we are going to be very, very happy."

"Well, I personally think you're trying a little too hard to convince me, but we'll drop it; for now. So what time does this little shindig start again?"

"Eight o'clock, Sierra," Hailey responded with irritation.

"Well, I guess I better go and get beautiful," Sierra said, rising from her comfortable spot on Hailey's loveseat.

Just as Sierra was about to open the door to leave, Hailey spoke and her mood along with the look on her face softened.

"Sierra, no pressure, but could you try to get there a little early? I'm meeting Melvin's sister for the first time. He doesn't have any other family and he and his twin sister Nelly are so close. I'm a little nervous about making a good impression. Melvin is so conservative, but him and I, we know each other. He's gotten used to me and accepts me as I am, but I'm just worried that his sister will think I'm not good enough for her brother. You know, the whole struggling artist thing and all."

Hailey never ceased to amaze Sierra. One minute she could be tough as nails, sprouting her radical views on love and physical attraction and the next minute she was like an insecure little girl wanting approval.

"Damn, girl, you're going to have me believing you love this man yet. You know I'd do anything for you; even be early. I'll be there by at least seven; not that you need me. You'll be fine on your own. You're beautiful, intelligent, a gifted artist and anyone would be lucky to have you."

With that, Sierra left and headed for her cramped apartment in East New York. The artist in Hailey wanted to wear something color-blocked and bright with raging colors, but she instead decided on a conservative black silky dress that skimmed her knee, exposing her shapely calves and the muscular tone readily apparent while wearing a four-inch pair of heels. She almost removed the dress and wore something else, because she could notice, even through the dress the deep valley between her legs, whenever the dress shifted back and forth. Melvin had once commented that the first thing he noticed when he met her three years earlier was the fact that she was wearing a pair of jeans and the tightness of the jeans accentuated this huge valley. He said it reminded him of a promise, almost like the gap between her thighs was beckoning him to enter. He might have liked it, but Hailey learned very early that that gap just brought her more male attention than she would have liked. After the rehearsal, the next stop was the rehearsal dinner, which was being held at Ashford and Simpson's restaurant, the Sugar Bar. Melvin and Hailey would arrive early to greet their guests.

"You're like a little kid on Christmas morning," Hailey said to Melvin.

"I know it's silly; it's just that my sister and I have been through a lot together and I really miss her. I can't wait to see her."

"No, it's not silly. I love that you care about another human being that way. It's what makes you the person you are."

Hailey softly touched her hand to Melvin's cocoa brown face and brought his face down to meet hers, running her fingers through his curly black hair, admiring the sexy cleft in his chin. It occurred to her, for the first time, that he really was sexy, but she never really seemed to notice that. Why? Maybe Sierra was right, maybe there was something not quite right about this union. Melvin and Hailey kissed briefly before he pulled away and gazed into her dark, haunting eyes, her similar cocoa complexion, the beautiful dimples that dotted her beautiful face. It occurred to him that they were perfect for one another.

"My sister is going to love you," he said. "I'm going to go and look for her outside."

Sierra had arrived impressively early and was now circulating among the guests. Sierra had always been possessing of more charisma than any one person needed. That was one of the things Hailey loved about her. Just as Hailey was about to cross the room to join Sierra, the look on her best friend's face stopped Hailey in her tracks and she turned to see what had Sierra's attention. Hailey could barely breathe. Taking strides across the room were her fiancé Melvin and the reason why Hailey had long ago reevaluated her take on love. It was Samantha (Sam for short), her lover in college and the last and only person she had ever gone completely "crazy" in love with. Hailey had been obsessed with Sam; that is until Samantha disappeared from her life never to be seen from or heard from again. It was suddenly as though she were that twenty– year-old college girl again. Melvin approached her; smiling.

"Finally, at long last," he began. "I get to introduce the two most important women in my life. Hailey, this is my sister Samantha Tonelle Wilson. Nelly, this is my beautiful wife to be Hailey."

"Hi," Hailey stuttered.

"Hello, Hailey. I've heard so much about you. My brother just goes on and on about you."

Hailey was amazed. She was as cool as a cucumber. No indication at all that she knew her. It occurred to Hailey that maybe she hadn't had all that much of an impact on her life, and maybe she truly didn't remember her. She should have been happy about the drama her not remembering would avoid, but she wasn't happy. She was a cross between sad and angry. How dare she not remember her! Hailey's anger spurred her on to play a game of cat and mouse with Sam, or Nelly, or whatever her name was.

"Nelly, huh? Has anyone ever called you Sam?" Hailey asked, knowing the answer.

"Everyone calls me Sam. That is, except for my brother here. He's been calling me Nelly since I was two years old."

Preoccupied with the rehearsal dinner and countless speeches and the like, Hailey had more questions than she could get answered sitting in this restaurant with all eyes and focus on her, the bride-to-be. Melvin insisted that he sit right in the middle of his sister and Hailey. However, Sam kept finding subtle ways to brush the back of Hailey's hair, her hands, even the side of her leg. The charge of electricity that accompanied each touch was more than Hailey could stand. She feigned a headache and Melvin insisted that he take her home. Instead, however, Sam offered to make sure that Hailey got home so that Melvin could stay and say goodbye to his guests.

The first five minutes alone in the car were silent. Then, finally Hailey spoke.

The only words she could muster were, "I don't understand. Your name was Hertz; not Wilson. Did you know it was me when Melvin told you we were getting married?"

"Well, the name Hertz was my adopted name. Melvin and I were separated when our mother died. My father only wanted Melvin. He didn't think he could care for a girl. So, I was put up for adoption. But after I grew up, I decided to change my name back legally, to my real name. And no, at first I didn't know it was you, but after a few months as he began to describe you, I knew it was you; not only by your physical description but the subtle things about your personality that Melvin mentioned. I know you probably think Melvin is this uptight brother with a stick up his butt, but Melvin takes your lead. He senses that there is some apprehension on your part but he loves you and he is willing to be patient and wait until you open up to him. I, on the other hand, know that will never happen; not because you are incapable but because you are living a lie. That is why I left. For all your liberal views, you are not true to the one person who matters the most; yourself. I'm sure you thought I was a bitch when I left you years ago when we were in college, but my reasons for leaving were not for lack of love. I left because I knew you would always ride the fence. You would never commit to being what you truly are. You, Hailey, are a lesbian, I know it, Sierra probably knows it and, God help him, I think Melvin knows it too. He just doesn't want to admit it to himself, because that would mean losing you. Unfortunately, the only person that doesn't seem to know you are a lesbian is you, and I couldn't live that lie with you, so I left."

Hailey thought of what they had shared back in college, the passion, the heat; something she hadn't felt since that time.

"So?" Hailey asked. "You seem to know so much about me. Tell me, what do I do now?"

Sam didn't answer her. Instead, she asked her about the art studio that Melvin had mentioned to her so many times; where Hailey displayed her work.

"I would love to see some of your work. You were always such a brilliant artist. Could I see your studio?"

"Yes," Hailey answered.

They traveled the rest of the way to SoHo in silence.

Her studio was housed in one of those old warehouses with the clanky elevators that you had to manually pull the gate on. As soon as they were ensconced in the elevator and the door was closed, Sam grabbed Hailey from behind, pulling at Hailey's pert, hardened nipples, struggling to free her from the dress that kept the two of them so far apart.

She had wanted her so badly, while sitting in the restaurant she actually thought she could smell her pussy beckoning to her for a taste. Sam engulfed her entire breast in her mouth, licking and sucking her breasts with such voracity. Hailey could barely stay on her feet. Shifting places with her feet, Sam could hear Hailey's soft, moist, hungry lips rubbing together; almost begging for her to love her. As soon as her tongue was inside of Sam's mouth, she remembered exactly what she tasted like, how sweet and hard yet soft the inner recesses of her mouth were; how she could be molasses sweet while being rough and sexually demanding. The two intermittently worshipped and battled with their tongues, licking and exploring every corner, while lashing tongues as if they were fencers in competition. Sam sought that soft place she had missed feeling so much, with her fingers she recalled what the inside of Hailey felt like. Sam sighed with pleasure as Hailey's walls contracted onto her fingers trapping her in place, while she tried to finger fuck her into the orgasm she so pleasantly remembered. Hailey remembered how much fun she used to have feeling Sam's inverted nipples grow by leaps and bounds inside of her mouth, telling her that she was satisfying Sam just as much as she herself was being satisfied. She needed to have that feeling again. Feeling her nipples grow inside of her mouth, caused her own nipples to swell to meet her lover's own desire. The two slumped to the floor, quickly shifting into the sixty-nine position. Neither could muster the patience to wait while the other was satisfied. Tongues plunged deep into each other's pussies, savoring their sweet juices, lapping up every dribble of nectar that fell, plunging their tongues as deep as physically possible, anxious to extract every bit of remaining sap. Sam remembered how much joy she felt in riding Hailey's plump, easily engorged clit and removing her mouth from her pussy, mounted Hailey, anxious to bring them both to simultaneous orgasm as they ground each of their clits together until they were red and ready to explode with wanting one another, and that they did.

As if in a trance, Hailey recited over and over again, "Oh, I love you. Oh, I love you," as Sam ground her pussy deeper and deeper into Hailey's orgasmic splendor. Numb with pleasure, they screamed out in unison announcing passion at its peak.

෨෬

Michelle Robinson is the mother of twelve-year-old identical twin boys and resides in New York City. She studied journalism at New York University and is planning to attend film school in 2008. Her erotic short story "Mi Destino" is included in Zane's New York Times *bestseller* Caramel Flava. *In addition to* Caramel Flava, *Michelle is also a contributing author to the Zane anthology collections* Succulent: Chocolate Flava II *with the story "The Quiet Room" and* Asian Spice *with the story "The Flow of Qi." She has recently completed work on four novels,* Color Me Grey, Pleasure Principle, Serial Typical *and* You Created a Monster, *and is currently working on the screenplay adaptation of "Mi Destino." Michelle can be reached at Robinson_201@hotmail.com as well as on www.myspace.com/justef*

The Time Tripper

Lucille Gayles

Pussy can make you do some remarkable, crazy, and unthinkable things, but travel across time for it? I don't know. Time travel just for a quick lay. Love maybe. Once in a lifetime love, definitely. Fucking? Eh, more or less the same in any time. Why stretch the laws of physics for that? I quickly changed my mind after I met Tempest. My name is Seshat, and I am a Black lesbian time-tripper. Nope, not a time traveler. That's actually a nobler calling. I mean, a sister might actually be able to help some people out and change the world. Or, on the flipside, be diabolical and gain world power. But like most people, I've never lived up to my full potential; one way or the other. Thus, I have often sought out brief moments of happiness through inefficient means, like material goods or drugs. Fortunately, happiness found me genetically and spiritually predisposed to the future.

Time-trippin' is kinda like traveling through time, but on a minor level. You don't have control over where you'll end up; in the future or past. Oh, and you don't get days, months, or even hours. Five minutes is the most I ever heard, and even then, that ain't in real time. 'Cause in real time it depends on the body. How long the body can remain in the little death. Time-trippin,' you see, is a high. But not everybody can do it. Not yet anyway.

But those of us who can do it, can only do so with others like us, time travelers or time-trippers. That's where Tempest comes in.

Usually when two people are connected like we were…will be, it's the past that connects them. But I couldn't remember her from any childhood memories, and my ancestors had stopped talking to me as soon as I'd begun to ignore them for my interests in the future. Yet, if anyone should understand how much the future is the past and the past the future, my ancestors should. Still, they weren't talking. Despite my being a sexual astrologist who writes horoscopes for a syndicated magazine column, I wasn't always the physical displacement of time that I am now. The spatialization of atomic matter is far removed from matters of the spirit that I'd been indoctrinated with. My family is from the south. Good Southern Baptists still clinging to the hidden chicken bones in our Vodun closet. But on a crisp December night, at a party (an overstatement of the evening) in Midtown Atlanta, bored and uninterested in the people that surrounded me, I glanced across the room at someone who seemed…familiar.

Tempest. Dark as midnight and just as beautiful. The white cashmere sweater that clung to her delicate curves illuminated her smooth and nearly flawless skin. Her thin, long dreads were sophisticatedly piled into a bun, with soft curly tendrils spilling from the twisted mane atop her head. As if the smile-induced sharp dimples in an otherwise soft face were not enough to excite, neutral lip gloss went a long way in drawing attention to her full plum-colored mouth. She donned black eyeliner and mascara to play up the shape of her eyes, while chocolate eye shadow brought out the already disarming color of them. I innocently watched as she gave a toothy smile to the Taye Diggs wannabe beside her, and he melted. Who wouldn't? She was captivating, and at the least, looking at her would be just what I needed to get me through at least another hour.

My attempts to drown out the tediousness of mundane and useless conversation were rewarded with what at first was a curious stare. She looked as if she were trying to place my face, but her inquisitiveness turned into amber waves of playful taunts. I smiled and dared her with my eyes to keep watching me. She did. I got caught up. Her eyes were luminous entries into a soul that seemed to be saying, "You looking at me? Look then, but be ready." Did she really have amber eyes? Or was it a trick of the light? Was it that her skin was radiant, deep and dark enough to make the brown iris glow? But Tempest wanted me to figure it out for myself. She didn't seem to care about feigning disinterest in me, or interest in the man still talking to her. I averted my eyes down to the drink in my hand, trying to hide the visceral response that she was eliciting from me.

There I was, a thirty-year-old woman who still looked twenty-something. Grown and sexy, caramel complexion with brown eyes. Confident in my casual short blazer, fitted white-buttoned top and mid-length skirt, but I could feel my face blush and stomach flutter from the way she flirted with me. I looked up again, and she gazed back at me from across the room, as if she had been waiting the entire night for me to see her look at me like…like I was naked, legs spread, and getting myself off just for her. Then, I really saw myself through her eyes: ten pounds lighter, sporting a bushy afro, in some killa ass black leather pumps, with a crazy fine outfit; the vision of me that I was becoming. Ump! I could feel myself slipping into the hiccups of time and space to be seduced by her. She turned her attention back to the dark-skinned brother who continued hanging at her side like a pocketbook.

I had been hoping that she wasn't straight. To say that Tempest was a fine-ass sister would be an understatement. It was clear that she possessed some unnamable magic that merely enhanced her physical beauty. Tempest was the kind of woman I hated seeing go to waste on account of some man. She was strong, comfortable, and poised. Powerful and graceful at the same time. Whatever she's got we all want to taste, to imitate, to be blessed with, and sanctified by! Men can't really appreciate a woman like that 'cause they'll always want only to own her and change her until she looks the same, but really is an inferior version of her original self. Yeah, when I saw Tempest all I could think about was how some other woman had been cheated out of her helping of the sexuality she exuded, and was walking around all womanless because she done got a second helping in the line.

I shook my head, took a swallow of my gin and tonic, and tried to lose myself in the conversation that had started around me. But she was glowing, and if I had wanted to ignore her, I couldn't. I caught myself gazing at her again. She continued conversing with a woman who had joined them. I spied her checkin' for me again. My heart raced excitedly to let my body know what my spirit had already figured out. For I literally saw my future in a universe of mysterious brown and flecked yellows of green; painted harshly by the hands of desire. In that color of time, we were not strangers as we were moments before. We were flesh melding and melting into each other. I was having visions of her that came with smells and sensations. My imagination was creating a sniff and lick Afronomical lesbian zodiac poster in my mind. I was drunk, but, thanks to her, the party was getting a lot better.

I walked over to the swarm of enamored men and women hanging on her every word and unceremoniously joined the crowd of admirers. She was an academic, a professor of physics writing a book on what she called "black people's future time paradox."

"The future has a way of gettin' all up in your face when it wants to get a message across, doesn't it," Tempest said directly to me, acknowledging my presence in a lazy manner that belied the intense way she had been ogling me before I'd come over. My mouth was dry so I didn't immediately respond to her. I nervously licked my lips, and she seemed to study that action before suggesting to her rapt audience that "the body is the ultimate future technology that humanity still has not mastered."

Technology was a force that had eluded me for some time. I was completely inept at any of the sciences and mathematics, but the future had come to me as a Black woman, not a computer.

"You're vibrating," she said, looking at me.

I know, I thought.

I was enthralled by her presence and the consideration she was now giving to me. I dumbly pulled my cell phone out of my interior jacket pocket. I looked down and attempted to collect a voice mail, but I saw only a symbol that I did not understand. Tempest must have seen the confusion on my face, and she boldly grasped my hand on its way to place the phone back into the inside pocket of the blazer I wore. Her touch electrified. Not unlike the rest of my body, my breast responded by offering a protruding and straining nipple to the brief contact she'd slyly insisted upon.

"It's not voicemail or a text message. Somebody sent you an image to download," Tempest said, using my ineptness as an opportunity to turn her back to the group of people she had just been talking to.

"Is that what that thing means?" I asked, and she proceeded to show me how to download the image. She stood close to me, at an angle, with her breast pressed against my arm.

"Black people kill me, getting technologically advanced shit and then they won't figure out how to work it." She spoke quietly, without looking at me.

"Thanks. I'll keep that in mind, next time I'm trying to download to that iPod that I haven't been able to figure out for a couple of months."

"Look at you!" she exclaimed, showing me the picture that one of my friends had taken of me a week ago. "I guess you look this hot all the time."

She openly took in my five-foot-five frame in much the same way she had my lips. She slid the phone back inside my pocket and deliberately brushed against my nipple this time.

"What's your name? I think I missed the introductions."

"Tempest. And you are?"

"Seshat," I answered.

"Egyptian goddess of the night sky and history," she said.

"Nah, sexual astrologist for the insomniac and psychic friends," I coyly revealed to her and she laughed, dimples and all.

Tempest was all fishnets, garters, and high heels with bohemian sex appeal that made me forget my ennui. Where I was crunk: unpolished, thick and curvy, she was jazz and soul: sophisticated, svelte, and shapely. I had already taken in every inch of her body. I knew that I would zig where she zagged. We would fit each other in the most utterly compelling intimacy.

"This is gonna sound like a line, but I swear to God that I know you."

She leaned into me and, with her lips pressed against my ear, whispered, "Maybe we're meeting in a past life or something."

I caught a whiff of her perfume, but under that light floral scent she smelled even more divine.

Forget the past and the present. The future was fucking me into oblivion. Tempest had invited me out to her car to, "Get high," she said. The backseat of the Chrysler 300 SI we slid into was roomy enough for two women to stretch out.

"Nice," I said, running my hand over the plush fabric of the backseat, but all nervous banter halted the moment I placed my hand on her stocking-covered thigh.

"I didn't come all across time for flirting, coy looks, and soft touches," she said, intrepidly unbuttoning my blouse enough to expose one of my naked B-cup breasts to the warmth of her small hands.

I responded by slowly pressing my lips to hers, afraid that once I kissed her she would be gone or I would wake up. And when I realized we were both still in the here and now, I brushed my mouth against hers, again and again. With each breathless kiss, my lips gently touched and demurely suckled Tempest's halfway-parted lips as she passionately whispered, "Fucking tease," repeatedly against the pressure of my lips. She caressed my nipples with the palm of her hands.

"You're a fucking tease," I moaned, right before my tongue tasted and fully parted her lips into a heady kiss that forced our bodies down onto the backseat.

What had slowly started as soft and sensual had quickly turned hard and nasty. Tempest expertly sought out my lips, and her tongue plunged in and out my mouth in a way that left me panting and hotter still. I tore away the stockings covering her legs so that I could feel the sweltering heat rising from her skin. My fingers inched toward her inner thighs, parting them until I came into contact with wet heat. Her hands were everywhere and nowhere. Not at all concerned about who might see through the fogged windows of the car, we undressed until we were both completely naked and writhing alongside each other. I rubbed my slick cunt against her hand in wild abandon, and she lowered her mouth to one of my breasts and ardently used her tongue to lavish my areolas with jolting sensations that made me wetter. As I crept nearer to the edge, I watched her from under hooded lids talk dirty to me and revel in my debauchery. This is what I'd seen in her eyes across the room. Desire and hunger that could consume and ignite at the same time. She'd seen it in me, too.

When I was as close as I could be, Tempest stopped talking. She ceased stroking, and she contorted us both into a position in which she could glide her sopping wet pussy against my eager mouth. She smelled like wet moss and musk. It was painful and uncomfortable, but the feel of her silken thighs on each side of my face made me ache for the taste of her, so much so that I didn't protest when she roughly bruised my mouth and suffocated me with the swollen lips of her cunt. She felt smooth. I caressed and palmed her ass while I lapped at her bald lips and girl-hood. Outside she tasted like good curry, flavorful and exotic. And the rest like oysters. I morphed my tongue into a spongy dick that she fucked so thoroughly, I thought it would shoot a load.

"Feels good," she gushed and whimpered in response to the way my tongue penetrated the inside of her. "Lick it. Lick it good," she hungrily commanded as my tongue lapped her protruding clitoris into a rigid and raw mass of painful longing. "Christ, there's never enough time with you!" she exclaimed, and I damn near choked; trying to swallow the juices from her climax.

It was all for her. Time had stopped just so that she could get off. At least that's how it seemed when she was approaching her third orgasm of the night. She was quick, but I had yet to be released from my state of sexual animation. I lay completely naked under her, feverish and animalistic, uninhibited in the way I reached up to touch her hair, face, and neck as she straddled my thigh. And when I thought I could get some control over the havoc she was wreaking on me, she bent over, leaned in and whispered in my ear, "You don't even know where you're taking me; where you're going."

I didn't understand her words. What I did know was the heat from her body, her breath against my ear, and the way her pussy had created a slip and slide of my leg, along with those words, made me feel like I was going to burst into liquid flames at any moment. I greedily lifted up and tasted the blackberry-colored nipples jutting from her breasts. My pussy jumped in retort to the stream of obscenities pouring from her mouth as she lost herself to the thigh-ride.

She seemed ready to hit her stride again, but paused a moment before maneuvering my body into a position in which she could slide between my legs. We half-lay, half-sat, scissor-like, opposing each other without moving. A wave of longing shot through my gut as I tried to catch my breath. I gasped at the feel of her engorged pussy, now delicately touching my own. I moaned at the agonizing stillness before losing myself to the first thrust against her. We fit each other in all the ways I could have ever imagined. It began as an unhurried steady grind. I could feel the definition of her outer lips, how they gave way to the cavernous hole of hot interior flesh. I felt my hood slicken and sloppily yield to the dewy velvet smoothness of her hood. Pussy to pussy, I lost track of time and found it again, using the throbbing and swelling heaviness of her clitoris mashed against mine. We gyrated strokes and cunt-fondled each other like the bitches in heat that we were.

The car felt like a sauna. The smell intoxicating. And nothing, not the impending cramps, nor the threat of being caught, could make us let go of each other until we let go of time.

I wanted to get under her skin, merge my whole body into the molasses that was Tempest's black hole. Nothing I did could get me as close to her as I wanted to be, but I didn't stop trying. She clawed at me and I reached for her, all without breaking the torrid connection of our timeless fuck. I caressed the nape of her neck. She tugged my hair while thrusting herself up and down against me. In my frenetic physical state and desire-clouded mind, I nonchalantly placed my fingers at the base of her neck. As she continued to buck against my pussy, the caresses of my fingers gave way to deliberate hands that pressured and encircled her neck each time she sighed "yeah" or groaned "fuck me." And when I decreased the force or moved my hand to tease an erect nipple, she would painfully gaze at me with want for the weight of my small hands wrapping around her neck. Through some unspoken communication delivered via her eyes, as well as her pussy popping and clamping down against my snatch, I applied and reapplied pressure and squeezed her neck, understanding that it would bring me closer to the orgasmic frenzy I sought.

My voice had become hoarse from begging, then harshly demanding more of the pleasurable swell. I ached for release. Pussy was too soft. Too hot. Too damn good. I wanted the good hurt to be over. I wanted it to never end. It was a frantic, ugly, and mean fuck…but she was getting me high. It was seeing my hands, that had just been squeezing her neck, fade and slip into her flesh, rather than against it, that tripped me out enough for me to grasp the meaning of the words that she had whispered to me earlier. My hands were no longer corporeal but rather ethereal energy with force.

I could not tell what was real. The only flesh that I could really sense was the hard pearl growing between my legs. I could still feel her against me, hear her screams when she came, when I too slipped toward my own peak in which I could not stop squeezing or choking. I felt my hands at the back of her wet throat and then solidly against the back of her neck. I was touching her everywhere but nowhere. There but not here. And as I pussy-fucked myself into intense multiple orgasms, I saw myself, her, and my future memory of her. We were in another time in a blue room, and I was delicately stroking the nape of her neck before undressing her.

"Damn, you trip-time better than I did my first time. You were almost there." She panted, our pussies still touching, each jumping at the disturbance of her voice.

"No, I came," I said, breathing heavily as if there were any doubt on the matter.

"But I wanted you 'becoming.'"

We weren't in love, but we were lovers. Desire is infinite. It stretches beyond existence. That first night with Tempest I discovered that I could travel through time. With the right lover, I learned that I could change the past, see the future, and enjoy the present. Yes. We were lovers who fucked up the time space continuum every single time we kissed, touched, or tasted the timelessness of each other. We were lovers, partners against the collapse of time. She had come to show me how.

ଽଠଔ

Lucille Gayles is the pseudonym of a teacher-critic-scholar and struggling novelist from Durham, N.C. She has been writing erotic poetry and fiction since she learned the alphabet. She currently resides and teaches at a university in Florida.

Jacqui
Jolie du Pré

Who knew I'd end up at Regina's Hair School? I thought I'd be at a top beauty academy, but one put me on a waiting list and another one flat out rejected me. Out of anger and desperation I enrolled, last minute, at Regina's. I rationalized that since it was located down the street from where I lived, it would be convenient and that it was just a stepping stone until I could transfer out to where I wanted to be.

There really was a Regina. Dark brown and big, everything about her was big. Big earrings; sometimes they were bright green. Big hair that, at last count, was five different shades. Big breasts that hung down to her navel. Regina didn't talk to her students much. She followed the "learn on your own" method. While we worked on the hair of clients, she sat in the back with a bucket of chicken and watched talk shows.

We each had pink booths that Regina bought to cheer the place up. On Mondays we didn't accept clients. Instead, we cleaned our tools and organized our stations. I stood next to Jacqui. Today she decided to pick me apart.

"Girl, we need to do somethin' about your hair."

"I like my hair!"

"Your clothes ain't right either. I'm gonna take you shoppin'."

ဆဂ

Shopping is fun, but going to the mall with a woman who wears furry baby blue boots would be a bad idea.

"Jacqui, I'm trying to concentrate here."

"You so damn snotty, Michelle! I'm just tryin' to help a sistah. I bet you ain't gettin' none either."

Actually I had, but it was nothing to brag about. Gina and I had been together for five years, but sex with her had lacked passion for months. We still shared a lot of the same interests, but even that was waning.

"That's none of your business."

"Oh, girl, don't tell me I gotta take care of that too."

"I'm not interested in getting fixed up with a man, Jacqui."

"Who said anything about a man?"

I stopped what I was doing and looked at her. She grinned from ear to ear, then she turned around and walked to the back of the room, her large ass stuffed in a pair of tight jeans. I had never told Jacqui that I was a lesbian. Was she into girls, too? My gaydar doesn't always work, but the way she had smiled at me and switched her big behind were evidence enough. I'm a black woman who is attracted to black women, but me and Jacqui? I shook the thought from my head.

ဆဂ

After school I grabbed some food, hopped on the bus and headed home, like I always do. My cell phone had been ringing nonstop, but I hadn't bothered to look at the caller ID, until now. It was Gina. I knew what she was calling about and she'd keep calling until I answered the phone. We had planned on seeing the Monet exhibit at the art museum. I hadn't confirmed whether or not I was going. The phone rang again.

"Well, I'm glad I caught you, since you don't seem to know how to return phone calls."

"I'm sorry. Are we on for tomorrow?"

"Yes, of course we're on, Michelle. That's why I'm calling. Why don't we do lunch at that cute little French restaurant before we see the exhibit?"

Oh great, I thought, another fro fro restaurant to waste my money on. I wish, just once, that Gina would choose a place less fancy.

"They've got really good hamburgers at that spot on the corner. That might be fun."

"Hamburgers? You know, you really should work on your diet. It's embarrassing. I'll see you at the French restaurant at one o'clock."

We hung up as I stared at the hotdog I was holding.

Then my cell phone rang again. It wasn't Gina calling back and I didn't recognize the number. I decided to answer it anyway.

"Hello?"

"Hey, Michelle! It's Jacqui."

Jacqui? How did she get my number? I had never given it to her.

"You comin' with me tonight?" she continued.

"Coming with you where?"

"The club?"

"What club? What are you talking about?"

"Surrender. You comin' out with me?"

I don't know what made Jacqui think I'd go with her. "No, I'm staying home tonight."

"Why you want to do that?"

"Why? Because I'm tired. How did you get my number?"

"Don't worry about it. Why won't you come out tonight?"

"I already told you. I'm tired."

"You need some excitement in your life, and then you won't be so tired. What time you want me to pick you up?"

I couldn't believe her persistence, even though she was right. I did need some excitement in my life.

"Jacqui, I'm going to hang up now. I'll see you Monday." I don't like to cut people off, but I knew Jacqui wouldn't let it go.

I'm certain that she looked over Regina's shoulder and got my number from Regina's records. That annoyed me. Yet, at the same time, I couldn't stop thinking about the club and the fact that Jacqui was on the pursuit.

How pathetic was my life? If I admitted it to myself, Jacqui was right about a lot of things. My hair sucked, my clothes sucked even more, and even though I had Gina, that relationship was fizzling fast. For a long time, I'd been feeling like I was on a treadmill that I couldn't get off.

I really couldn't picture myself with Jacqui, but it certainly couldn't hurt to get the hell out of the house and go to a club for a change. So I looked for Jacqui's number on my cell phone and I called her back. I'd have to watch how late I stayed out. Gina would hate it if I was yawning on her all day.

"Now you're getting some sense in your head. I'll get you at ten. Cool?"

"Yes, Jacqui. That's cool."

&⁂&

I looked through my closet, trying to find something decent to wear. I found some black slacks and a colorful blouse. A pair of black shoes completed the outfit. I put makeup on, for the first time in months, and combed my hair into a style. Then I sat in a chair and waited for Jacqui to arrive.

Ten o'clock got there and then ten-thirty. If there's one thing I've always been it's punctual, and if there's one thing I can't stand, it's when people are late. But at around a quarter to eleven, my cell rang.

"Come on down, bitch! I'm ready for you."

Well, it's about time, I thought. My nerves were at full tilt as I descended the stairs. What was I getting myself into?

When I opened the door to the car, I saw that Jacqui's full-figured body was barely covered. Her blouse was extremely low-cut, exposing much of her very large breasts, and she had on one of the shortest skirts known to woman.

She looked me up and down.

"Well...I guess I should have worn a different outfit," I said.

"That's okay, baby, you ain't gonna have it on that long."

I guess that comment should have bothered me, but it didn't. In fact, I started wondering what her breasts looked like under her blouse.

As soon as I sat down, she peeled out onto the road as if she were being chased.

"Slow down, Jacqui!"

"Don't worry, baby! I got control!"

"Just don't kill us. I'm too young to die!"

She laughed at me and just kept on driving fast. Consequently, we got to the club in record time.

Surrender. I had never been there before. Dark lighting, very crowded, loud and upbeat music and black lesbians everywhere—some butch, some femme. Women were dancing together; it seemed, in every inch of the room. The energy was thick. As soon as we entered, Jacqui grabbed my hand and brought me to the bar.

"Hey, Lekisha!"

"Hey! How you been?"

It was obvious that Jacqui was a regular customer. Lekisha looked at me and smiled.

"Two rum and Cokes," Jacqui said. "Put a lot of rum in hers."

"Jacqui, I don't drink!"

"Well, you need to start!"

Jacqui handed me the drink. "Here," she said.

"Well...okay." I took some sips. "It's strong!"

"Good!" She took our drinks and put them over to the side. Then she dragged me to the edge of the dance floor. I started to panic, because I never dance. But Jacqui didn't care, and before long we were standing in the middle of it. But we weren't alone. We were surrounded by what seemed like a million lesbians, all moving to the beat.

Jacqui put her hands on my waist while she wiggled her hips. The alcohol I had consumed was beginning to take affect. Her large breasts bounced inside her top. Her big behind moved up and down to the music. She pulled me close to her. I began to move a little, at least as best as I could.

"Girl, you got it!" Jacqui was being kind, because she could tell I was hopeless. Yet dancing with her was really fun. Later she pulled me off the floor and we walked back to our drinks.

At much as I hated to admit it, I was falling under Jacqui's spell. And the truth of the matter was, my panties were wet, too. Before long, Jacqui put her lips on mine. They felt so good. Our lips seemed to melt into each other.

She looked me dead in the eyes. "I'm taking you to my place now, and you're gonna let me do whatever I want, understand?"

"Yes, I understand."

She was in charge and that was fine by me. I didn't think it was possible for my pussy to gush anymore than it already had. She grabbed my hand and led me out of the smoky bar to her car. Before she put me in the car she pushed me against it and pressed her body into mine. I could feel her large breasts on my small ones. We put our arms around each other and hugged each other tight. Then we kissed again, out in the open, for a long time.

"Come on, girl! It's time to go," she said.

"Are you sure you can drive? I'm feeling sort of light-headed."

Jacqui laughed. "I told you, baby, don't worry. I got control."

∞∞

Jacqui's bedroom was a mess and a pile of clothes topped her comforter, but she threw all the stuff that was on her bed onto the floor. Then she threw me on the bed and straddled me, her knees by my ears and me with a clear view of her blue panties under her skirt. She was wet, very wet. Her sweet musk wafted into my senses.

She reached down and kissed me. Our tongues rolled over each others. Maybe it was the fact that I hadn't had good sex in a long time, or the fact that I was still tipsy, or just the fact that Jacqui was really turning me on but I wanted to be the one in control.

I rolled Jacqui on the bed until I was on top of her. Then I reached under her skirt and pulled her panties off. I wanted more than her scent; I wanted her in my mouth. I pulled the skirt up to her waist. She had shaved her hair completely off. I dropped my mouth to her pussy, spreading her thighs with my hands.

"Damn, girl!" she screamed as I ate her. I wanted all of her. I wanted to push my face into her and that's what I did. Jacqui was so wet that my face was covered with her juices. I sucked her thick clit into my mouth. I couldn't get enough of it. I knew it felt good for her and I knew she had to be close to coming.

I pulled Jacqui's blouse off. I guess I should have been more careful, because I ripped it in the process. She didn't seem to mind. I continue to lick her pussy while I squeezed her breasts in my hands. She grabbed my head and brought my mouth to one of her large nipples. I smashed her breasts against my face. Her nipples were so big and round, I just wanted to lick them for a very long time.

I reached between her legs and stuck my finger into her slick pussy. At the same time, I played with her fat clit.

"Yeah! That's it!" she screamed. Jacqui came like a fountain.

∞∞

After two hours of lovemaking, I lay next to Jacqui in her bed.

"Tomorrow, I'm taking you shoppin'," she said.

"I can't go shopping. I have another engagement."

"You have another who? Girl, we going to the mall!"

She rolled on top of me and kissed my lips again. One thing was for certain, there was no way in hell I was spending my day looking at Monet.

∞∞

Twenty minutes later, Jacqui was asleep. I hadn't planned on staying the night, but it felt very comfortable in her bed. As I lay, I realized how relaxed I was.

I kissed Jacqui on the cheek. She smiled a little; even though she wasn't awake. I looked around the room and tried to remember where I had put my cell phone. Once I spotted it, I got out of bed to get it and then I got back in bed to make the call. Gina stayed up late. It was better to contact her now rather than later.

"Gina?"

"Michelle? What's up? Do you know what time it is?"

"Yes, I know what time it is. I didn't wake you, did I?"

"No, no. What's the matter?"

"I can't make it tomorrow."

"What? You can't? Why?"

"I…." The words didn't want to come.

"You hungry?" Jacqui wasn't asleep anymore.

"Who is that? Are you with a woman?" Gina asked.

I was frozen. Jacqui was hungry, and frankly, so was I, and Gina wanted to know what was going on.

"I gotta go. I'll call you later," I said.

"What do you mean, you'll call me later? Where are you?"

Jacqui started kissing my neck. She didn't say it, but I think she knew that I was on the phone with my girlfriend. It was as if she was testing me to see who I wanted. I knew who I wanted. It was time to make a change.

"Gotta go," I said.

Jacqui looked at me and smiled a wicked little grin. "Who was that, your girl?"

"No. Where are you taking me tomorrow?"

"I told you, the mall. I saw this orange dress that would look sharp as hell on you."

There wasn't anything in my closet that came close to orange. This was going to be quite a change. I kissed Jacqui on the lips. "Sounds good to me!"

ഇൻരു

Jolie du Pré is an African-American author of erotica and erotic romance. Her work has appeared on the Internet, in eBook and in Best Lesbian Erotica 2007 *and other print anthologies. Jolie is the editor of* Iridescence: Sensuous Shades of Lesbian Erotica, *published by Alyson Books. She is also the founder of GLBT Promo, a promotional group for gay, lesbian, bisexual and transgender erotica and erotic romance. Visit her website at www.joliedupre.com.*

At Last

Kimberly Kaye Terry

Serena gratefully lowered her aching body into the bar stool and closed her eyes, blowing a tired breath of air from her partially opened lips. With a sigh, she raised two fingers to her temple, massaging away the nagging headache that had been hovering for the last hour. Her back and feet ached from standing all day at the convention, talking to various company execs, trying her damndest to keep the smile and the charm flowing as she attended the marketing convention the pharmaceutical company she worked for had sent her on.

She glanced around the deserted bar before she eased her feet out of her pumps.

As soon as she'd been able to escape the convention, she'd driven the small rental back to her hotel, one she'd chosen that was far away from the convention site, having no desire to mingle with the conventioneers, to snatch off the itchy pantyhose, conservative navy blue suit and matching pumps. After undressing, she'd taken a long, leisurely shower, allowing the hot water to sluice over her skin and ease the hard knot of tension away from her aching muscles.

The tension she felt came from both the hassle of networking at the conference, as well as from the doubts she'd been having of late, with increasing frequency, about her relationship with Reggie. Doubts she'd tried to express to her mother which had, in turn, caused an ugly fight between them. Her mother, as usual, reminded Serena that Reggie was a man any woman would beg, borrow, and steal to land.

He had everything a woman could ask for in a man. Her mother had scolded her, as though she were a child; her lips pinched, her brow furrowed in anger.

As her mother ran down his dossier, Serena had turned away, tuning her out, and refrained from telling her to mind her own business for once and allow her to live her life, to choose her own mate, without her mother constantly trying to arrange her life.

Yes, Reggie had it all. No doubt about it. Fine as hell, intelligent, U.S. Naval Captain with a bright future ahead of him, chiseled, sculpted body—and a dick the size of Mt. Everest.

And the man knew how to wield that beautiful thick cock like the soldier he was, Serena thought, remembering their previous night's marathon sex session before she left for her convention.

Yes, the man *definitely* knew what to do to get a woman wet, willing, and ready. But for all of that, there was an ache, an unfulfilled need in her that Reggie hadn't been able to fulfill. One that no man ever had.

No. It wasn't Reggie. Damn. If only it were that easy, Serena thought glumly.

It was her. All her. She'd shrugged off the disturbing thoughts and had raised her face to the stinging water raining down on her from the shower head.

Once the water began to cool, with reluctance, she'd turned the shower off and stepped out of the tub, wrapping her body in one of the thick, monogrammed hotel towels. Padding over to the small mirror mounted above the sink, she'd allowed the towel to slip from her body and stood naked in front of the mirror, examining herself.

She'd stared at her reflection, scrunching her nose at the image that stared back. She ran her fingers over her face, run along the tired lines that softly bracketed her wide mouth and noticed that—despite her deep chocolate-brown complexion—dark shadows underscored her eyes.

She needed to make some decisions about her life, and the longer she waited, the harder it would be.

Slowly her hands dropped away from her face and she lowered them to her breasts. Her breath quickened as she lightly cupped the small mounds, running her thumb over her nipples. She gazed at her breasts in the mirror, watching the twin, plumb-colored nipples tighten as she manipulated them.

She eased one hand away from one of her breasts, sliding over her moist skin, down to the V of her legs, her fingers delving between her moist folds. As she rubbed her clit, she continued to stare at her reflection, her lids dropping low, her tongue coming out to moisten her lower rim. Her skin grew uncomfortably tight, her breathing increased as she worked her clit, dipping two fingers inside and pumping them in and out until she felt the unmistakable sensation of an orgasm swamp her body.

With a small gasp, Serena came, her body jerking as she released, removing her hand from her pussy and planting both on the edge of the counter, gripping the basin tightly as her self-induced pleasure washed over her. Once her body relaxed, her breathing back to normal, she'd turned on the faucet and washed her trembling hands.

Blowing out a breath of air, she'd unclipped her hair, allowing the freed strands to tumble to her shoulders. She picked up the brush lying on the ceramic counter, and ran it haphazardly through her hair before securing it with a coated band.

She quickly left the bathroom and slipped into a short black skirt and silk blouse, and with key and purse in hand, headed to the bar downstairs in the hotel lobby. She needed a drink. Badly.

"Miss…can I get you something for that?"

Serena's eyes snapped open when a soft, yet husky voice asked the question.

She followed the sound of the voice and instantly felt her heart slam against her chest. Serena's breath caught in her throat as she stared for what seemed like an eternity into the face of one of the most beautiful people she'd ever laid eyes on, standing behind the bar counter with a smile on her bow-shaped, pink lips.

Serena's gaze traveled over the bartender. Over her close-cropped, inky black straight hair, multi-pierced small ears, to her whiskey-colored, almond-shaped eyes, which were fringed by lashes so thick and dark, so long, they appeared unreal.

Her nose was aquiline, small, with just a hint of a tilt at the end that added to her overall beauty instead of distracting from it. Her skin, which was the color of warm honey, was flawless, without a hint of makeup to mask her natural beauty. A small mole graced the corner of her mouth, and as she smiled at Serena, her small white, even teeth flashed.

Three of the top buttons on the white, starched uniform blouse she wore were undone, the crests of her plush, creamy breasts exposed, and Serena saw the outline of her small nipples pressed against the blouse, and realized she wasn't wearing a bra.

When Serena didn't answer, but continued to gaze at the bartender, a look of concern appeared in the bartender's beautiful eyes and she pulled the corner of her lower lip into her mouth by her top teeth.

Serena's tongue snaked out to lick suddenly dry lips.

With a start, she realized she was staring with her mouth slightly open and quickly snapped her lips shut and cleared her throat.

"Oh no, I'm fine," she croaked out the response and released a nervous sounding, dry laugh.

"Hard day?" the bartender asked, smiling at Serena as she reached out and took her empty glass.

Without asking, she refilled Serena's glass, her small hands wrapped around the neck of the bottle of wine, and images flashed in Serena's mind like a slideshow of the woman's small hands wrapping around Serena's breasts, her short nails scraping over her nipples as the two of them writhed together, bodies entwined, on the bed in her room upstairs in the hotel.

The image came out of nowhere, as startling in its intensity as it was appealing. Serena shook her head to clear the ridiculous images away, surprised and somewhat uncomfortable with the responding wetness she felt between her thighs because of her wayward thoughts.

What in the hell was wrong with her, she thought, shaking her head, forcing the hot visual out of her head.

She wasn't into women.

Once, in college, curious, she'd experimented with one of the other girls in her dormitory after a frat party, high and feeling reckless. Neither she nor her partner had known what the hell they were doing as they'd fumbled their way to orgasm, and in the morning they'd woken up, embarrassed and vowed to never talk about what they'd done the previous night.

But that had been the sum total of her experimentation and one she'd never repeated. She'd forced to the back of her mind the way it had felt to have a woman's soft body and sweet curves beneath hers, the way it had felt to taste another woman's essence.

"What's your name?"

"Serena. And yours?" Serena asked and laughed sheepishly when the bartender pointed a small, neatly manicured finger to her name tag. *Cree.*

The name fit her. Unique, somehow exotic. Just like her.

Not knowing what else to say, she glanced around at the empty bar. "Is it normally this quiet around here?" Serena asked, reluctantly turning away from the bartender's—Cree's—mesmerizing eyes.

"Actually, it can be pretty lively around here; especially during conventions. But the Hilton booked the last two conventions, so we're a bit slow. Plus, it's closing time."

Serena whipped her head around, her eyes going to the mirrored Heineken clock mounted above the wine rack over the bar. "Oh, God, I'm so sorry! You probably want to get out of here. Didn't know it was so late," she said and hastily moved to stand from the barstool, a sting of disappointment flooding her.

"No, you don't have to go. I just need to lock up, so no one else comes in," Cree quipped with a small laugh and a wink, and Serena felt a curious happiness, despite the butterflies that settled in her stomach. For some reason, the thought of being alone with Cree sent shivers of fear—and anticipation—racing down along her spine.

When the main lights in the bar flickered off, leaving the only luminosity from the lit bar, Serena turned around and took a fortifying drink of her wine.

Moments later, she felt fingertips feather down her neck and turned in her stool, her mouth open, and stared into Cree's smiling face.

"You're tense. Why don't you let me help you get rid of that headache," she murmured. Serena's heart pounded a little harder against her chest and her mouth went dry, yet she turned back around and allowed the woman to run her fingers over her neck and shoulders, her small hands surprisingly strong as she kneaded Serena's tense muscles.

"Hmmm," Serena murmured, closing her eyes.

"Feel good?"

"Yeah, really good," she answered, feeling her body melt under the woman's talented fingers like hot butter.

"Here, why don't you take off your blouse? It'll feel better," she said and Serena glanced over her shoulder at the woman.

"Uh, I don't think that's necessary," she laughed nervously. "Besides, anyone could walk by and see," she finished, swallowing the melon-sized ball of fearful anticipation of what could happen.

"No worries. The door's locked, windows tinted. Just relax. And enjoy," Cree replied easily, moving in front of Serena.

With their eyes locked, with the clarity in Cree's eyes easy to discern, her hand grazed the top of Serena's breasts, fingering her through the silk of her blouse before slipping the buttons free. Her gaze remained steady on Serena's as she slowly unclipped the front closure on Serena's bra, allowing her breasts to tumble free. Serena felt ready to explode from the sheer eroticism of what she was allowing—freely participating in—to naturally unfold.

The corners of Cree's lips lifted in a smile of appreciation as she thumbed one of Serena's turgid nipples, teasing them to tighten to the point of near pain. She leaned down and captured one of the erect, stiff buds, swabbing it with her tongue, before carefully taking it in her mouth and suckling the nipple, deeply.

Serena grasped her by the back of her short cropped head and pulled her closer as jolts of electricity wildly arced from her nipples to her pussy, while the woman milked, pulled and tugged, alternating her attention from one breast to the other.

Releasing her suctioning hold on her breasts, Cree stepped in closer between Serena's legs, bumping them further apart, her hands coming to rest on the top of her thighs as she continued to minister to her breasts.

With her breath caught in her throat, nostrils flaring as she inhaled the woman's unique scent deeply into her lungs, Serena released appreciative moans of delight. In heated anticipation she felt Cree's small hands, caress up the length of her thighs before shoving her skirt to her waist. Cree leaned close, her upper body pressed against hers, and whispered hotly in her ear, "What do you want from me, Serena? Say it," she demanded, softly. "Say what you want. What you need. Just once. Say it... Just once," she encouraged.

"I need to feel you," Serena bit out, harshly, her body trembling, so desperate was her need.

"Then show me," Cree replied and grasped her earlobe between her teeth, sucking the flesh. Serena cried out in passionate disbelief at the flood of cream from her pussy as it ran down her thighs, from the simple act.

Serena reached between their bodies and clumsily unbuttoned Cree's starched white blouse. Cree laughed a tinkling laugh when Serena mumbled an apology as several of the buttons got torn away in her haste to rid her of her blouse.

The minute Serena felt her large perfectly round breasts spill from beneath the blouse, she groaned and pushed away from the barstool, allowing it to tumble back with a clang to the floor as she moved as close as she could to the other woman, their breasts pressed tightly against each other.

Cree placed her hands beneath the globes of Serena's buttocks, squeezing and kneading the twin spheres. Mouths met in a desperate clash of need and lust and the women tumbled to the carpeted floor of the bar, Cree landing with a laugh on top of Serena. She leaned away and reached behind her body, unbuttoning her skirt and shoving it from her body before returning to straddle Serena.

With a sexy smile on her pretty lips, she bunched Serena's skirt up higher, exposing her further, and one of her fingers pulled at the elastic band of Serena's panties. She kept her eyes locked on Serena's as her hand slipped further inside her panties, tunneling through the trimmed hair surrounding Serena's mound.

When her index finger found the pulse of her pussy and swirled around the slick, stiff, blood-filled clit, Serena released a small mewling cry from behind clenched teeth, her body humming with desire.

Cree kept her gaze locked with Serena's and slipped her fingers between her drenched folds.

"Oh, God. This feels so good," Serena whispered, barely able to speak past the lump in her throat as Cree's fingers dipped in and out of her slick core, stroking her clit, rubbing her juices over and around the plump bud.

While Cree's hand continued to toy and play with her pussy, the other hand wrapped around the back of Serena's head, and she lay down on top of her. Serena had been expecting a rough, hard kiss, but when their lips met in a kiss so soft, so sweet, Serena felt tears sting the back of her eyes, forcing her to close them in near sensual agony. She felt one lone tear escape and travel down her face.

Cree released her lips and whispered against the corner of her mouth, "Sssh, it's okay." And her tongue snaked out to kiss the tear away, before she licked the corner of Serena's lips, easing between the seam of her mouth, stroking her lower lip in soft scissoring movements, silently asking for admittance into her mouth.

This close to her, Cree's scent, both feminine and sweet, while at the same time earthy and raw, wrapped around Serena, sealing them in a heady cocoon of lust, want and desperate need.

"I'm going to make you come. Do you want to come, Serena?"

Mindless, Serena tossed her head back and forth, mewling and crying as the woman continued to finger-fuck her, the look in her whiskey-colored eyes intense, passionate…*primal*.

At the same time she whispered the demand, she eased her fingers from Serena's dripping pussy, despite Serena's cry of denial, and snaked her body down until she reached the V of Serena's legs.

She ripped Serena's panties from her body, and shoving her legs up, until her feet were planted on the floor, she placed her entire mouth over Serena's pussy, shoved her tongue deep inside her cunt and licked, laved, and nibbled at her.

"Yes!" Serena screamed, clamping her legs close together alongside Cree's face, bracketing her, keeping her right where Serena wanted—*needed*—her to be.

Cree separated Serena's slick folds, spreading her pussy lips wide and pulled her closer. The heel of her other hand above her pelvic bone pressed lightly, while she paid homage to her pussy, lapping up the cream that now so freely streamed down the insides of her thighs.

Dear, God, Serena thought, she was lapping it up like it was some type of nectar straight from heaven.

She bucked against her talented tongue, squirming and rooting on her face, trying to get closer, urging, no, *demanding* her, to take it to the next level and give her the completion she needed.

Cree ignored her.

Instead, she continued her sensual teasing, paying no heed to her silent plea, taking her time with Serena, stroking her cunt in smooth easy glides. Serena wanted to cry, die, *something*. Her body was taut like the strings on some forgotten old guitar, the pleasure was so intense. She didn't know how much more she could take. On and on she lapped in slow, leisurely caresses, her face buried deep between her legs.

"Oh, please…" Serena begged and took in deep, desperate breaths of air.

Cree finally pulled her hood deep into the hot cavern of her mouth. She used her tongue to swirl and ferret out her pulsing, throbbing clit with such delicate ferocity, Serena thought she'd lose her mind.

As she licked and gobbled, laving her cunt, she removed the hand pressing down on her pelvis, and used both hands to separate the cheeks of Serena's ass. She rotated them in counter-clockwise motions, delving her tongue deeper and deeper into her core at the same time.

"Yes, that feels *so* good, please—*please* don't stop," Serena shamelessly begged.

When she felt one, then two fingers press into her ass, pushing past the puckered resistance, she groaned in a mixture of pain and pleasure so intertwined, she didn't know where one left off and the other began.

The laps of Cree's smooth, velvet tongue and press of her fingers inside her ass, was an erotic feeling unlike anything Serena had ever experienced.

Serena exploded.

She reared her body up, grabbed the woman's hair between her fists, but Cree continued to lick, eat and consume her pussy with greedy laps of her tongue while carefully moving her fingers in and out of the tight walls of her anus. Serena's body broke out in a fine sheen of sweat, her body shook and hips bucked against her mouth, and fingers.

Serena fell back down on the carpeted floor, her body writhing in violent trembles. Cree removed her fingers and shoved Serena's legs up, spreading her as wide as possible and climbed on top of her.

Grinding her body on hers, Cree rubbed and pumped her pussy against Serena's until Serena screamed. Plunging her tongue inside her mouth, swallowing her screams of passion, Cree continued to work her body along Serena's until the orgasm slammed into both of them, flames licking through Serena's body like a brush fire, devastating and complete.

Cree wrapped her arms around Serena and allowed them to ride the crest of orgasm together. When it was over, when her body was limp, completely boneless, and Cree lay quietly on top of her, she closed her eyes and smiled a tired yet satisfied smile, and gently reached a hand up to wipe away the soft tendrils of hair from Cree's sweaty forehead.

At last she'd found what was missing from her life.

෮෬

Kimberly Kaye Terry is a multi-published author who pens interracial, delicious tales that expertly blend eroticism and true romance for Kensington Publishing and Ellora's Cave. She lives with her husband, a Lt. Colonel in the U.S. Army, and their beautiful child in a suburb in Texas. Kimberly has a bachelor's degree in social work, a master's degree in human relations and counseling, and is a proud member of the one and only Zeta Phi Beta Sorority. Kimberly invites you to relax while you curl up with one of her scintillating tales of vivacious women and the amazing men who love them as they make their journey to finding true love. For more about Kimberly Kaye Terry check out www.kimberlykayeterry.com

New Orientation
Delilah Devlin

I sped down the steps, my backpack bouncing wildly against me, spotted my gate, and slowed. I rechecked the rail time-table for the hundredth time—"22.20," it read. Not trusting my own Timex, I glanced up at the large overhead clock next to the gate number. If I calculated the time correctly, the train should be rolling in right about now.

"Damn, I just made it."

Already warm from too much cognac sipped at a tavern not far from the station, the sprint from the taxi stand had me wishing for good old air-conditioned air—a rare commodity in Strasburg. Instead, I fanned myself with the travel guide and peered down the tracks into the darkness stretching beyond the covered platform.

"You're American," came a crisp, nearly accentless voice from behind me.

"What gave it away? The dreadlocks or the Nikes?" I grumbled without looking back.

"The guidebook, actually. You're always so worried about time when you're on vacation—one might think you're German."

The amusement underlying her tone made me feel a little embarrassed for my rudeness, so I drew a deep breath, plastered on a smile, and turned.

I had to raise my gaze. The woman was taller than my own five feet four inches. Her angular shoulders, straight, boyish figure and chin-length hair were made more feminine by large, luminous blue eyes.

About my age, mid-twenties, she looked a world removed from mine—blonde hair, cream-colored skin, poised and polished like a shiny new doll. My clothing was rumpled and too casual for anyone from around here, except the teenagers.

I lifted my chin. "And how'd you know I'm on vacation?"

She shook her head, which sent her wispy hair shivering around her cheeks. "I'm not saying anything else, or you'll think I'm pretending to be a psychic." This time the slight accent sounded like a soft lisp. *Nice…*

The sound seemed to tickle down my spine.

"Your English is very good."

She wrinkled her short, straight nose. "But not so good you didn't think I might be American myself."

My snort wasn't very elegant. "That's 'cause you speak it too well."

She nodded toward my book, her expression friendly. "Do you need help with your schedule?"

"I just need to know if the train I hear comin' down the tracks is the Orient Express."

"It is. Are you going to Vienna?"

"If that's Wien on the map, then yeah."

"Not to worry, you're in the right place and that's our train. Are you in a sleeper car for the night?"

"I paid for a couchette."

Again, her nose wrinkled—an affectation that made her seem younger. "You do know you'll be sleeping with five other people."

"I'm carrying a backpack," I said, my tone dead-panned. "You know this isn't a luxury vacation for me."

"I've reserved a sleeper car. It's about eighty Euros extra, and I only have to share it with one other person…" Her voice trailed off, but a question glinted in her pale-blue eyes.

Realizing I'd just had a longer conversation with this woman than I'd had with anyone since I'd set down in Paris a week ago, I felt reluctant to dismiss her suggestion. "You said you reserved yours…"

"If no one else has reserved the space, just sit in the car with me and you can pay the attendant when he comes."

"I'm Nicole, by the way," I said, adjusting my pack on one shoulder to hold out my hand.

Her firm grip surprised me. "Annegret."

She continued to hold my hand, and I fought my natural inclination to pull away first, not understanding if this was just one of the many European customs I didn't get.

When her thumb caressed my palm, my breath caught. Again, an unspoken question lay in the intensity of her intelligent gaze.

"Annegret…" I began, but the train finally arrived, pulling to a halt next to our concrete platform.

She released me, picked up the small overnight bag at her feet, and walked to the doors sliding open on the car marked "1."

First class. The cut of her thin wool suit—a short, body-hugging jacket, a slim skirt that reached mid-thigh—snuggled close to her lithe figure. Definitely first class. My eyes trailed down her body, past the swell of her small bottom to her nude legs, and then snagged on the clunky leather and cork sandals she wore.

"Strictly for comfort. Like your Nikes," she said, catching my startled glance and sounding just a bit breathless, perhaps even anxious. "Coming?"

Maybe I'd read more into that little caress than I should have. Or maybe she worried that she'd really offended me this time.

Fact was, I wasn't so much shocked as secretly thrilled. Annegret with her straight blonde hair and tall lean body was an attractive woman, and while I'd never had a sexual encounter with a woman before, it wasn't like I hadn't ever entertained the thought.

However, back in my own neighborhood, the opportunity had never presented itself, and frankly, there was no way in hell I'd let word get around that I swung like a pendulum. Here, I could take a chance. After all, I'd come to Europe seeking adventure and an expansion of my narrow horizons.

I followed her up the steps into the sleeper car, trailing behind her down the narrow corridor as she checked the numbers on the doors until she came to hers. She glanced over her shoulder, excitement shimmering in her eyes, and entered the tiny cabin.

Two red upholstered chairs sat side-by-side under a window. A wall with seams running down its length must be where the fold-down beds lay hidden.

"Stow your pack in the bin over the door," she said, as she chose another compartment.

We took our seats. My gaze roamed the narrow room, taking in the amenities—the sink, the linens and towels stacked in a cupboard. All the while, I felt her glance burning over my skin as the sensual tension escalated in the room.

The attendant arrived just as the train lurched out of the station. Annegret presented her ticket; I gave him my flexi-pass and enough Euros to secure the berth. After arranging for snacks and tea in the morning, I sat while Annegret pulled down the shade over the window and at the door, and turned the lock to assure our privacy.

All the while she moved about in silence, I felt my palms sweat and my heartbeat thud against my chest. Was this really what I thought this was all about?

When she turned back, she smoothed her palms down the side of her skirt and cleared her throat. "You don't have to do anything, Nicole. We can just talk."

"Tell you the truth, I'm not a hundred percent sure what you want from me."

"What I want?" She licked her lips nervously, and then sat on the edge of her chair, leaning toward me. "I think you know."

"This is kind of quick for me."

"Sometimes, you see someone…and you just know."

"What about me made you think…*that*?" I said, knowing—coward that I was—that I was talking in circles around a very delicate question. An uncomfortable one, if my intuition wasn't right.

"I wasn't certain whether you would go for a girl, but I was attracted. *Immediately*." Annegret lifted her shoulders, a hint of hopeful vulnerability stealing across her face. "Since we aren't likely to see one another ever again, I thought I'd take a chance."

I swallowed, understanding exactly what she felt. Maybe it was the cognac lowering my reserve. Maybe I'd had a secret itch to be with a woman and thought I'd never have the opportunity, but she looked like the kind of person who wouldn't mind me fumbling all over her body while I learned a thing or two.

This trip was all about adventure…and seeing things I'd never see back home. A white girl's clit, up close and personal, well, I thought I might want me some of that if the melting heat of my pussy was any indication.

She reached across the space between us and placed her hand on my knee.

Even through the denim, my skin burned.

"I would like to make love to you. Are you shocked?"

Without replying, I lifted her hand from my knee, watching as her fingers curled. A glance at her face, and I saw her features tighten. She thought I was rejecting her.

With my free hand, I pulled out the hem of my T-shirt and slid her hand beneath it, pushing it up toward my breast.

Her lips parted, her fingers splayed wide to cup my large breast, then curved over the top edge of the bra to drag it down.

As her hand reached inside to caress me, I couldn't help an excited little shiver. "No one's gonna come barging in on us?" I asked, my voice tightening up.

"We're alone," she said, her accent growing thicker. "No one will interrupt us."

"That bed gonna be big enough for both of us?"

A fingernail scraped the tip of my breast. "My ass is slender, and since I'll be on top of you, we'll fit."

She pulled her hand free, grabbed the hem of my shirt and pulled it over my head, then reached from my bra and flicked the front clasp open, smiling as my breasts sprang free.

She'd accomplished it all so quickly, I sat blinking stupidly.

"I love the color of your nipples…brown and purple," she said, tracing around them with her forefingers, then looking up to catch my gaze, perhaps to gauge my comfort.

I gave her a short nod.

She clasped my nipples between her thumbs and forefingers to tug gently until they peaked.

Feeling awkward and off kilter, I summoned my courage. "Maybe we should get ready for bed," I said, my voice roughening as my arousal spiked.

"Mmmm…" Her gaze didn't lift from the nipples she tweaked. "Maybe we should. I'd like to see all of you."

We both rose and began to undress. I watched as she draped

her jacket and blouse carefully over the back of her chair. The lace-edged camisole went next. She was braless beneath it. The points of her small round breasts were engorged and tilted slightly upward. Like they were meant to be sipped standing.

The cognac made me brave, gave me an excuse to act without thinking. Before I even got to my jeans, I leaned down and latched onto one of her little pink nipples, suckling hard, curving my hand around her breast to squeeze it as I drew on it like a straw.

"Let me see," she groaned, pushing back my head just enough so my locs didn't impede her view.

With her watching, her breaths deepening, I felt powerful, sensual, knowing how my full, dark lips must look against her pale breast. I pushed them out a little, exaggerating the pucker as I mouthed her soft, velvety nipple.

"Our clothes?" she reminded me breathlessly. "I want to see all of you."

So did I. The taste of her skin, the smell of her light perfume and lighter musk was beginning to do nasty things to my cunt.

I let go and straightened, not daring to look her way again, until I'd toed off my shoes and pushed my jeans and panties to the floor. When I finally looked up, she stood close, her gaze traveling down my body.

"Did you wax it?" she asked, sounding breathless, her gaze glued to my naked pussy.

"I like it smooth," I whispered.

Her pale wispy bush didn't do a thing to hide her pinkening labia.

My tongue swept out to lick my dry mouth.

Annegret turned to the wall and maneuvered the bed down from the hidden cubby. Smaller than a twin mattress, still, I thought we'd have room. Images of us clit-diving had me almost smiling.

"The linens," she murmured.

I gathered them and we made the bed, all the while looking each other over. Once when she bent to tuck a sheet beneath the mattress, I got a glimpse of her pussy from behind and was tempted to slip my fingers inside to fuck her, but I was afraid I'd move too fast. Appear like an eager puppy begging for a meal or scratch.

"Lie down," she said, and reached for the switch to dim the lights.

I didn't feel comfortable lying with my feet toward the door. I didn't quite trust the attendants wouldn't enter, so I faced the window and lowered myself, making room for her between my legs.

When she climbed over me and her knees scraped softly along my inner thighs, I gasped, but opened wider beneath her. When the soft, curling hair on her mons brushed my smooth cunt, I planted my feet in the mattress and tilted my hips up to rub my pubic bone hard against hers.

She came over me, resting on one elbow, her tight nipples dragging over the tops of my breasts.

I'd never felt anything like it, surrounded by her sweet scent, blanketed by her soft skin… Added to the gentle vibrations coming from the speeding train, and my whole body hummed with pleasure.

Her fingers cupped my cheek; a thumb rubbed my lower lip, then the upper. "You know, you can touch me too," she said with a small smile.

Her invitation unlocked me from my small moment of indecision. I lifted my arms and brought them around her, smoothing my hands down her back to cup the globes of her small ass, pressing my fingers into softness.

I glided my fingers down her cleft, touched her little asshole, making her gasp and grind her pubic bone against mine.

Feeling a little more confident that her body might react the same as mine, I reached lower, sliding between her moist folds to rim her opening. "I've had this image in my mind...," I whispered.

"Of what, Nicole?" she said, bending down to slide her lips along my cheek.

"Me, eating you out."

Soft laughter gusted against my ear. "I like where your mind is going. Do you want to try it?"

"Please. But I want to do it from behind you."

"Then I won't be able to touch you," she said, raising her head to give me a pout.

"Plenty of time for that, huh? We don't get to Vienna until eight."

Her eyes glittered with excitement. Her cheeks flushed. "All right, then."

After a few breathless, laughing moments, we repositioned ourselves. This time I didn't even mind my ass pointed right at the door, because her ass raised high in front of me as she fell forward on her hands.

"Put your face on the mattress," I said, wanting her pussy tilted at my mouth.

Her pussy, already glistening and slick, lifted higher.

So, this is what it looked like, when a guy knelt behind me. Other than the colors—creamy, pink outer lips, the thinner inner lips a deep rose, there wasn't much difference between hers and mine. I parted her with my thumbs, bent close to breathe in the rich scent of her arousal and stuck out my tongue for a taste.

My first hesitant touch had her entrance convulsing—opening, then closing, her thighs tensing.

I dove in for more, licking from the bottom of her slit upward, past her cunt to the sensitive perineum, then stroking over her asshole.

I didn't know why I did that last bit, had never been comfortable with a man exploring me there, and was glad she faced away because I don't think I would have tried it with her watching me.

Annegret moaned and pulsed her bottom up and down, encouraging me to continue.

My hunger growing stronger, I rolled my tongue at the bottom of her slit, feeling my way. Finding the hard knot of her clit, I rubbed over it again and again.

Her bottom trembled, and she widened her knees on the narrow bed.

When her entrance clasped wetly, I drew away to watch as I thrust two fingers inside her. She swallowed them easily, scooting back a little to take them and rotating to screw me deeper.

Three fingers seemed to stretch her silken walls, and cream seeped around me, easing me inside. I pumped my hand into her, slowly at first, rotating my fingers to scrape my knuckles against her passage, then stroking faster as her moans deepened.

"Nicole!" she rasped. "I have to see, please."

Suddenly, I realized I was the one in charge and loving it. I withdrew my fingers, lapped her once with my tongue and helped her turn to lie on her back.

I came over her, my lips latching on to a quivering tit and my fingers searching between her legs again for her entrance. I slid inside, toggled her clit with my thumb and started to move as though I was fucking her, pulsing up and down, dragging her breast with me, moving my hand in and out in rhythm with my body.

With my pussy high and open, the cool air of the cabin sweeping over my moist, heated flesh, soon it wasn't enough.

Without asking, without looking for her approval, I turned and climbed backward, inching my knees toward her head.

Her hands guided me higher, helping me to place them on either side of her shoulders. When her lips lifted to my cunt, I gave a little growl and lowered myself onto her face.

Her arms wrapped around my hips, her hands found my fleshy ass and massaged my cheeks as I dipped against her mouth.

Her lips closed around my clit, latching firmly, and she sucked and tongued me until I was the one trembling.

Arching over her, I slipped my hands beneath her ass, bringing one between her legs. I slid my fingers inside her and rolled my mouth between her folds until my lips found the little pea-sized kernel. I fucked her with my fingers I suckled her clit until her hips jerked upward.

Together, we moaned and ground our sexes against each other's mouths. The tendril of arousal curling around my womb tightened. I pumped my hips up and down, forcing her to follow with her lips.

When my release washed over me, I thrust my fingers hard inside her and teethed her clit until I felt her helpless little jerks become more frantic.

Her mouth broke from my clit and a thin wail echoed in the tiny room.

For long moments afterward, I kissed her pussy, her inner thighs, wet my cheeks and chin in the well of her femininity.

Annegret stroked my cunt with her tongue and fingers, drinking my release, until at last, she drew a deep breath and hugged my hips. "And I thought I would be on top, little virgin."

My short, breathless laughter shook us both. I rolled off her, lying on my side snuggled close to her warm body. I glided a hand over her soft belly and combed my fingers through her thatch.

Annegret sat up and gave me a caress that stroked along my

shoulders and back. "I have Schnapps. Would you like a drink? We'll make a toast."

As she climbed off the mattress, I collapsed face first on the bed, completely undone, but feeling that warm, enervating afterglow. I turned my head and watched her bend over to reach into the cupboard where she'd stowed her bag. "Was I okay?"

I winced, wishing I could take it back. I sounded like I had after the first time I'd screwed a boy, but I felt every bit as unsure. This was new territory for me.

Annegret lifted a bottle from her back, unscrewed the top and held it high. "I'm ready to celebrate, aren't I?" She held out the bottle to me, and sat on the edge of the bed. "If you hadn't been everything I dreamed, I'd probably be dressing now, and wondering how long I'd have to hide in the bathroom down the hall until you fell asleep."

Her expression, happy and flirting, was so much easier to read than a man's. I took a long swallow from the bottle, wrinkled my nose and handed it back.

"Too sweet?" she said, laughing.

"Yeah, but it is warming me all the way to my toes."

Her eyebrows rose. "I thought that was supposed to be my job."

"Well, if you'd like to give it another try…"

Her wide smile drew my mouth into a grin. She bent and kissed me. "I think I've never enjoyed a business trip quite so much."

I tugged her hair, bringing her closer. "And I never saw this one listed in the travel brochures. But I think I like it."

Her glance slid away, and her head tilted. "You know…I have this room reserved at a little hotel, not far from the Opera House…"

"Hmmm…That's right on my itinerary," I murmured, knowing where this was headed.

"I'll show you the sights after I finish with my business."

"I'm seeing them just fine," I drawled, and reached to cup her breast, playing with her nipple until it lengthened.

Maybe this wasn't exactly how I thought I'd spend my week in Austria, but then again, I'd packed light, wanting to be free to linger where I chose.

I chose Annegret.

ဢ

These days, award-winning novelist Delilah Devlin is missing the wide-open skies and starry nights of South Texas but loving her dark forest in Central Arkansas, with its eccentric characters and isolation—the better to feed her hungry muse! Her personal journey has taken her through one war and many countries, cultures, jobs, and relationships to bring her to where she is now—writing sexy adventures that share a common thread of self-discovery and transformation. For more about Delilah, check out: www.DelilahDevlin.com.

The Private Room
Allison Hobbs

Astra and Lanie, my girls since high school, invited me out to celebrate my divorce.

Celebrate! Yeah, right. Getting untangled from my marital mishap wasn't easy and it most certainly wasn't cheap. I get nauseous just thinking about all the money I had to spend. So, when Astra and Lanie came up with the divorce celebration idea, I felt more like puking than raising a glass in cheer. But I decided to grin and bear it, pretending that a failed marriage and the high cost of being free had not taken a terrific toll.

We bar-hopped on South Street and I really got my drink on, throwing down Cosmopolitans like I was guzzling fruit juice. *Hell, I deserve to get pissy drunk*, I grumbled to myself. My divorce settlement sucked. What kind of backwards society would demand that a woman pay spousal support to a big, strapping man? Why should I be penalized just because I work hard for a living and he chooses to loaf around? What a fool I'd been. But you know how the saying goes. Love makes you… No, scratch that—good dick makes you do foolish things.

After Astra and Lanie were sufficiently inebriated, the three of us—dignified (when sober), wage-earning, home-owning, church-going women—boldly sauntered inside one of those sleazy, adult novelty shops on the South Street strip. Emitting drunken giggles, we shook boxes of penis-shaped pasta, fondled feather ticklers, squeezed the pumps of nipple suckers, and ogled pussy pound cake and other naughty novelties.

Tipsy and having a good time, I actually forgot my troubles for a little while. But in the midst of laughter and frivolity, while watching Astra try to squeeze into an extremely small, satin-padded corset, I was hit with a sudden feeling of being utterly alone. No longer happy and carefree, it was obvious that the liquor was wearing off. A lump in my throat took form when I caught sight of an attractive couple holding hands as they browsed, stopping ever so often to express their love with an open-mouthed, fervent kiss.

Viewing this passionate pair pierced my heart so deeply, my knees practically buckled from the pain. Envious and close to tears, I was unable to continue my happy-to-be-free routine. I turned from the couple and briskly walked away.

"Where are you going?" Lanie tilted her head to the side.

Looking over my shoulder while walking quickly, I mouthed, "Restroom." In my haste to get away from my friend and be alone, I mistakenly wandered into a deserted aisle that showcased hard-core sex paraphernalia. My mouth dropped open at the startling sight of vibrators, life-like dildos of varying sizes, Jock-Strap harnesses equipped with realistic penises and scrotums attached. A thigh harness with a protrusive phallus made me gasp out loud. I squinted at the advertising on the package that boasted that it was great for lap dancing.

Sobered by the jolting sight of dicks and dangling balls, my lips parted to call my friends over to share the shock of the scandalous display. But before I spoke a word, I heard someone murmur, "Mmm. Nice ass."

Just because it appeared that I was appraising the strap-on dildos, didn't make me fair game for some horny bastard. With my face

set in mean mode, and feeling justified in expressing my indigna-
tion, I jerked my head upward. But my hateful expression swiftly
changed to a look of bafflement when I discovered the person who
crudely assessed my body was not a lecherous man, after all.

The voice belonged to a young woman. Early twenties. Muscular
and lean. She was a lesbian, no doubt about it, but not the feminine,
curvy, girls-gone-wild, come join me in a ménage-a-tois, porno-
flick chick. She was a rough and rugged type of dyke. It took a
few seconds to mentally shift gears. But I got it together because
this thugged-out, hussy needed to know, I'm not the one! Dramat-
ically, I scanned the aisle, turning my head back and forth, looking
around me as if to say, '*I know, you're not talking to me!*'

She ignored my theatrics and nudged her chin toward the fake
dicks. "Which one do you like?"

Too appalled to speak, I twisted my features into a severe scowl.
No she didn't! I wanted to chastise her, but being alone in the
aisle with this brazen she-male, I didn't dare antagonize her. God
forbid if she developed an attitude and got all up in my face. I've
heard that *those people* are easy to anger and prone to violence.
Unwilling to risk a physical confrontation, I held my scolding
tongue. I pictured myself wind-milling her wildly and it wasn't an
attractive sight. Even worse, was the image of the muscle-bound
dyke using one hard-ass, well-aimed punch to knock me the hell out.

Still, despite my fear of her brute strength, I had to let her
know that I felt offended. With carefully chosen words, I spoke
ever so politely, gesturing with my hands to make my point.
"Your behavior is crude." I took a deep, huffy breath. "Now, my
motto is to live and let live, but I don't appreciate being hit on by
a woman." I gave a huge sigh, and then added smugly, "For your
information, I'm not gay."

"For real?" She took on a feigned expression of innocence.

"For real!" I sucked my teeth in disgust.

She nodded her head toward the sex gear. "So, why are you checking out the strap-ons? You thinking about switching teams?"

"Not hardly," I tossed back. "Unlike you, I am not confused about my sexuality. I'm straight as an arrow—one hundred percent, heterosexual," I asserted, fired up and mad as hell.

Paying no attention to my angry words and tone, the dyke chick's eyes roamed my body. It creeped me out when her roving gaze settled on my breasts. Silently admonishing myself for wearing such a low-cut top, I folded my arms across my chest to shield my innocent twins from her perverted stare.

"Oh, excuse me, was I staring?" She shook her head as if to break the captivating spell my extra-large boobies seemed to have on her.

I dropped my arms, prepared to leave the vicinity of the dyke and the triple X-rated sex toys.

"Yo, are they real?" There was amusement in her voice as her eyes again zoomed in on my deep cleavage.

"Of course, they're real." I rolled my eyes. "Not that it's any of your business." Finished with the vile chitchat, I gave her my back and took a few steps in the opposite direction. Suddenly, I heard the sound of a package being torn open.

"Yo, hot chocolate," she called out, referring to my dark-brown complexion.

My gut reaction was to ignore her and swiftly rejoin my friends, but curiosity got the best of me. I refused to acknowledge to myself that it was *she* who intrigued me. Brushing the thought aside, I stopped and slowly turned around.

"What do you think about this one? Big enough?" At her groin, she'd placed a replica of an erect penis. It had the fullness, shape, and appearance of the real thing.

It was vulgar, a revolting contradiction—a chick with a dick. Blatantly disrespectful, the virile-looking young woman caressed the length of the heavily veined shaft. The gender dichotomy had my mind spinning. The imagery was surreal.

And intriguing.

I felt a quick rush of uncomfortable heat. I wanted to whisk myself away from the tawdry aisle of dangling fake appendages. It was time to end this lurid interlude, but my feet refused to move.

In the distance, I could hear Astra's and Lanie's excited, slurred voices as they undoubtedly stumbled upon another provocative conversation piece. They were too sloshed and too caught up in the marvels inside the South Street sex shop to concern themselves with my whereabouts.

"Think you can you handle this?" The dyke chick used her thumb and forefinger to fondle the mushroom-capped head. Her behavior was lewd; her words were coarse and lustful, bringing me to my senses.

Then she smiled at me, disarming me with the appearance of a dimple in her left cheek. That dimple, so non-threatening, so adorable, came from out of the blue. The charming indentation in her cheek threw me off balance, skewed my sensibility, and caused me to inadvertently take notice of her smooth, flawless, ginger-colored skin. To be honest, she wasn't as tough-looking as I'd first thought.

In fact, she was really cute with perfectly arched brows, and almond-shaped, brown eyes that sparkled with sexual mischief as they once again glanced downward and penetrated the satin fabric of my black bra. In an instant, my nipples hardened against my will.

Whoa! This woman was a predator. She sensed my emotional quandary and smelled fear.

Astra and Lanie were a few aisles over; I could hear them giggling at some outlandish discovery, but instead of rushing to rejoin my friends, instead of returning to the safety of the real world where wounded women assumed stiff upper lips, and banded together to celebrate the overthrowing of yet another mistake-of-a mate, I stood transfixed in a surreal space, disturbingly mesmerized by a masculine female.

She cradled her hairless chin between her thumb and forefinger, stroked it thoughtfully, clearly realizing that I was experiencing a bout of sexual confusion and the ball was now in her court. Then, with the aggressive posturing of a man who is confident that he can have whatever he wants, she took a few steps toward me. "My name is Tristan."

"Nina," I replied, eyes downcast, nervously brushing back wayward strands of hair.

Her eyes darted to my voluptuous behind. "You're sexy, Nina. You know I wanna tap that ass, right? And yo, I can't wait to wrap my lips around that big chocolate mound," she replied with a wink.

Without warning, completely unexpected, I felt an outpouring of liquid heat, saturated the thick thatch of hair that curled near the lips of my womanhood. My cheeks felt hot and flushed, they would have been blazing red if it weren't for my deep-brown skin tone, which concealed my embarrassing and unexpected arousal.

Wearing a satisfied smile, she stuffed the strap-on inside the box and returned it to the shelf. Her swagger, her demeanor was masculine. That cute dimple and something else that was hard to identify gave her softness. The intermingling of male and female energy was surprisingly sensual.

"Come here." Tristan moistened her lips as if preparing to kiss me. I hesitated. "Get over here, girl. I won't bite you."

As if hypnotized, I took a few steps toward her. The moment I got within reach, she wrapped her arms around my waist. Her hands briefly rested on the cheeks of my buttocks and then began a gentle, circular massage, causing the liquid heat to increase between my thighs, as her fingers trailed down the crack of my fabric-covered ass. Caught up in the pleasure of her forbidden touch, an anguished moan escaped my lips.

Her lips brushed my neck. She inhaled my scent. "Mmm. You smell good. Whatchu wearing?"

"Um…." My mind was mush, hell if I knew.

"Does your pussy taste as good as you smell?" Tristan's inquiry made me shudder. I grunted an unintelligible response.

"You gotta let me sample some of that. You wanna get with me?" Her voice was a low, sensual rumble.

Unable to speak, I said nothing, unsure what to say, what was going on with me that I was attracted to this woman. There I stood, in a public venue, captured in the arms of a strange woman, fighting the strong urge to drop my pants and get down and dirty right there on the tiled floor.

It dawned on me that security cameras were rolling, but I was beyond caring. It was difficult to summon rational thought and proper behavior with a vagina clenching up and pleading to be fucked.

Tristan released me. She peeked at her wristwatch, which was big, round-faced and manly. "Get rid of your giggly girlfriends. It shouldn't take you more than a couple minutes to kick it like you have a headache. Tell 'em you have to bounce. After you get your situation straight, swing back by here."

"Uh, okay," I stammered but lingered, feeling as if I were in a dream-like state.

She frowned at her watch again. "Go handle your business." She gave me a quick kiss on the lips. It was more a dismissive gesture than one of affection.

Following her order, I walked away and bumped smack into Astra and Lanie. Their sour expressions indicated that they were not pleased with my lengthy visit to the restroom.

"What took you so long? It's late. We're ready to go." Astra's mouth was set in a firm no-nonsense line.

"I was sick." I touched my stomach. "Too many Cosmos."

We walked to the parking lot on Bainbridge Street, exchanged air kisses and got in our separate cars. I paid my parking fee, pulled out of the lot and drove around the block, and then parked on a dark residential street.

Walking fast and cautiously looking over my shoulder in case Astra or Lanie caught me trying to get my creep on, I hurried back to South Street.

Inside the brightly lit sex shop, I craned my neck, looking for Tristan.

"Are you Nina?" a man working the register inquired.

I nodded, wondering how he knew my name.

"Your party is in the private room," he said, using a discreet tone.

"The private room?" My whispery voice was squeaky and confused.

He pointed to the back of the store. "Walk straight back and knock on the door."

For the love of God, why didn't I just turn around and go home? Tristan was waiting for me in the stock room with the approval of the establishment. This twisted liaison was getting raunchier and stranger by the second. But I finally admitted to myself that I was bi-curious, so I mumbled a "thank you" and took awkward steps toward my illicit rendezvous.

Knowing that I was making an absolute fool of myself, I paused at the door with a plate that actually spelled out the word, "Private." Never had I felt so out of control, so out of my element, but Tristan's sexy murmurings and her earthy sexiness had piqued my interest. My libido was fully charged. There was no turning back.

Nervously, I raised a balled fist and rapped on the door.

Tristan cracked the door open. "Hey sexy," she welcomed me, dimple on display, motioning for me to enter.

To my astonishment, there were no stacked boxes filled with sexual gizmos. The room was furnished with a plainly made bed and two metal folding chairs. Framed prints decorated the walls. I had stepped into a hidden, underground lifestyle. I felt disoriented, but before I could verbalize regret, before I could bow out gracefully, Tristan's mouth claimed mine.

Her aggressive tongue parted my lips, snaked in and out of my mouth. She clutched handfuls of my hair and pulled until I cried out from the sweet pain. She pulled her mouth away. "You want me, baby?" she asked and smiled when I gasped a desperate, "Yes!"

Satisfied with my frantic state of sexual need, she slid her hands around my waist and roughly pulled me closer until we were groin-to-groin. Holding her tight, I positioned my clit against the hard rod hidden in her pants that felt exactly like an erect penis. Our gyrating hips rocked in sync. My breathing became harsh as desire mounted.

"Take your clothes off, baby." Tristan tugged at the waistband of my pants and then began removing her own clothing.

Quickly, I kicked off my shoes and stole a glance. Standing sideways from me, Tristan skimmed off her top. Her small breasts, topped by tiny brown nipples, jiggled deliciously as she moved. She turned away and removed her denim pants, shed her boxers.

Her naked ass was toned and tight. The contrast of soft and feminine and rock-hard made my pussy burn.

But when she turned and faced me, I nearly lost my breath. She was wearing the hell out of the harnessed, medium-brown colored dick. She looked so damn sexy with that big brown cock, I almost tripped trying to get out of my pants.

Completely nude, I stretched out on the bed. Sexual tension knotted inside my creamy core, but I squeezed my legs together to alleviate the pressure.

She sauntered over and straddled me. "Pretty titties," she murmured in a husky voice. At first, Tristan flicked her tongue against my firm nipples, and then she sucked each dark bead.

I felt my body flush with arousal, began to feel a recognizable ache as intense heat flooded through me; my juices—hot and syrupy—ran down my thighs. She cupped both breasts, pushed them together and sucked the plum-colored nipples until they became sensitive, glistening peaks. I winced when she grazed her teeth against my pebbled flesh, which was now painfully engorged.

"Turn over and let me see that round, kissable ass."

I flipped over on command.

She gave my behind a couple of soft smacks. "Mmm. Look at all that jiggle." Lying on my stomach, I was in a sexual frenzy as Tristan alternated smacking and kissing my butt cheeks.

A bundle of pent-up anxiety had me humping and pressing my clit against the mattress. Noticing my distress, Tristan spread my legs, lifted me to a slightly raised position and licked my honey pot from behind. "Oh, God," I cried out as she inserted her tongue deeply. The slurping sounds along with her tongue lashes inside my hot tunnel sent me to the brink of arousal.

She rearranged herself, and I felt the plastic shaft press insistently against my smooth backside. I assumed that beneath the male appendage, Tristan's own vagina was wet and burning hot. I wondered if she needed me to probe her with my fingers.

With an arm draped over my side, Tristan used her longest finger to caress my clitoris. Slowly, sensually, she penetrated my soft, honey-coated passageway.

"I'm ready to fuck, baby. You want this dick?" she asked.

I replied with a long, tortured groan.

Enjoying the heightened sensation of dual stimulation, I rotated my hips and moaned softly as I rocked back and forth against Tristan's finger while simultaneously accepting penetration from the plastic penis. Tristan's penile thrusts were slow and steady.

"Deeper!" I moaned.

"You sure? I'm trying to be gentle. I don't want to hurt you."

"Harder!" I insisted, losing control, pushing back as my body demanded more.

Tristan squeezed my buttocks and obligingly drove the dildo in to the hilt. She released one buttock and wound her hand around my belly to reach for my pussy, then took hold of my labia, pulling on one slippery lip and then the other. Her grunting sounds made me aware of her unfulfilled hunger.

"What do you want me to do?" I whimpered.

"Just let me fuck you, I'll get mine," she assured me.

With the intention of satiating both of our desires, Tristan plunged her male appendage in and out of my vagina with speed and intensity that had me perspiring as I struggled to match her rhythm. In the next blissful instant, we exploded together, bucking, shaking, shuddering. Crying out, our voices rang in shared passion.

As we dressed in silence, I took small peeks at her from beneath lowered lashes, my stomach dropping as reality crashed down on me.

What had I just done?

She opened the door for me, gallantly allowing me to go in front of her. I patted my hair in place, checked my clothing one more time and slipped past her, without giving her a glance.

We passed the register. "Good looking out," Tristan said to the manager.

I bit my lip, not meeting his eyes. As we approached the door, her hand swatted my ass.

I glanced up at her. "You could be more polite," I chastised her. "And anyway, how do you know about that room?"

"I work there part time," Tristan divulged with a grin. "I stock the shelves after hours. Yo, Nina. I want to get to know you better. You down with that?"

I pressed my lips together, wondering if I dare take it to the next level with her. Was I out of my mind to even consider it?

I stared at her, torn, and that sweet dimple deepened in her cheek.

I reached out and grabbed her hand. Tristan turned, and moved my hand into the crook of her elbow, tucking it and me close to her side, and we ambled down South Street.

My decision was made.

৪০৫৪

The Queen of Seduction, Allison Hobbs resides in Philadelphia, PA and is the protégé of Zane, who believes that Allison will be the next erotic author to break out and sell millions of books. Her writing is unique, as proven with her vast collection of novels, all published by Zane: Pandora's Box, Insatiable, Dangerously in Love, Double Dippin', The Enchantress, A Bona Fide Gold Digger, The Climax: Insatiable 2, and the upcoming Big Juicy Lips: Double Dippin' 2, Pure Pleasure: Gold Digger 2, and The Sorceress. You can visit her on the web at: www.allisonhobbs.com

In My Mind
Zane

Twice a week, when I entered the classroom, I would always see her first. Well, actually, the back of her as she prepared all of her materials for class. She sat in the first row, obviously a serious student who wanted to make the best impression. I admired that.

As I walked from the rear to the front, I would brush past her and catch her distinctive whiff. She wasn't the perfume type, but she always smelled great. I recognized when she changed to the featured scent of the month at Bath and Body Works; I always did the same, but Moonlit Path would always be my favorite.

A few times I said hello to her. She whispered a soft response but never engaged in conversation with me after class, like many of the other students, especially the male students. All of them wanted to sample what they had come to know so well visually.

Never in a million years would I have imagined becoming a nude model, even though I had sketched and painted many of them when I had been an art major at the same university where I now worked. Times were hard since my mother had passed away, and I needed to pay my bills. I had obtained a little success as a painter, but no one would ever take me seriously until I was dead.

Shane was her name. One of the other students had mentioned

that she was originally from Atlanta and had moved to Washington, D.C. for college. She was taller than me but, then again, so were most women. Since I measured four feet eleven inches, most girls were taller than me before they finished elementary school. Shane had long brown dreadlocks, coconut flesh and a gap between her front teeth. She wore glasses and tried to hide the fact that she was beautiful by wearing frumpy clothes and no makeup.

I did not become a lesbian until I was in my late-twenties. In retrospect, I probably always should have been one. No man had ever truly appreciated my value or respected me, not until after I was gone and they were trying to convince me to come back. Pain recognizes pain, though, and I often saw agony on Shane's face during class. I had nothing else to do but stare at everyone while they stared at my body.

The routine was always the same. I would come in, go up on the small riser, disrobe and then strike a pose, which changed weekly. The first week, the instructor had me lie on a Victorian chaise and strike a historical pose. The second week, I had to stand with my back to them and my head bent to the right so they could see my profile. I hated that. My neck had such a crick in it that I had to go home and use a heating pad. The third week, I sat on a stool with my hands folded on my lap. Now we were into the fourth week and I had to stand erect with my back slightly arched, my arms raised over my head grasping a pole, with my chin pointed a little down and to the left.

Class began and all eyes were on me. Pencils were out and the only sounds were the tips whisking across the paper and the low music playing in the background. "Bed" by J. Holiday was currently playing and all I could think about was putting Shane to bed. I had often wondered if she had ever noticed how much I stared at her over others in the class. My gaze would remain fixed on her while I made love to her over and over again in my mind. I imagined her hands running through my curly, black hair and her tongue on my nipples, that would often become hard just from the fantasy. The third week, I had actually climaxed while posing. In my mind, I had been eating Shane's pussy and she was screaming out my name: "Emile! Emile!" I hoped no one had seen the wetness of my pussy dripping down the legs of the stool. Then again, it was what it was. If I was going to sit there in the same position for three hours, twice a week, my mind had to do something. Shane had been not on my mind, but *in my mind* for so long and I decided that it was time to do something about it.

"Hello, Shane," I said while she was packing up her supplies.

"Hey, Emile," she whispered back.

"How are things going?" I asked, which took our normal conversation further than it had ever been.

She looked nervous. "I'm fine. Why do you ask?"

It was like she was trying to hide something, or feared that I had found out something. I knew next to nothing about her.

"I was just asking. We spend six hours a week together, so I was only wondering."

Shane scanned the room, full of others. "But everyone is here every week."

I shrugged, standing there in my plush robe and flip-flops. "Everyone else has at least held one conversation with me; everyone but you." I started to walk away, admitting defeat way too easily. "Sorry if I bothered you."

She grabbed my arm and, even through the thick fabric, electricity shot up my spine. My fantasy had touched me—for the first time but far from the last.

"Emile, I didn't mean to come off the wrong way. It's just that, well, it's been a rough month for me."

"I'm a great listener. Would you like to go have a drink and talk about it?"

"Oh, I wouldn't want to impose on you."

Was that a blush?

"Shane, it's not an imposition. Everyone needs someone to talk to, and I've had a rough year, not just a month."

"Really?"

"Yes, we all have issues, and it's important not to keep things wrapped up inside."

Shane giggled. "A drink would be nice, right about now. But only if you have the time."

I brushed one of her dreadlocks off her cheek. "Just give me ten minutes. I'll meet you out front."

"Um, okay."

༄༅

While I was getting dressed, I hoped that my touching her cheek like that hadn't scared her off. I had no idea if Shane was into men, or women, or both. I only craved for her to be into me.

When I pulled up in front of the building in my red BMW, left to me by my mother, Shane was standing on the steps.

"Get in," I said, as I pushed the passenger door open.

Twenty seconds later, we were headed to the campus exit gates.

"So what do you like to drink?" I asked.

Shane shrugged. "I'm not a big drinker, so anything fruity is cool."

"Great! I know a place in Georgetown that sells marvelous frozen drinks—all flavors of Daiquiris and Margaritas."

"Cool."

"They also have a smokin' DJ. You like go-go music?"

"I really don't know that much about it, except for 'Da Butt' by E.U. Have you heard that?"

"Damn, girl, everyone's done da butt!"

We fell out laughing.

I continued, "I guess they don't have a lot of go-go in Atlanta."

There was that nervous look again. "How did you know that I'm from Atlanta?"

"Someone mentioned it." I sighed. "Can I ask you a question?"

"Um, okay," she replied hesitantly.

"Are you seeing anyone right now?"

A frown came across her face. "Why do you ask?"

"Just wondering. You seem kind of on edge and most of the time when women are on edge, it's because of relationship problems."

Shane laughed. "You're very astute. Actually, the person that I've been seeing has been tripping lately. They've been spending time with someone else, I think."

There it was. She was definitely into women. The use of "the person," "they've," and "someone else," instead of "the man," "he's," and "another woman," had said it all. It takes one to know one. I grinned like a Cheshire cat. Since she was into kitty kat, half of the battle was already won.

I decided not to fake the funk and turned the car around to head to Southeast. "I just thought of another place we can go. You'll like it a whole lot better."

৪৩য়

We entered Too Deep, my regular spot near the Navy Yard, and Shane's eyes almost popped clear out of her head. Wall-to-wall fine women were socializing, drinking, and engaged in public displays of affection. I did not ask her if she was down with the program, but simply led her to the bar and ordered two frozen Pina Coladas.

A blob of the drink landed on Shane's chest when she picked up the overflowing cup. She was about to wipe it off with a cocktail napkin but I stopped her, leaned in closer to her and licked it off. I took my time and ran the tip of my tongue down the middle of her breasts, as much as I could with her shirt still on. I couldn't wait until I could suckle on them for hours at a time. My breasts are my most sensitive part, and thus, I like to suck on them the way I want my women to reciprocate. Knowing how much pleasure I derive from it makes me want to pleasure others.

I sat back and gazed into Shane's eyes, to gauge her reaction. Her mouth was hanging open but she didn't look upset. While her mouth was already open, I took advantage of it and slid my tongue into it. At first, she did not move hers as I explored the inside, flicking my tongue over the roof of her mouth. Then she got into it and it was on; we were making out like two teenagers and Shane was a fantastic kisser. The thought of her moving her tongue like that inside of my pussy had my panties on fire.

"U Got It Bad" by Usher started playing and I asked Shane to dance. We ended up in the middle of the dance floor, grinding on each other and my head only came up to her chest, just like a normal size woman's would to a normal-sized man. We were the perfect fit. I got lost in her, laying my head on her breast as she wrapped her arms around me and we got caught up in the words. I had it bad and I knew it. I only hoped that Shane was feeling me as much. Whoever had fucked up with her was a dumb-ass sister!

Shane had on a skirt. I reached down between her legs and worked my index finger inside her panties, which felt like cotton.

"You smell so sweet," I told her as I gazed up into her eyes.

She flinched as I started fingering her pussy. It was so wet.

"You smell sweet yourself, Emile."

I pulled my finger out and licked it. "And you taste even sweeter."

I dove back into her panties, with two fingers next, and worked her damn near into a frenzy for the remainder of the song and the next: "No Love" by Kevon Edmonds.

ঙেঞ্জ

We left the club an hour later and headed to my apartment. Shane never asked me if I was seeing anyone and I never bothered to offer the information. For the past three years, I had been living with Madonna, but she was out of the country for four months on a contract assignment. It was my intention to end the relationship as soon as she returned. I needed a lot of attention, more importantly affection, and Madonna was too caught up in her profession to sustain me as her woman. She saw it exactly the opposite. Madonna felt that I was wasting my life away on a silly dream and that I needed to do more to contribute to the household. That was one of the reasons that I had reduced myself to nude modeling.

When we got to my place, luckily I had taken down all the pictures of Madonna and me cuddling and grinning from ear-to-ear, back when we had been happier. Sure, all of her clothes and belongings were there, but unlike a man, who has to hide hair bows and perfume bottles when a chick comes over, I was expected to have feminine items at my place.

"Wow, you're an artist!" Shane said when she noticed the easel, all the paint brushes, charcoal pencils and other supplies.

"Yes, I have an art degree from the university," I said. "That's how I knew that I could get a job there. Professor Andrews used to teach me back in the day."

"Oh, that's wild." Shane snickered. "I never would have guessed."

"Being that all you ever knew about me before tonight was my nude body, there was no way for you to have guessed."

I should not have said that. I could tell that Shane was beginning to ponder the fact that we really did not know each other. Plus, Shane had someone else. And even though her lover was probably cheating, Shane obviously still cared. I could have backed off, but Shane was *in my mind* and I had to have her—all of her.

"Why don't you make yourself comfortable on the couch?" I suggested. "I'll go get us a bottle of wine."

"Oh, I don't know if I should mix liquors," Shane said in protest.

"It'll be okay. If you don't want any, I could still use some."

I got a bottle of Chardonnay and two wine glasses from the kitchen and when I returned, I was shocked. Shane wasn't on the couch. She was standing in the middle of my living room…naked.

"I realize that my body is nowhere near as great as yours, but this is who I am," she whispered.

"You're stunning!" I set the bottle and glasses on the coffee table and started taking off my clothes. "I know you've seen this all before," I joked.

"Yes, but now I get to touch it, and lick it, and suck it."

No, she was not turning the seduction table on me!

"Oh, so it's like that, Shane? I never took you to be a freak!"

"Like you said, before tonight, who could have known what?" She paused. "I've wanted to suck on that pussy of yours since day one. It's always glistening, and it's shaved into a heart." She spread her legs and pointed to her own pussy. "See, we're twins."

Shane had shaved her pussy hairs into a heart, just like mine. *Damn, I was in love!*

I had first started doing it to prove to Madonna how much I

cared for her, and often asked her to let me do hers, but she balked at the thought. *Fuck that bitch!*

Before I could even get over the fact that I had been in Shane's mind as much as she had been in mine, she was lifting me off the floor and carrying me to the bedroom. Yes, carrying me. She laid me on my back, spread my legs, and her warm tongue invaded my walls as I moaned in pure delight. I played with my nipples while she sucked on my hardened clit. My thighs began to shiver as she slid her finger into my asshole and started working both my holes. I grabbed a pillow and started biting on the corner to muffle a scream as I came for the first time.

Shane looked up at me. "I've wanted to taste your cum since the day you came on that stool."

I tried to catch my breath as I let go of the pillow with my teeth. "You saw that, huh?"

"Not only did I see it, I yearned to come up there and lick every drop off the stool. That was one lucky stool, to have your pussy sitting on top of it. All I could think about was that it should have been my face."

"Damn, Shane!" I said. "This is going to sound absolutely crazy, but I think I love you!"

I jumped up and pushed her on her back, demanding, "I have to taste you. Right now."

I dove in with my tongue, having never wanted to explore a woman's pussy more in my entire life. Shane tasted like the Pina Coladas we drank at Too Deep, but I could tell that she had a healthy diet, like myself. I ate her like my life depended on it. In many ways, it did. I needed her in my life and I had to do whatever I could to make sure that she would never want another.

೮౧౪

We spent the next four hours pleasuring one another. I ate her from four different angles: spread eagle, from the back, with her on top of my face, and in the shower with her foot propped up on the side of the tub. Each time that I tasted her, it only got better and better.

When we were in the shower, I sucked on her breasts so erotically and so passionately that I came twice just from doing that. Shane gave as good as she got and turned me out in ways that I had never even imagined…*in my mind*. She ate me out on the kitchen table off a canvas and later, she shellacked my juices onto it so we could always remember our first time together.

ಹಾಃ

By the time Madonna had returned from her business trip, I had moved out and in with Shane. The woman she had been tied up with had left her. As suspected, she had been cheating all along. Hell, she dropped her dime and I picked it up. Shane and I often paint and sketch each other. It had been years since I had sketched a nude and I never wanted to sketch another one outside of her.

Shane will forever be…in my mind.

ಹಾಃ

Zane is the New York Times *bestselling author of more than ten titles, the editor of numerous anthologies, and the publisher of Strebor Books, an imprint of ATRIA Books/Simon and Schuster. She is also the executive producer of several television and film projects, including* Zane's Sex Chronicles, *an original Cinemax program loosely based on her life. You can visit her online at: www.eroticanoir.com, join her mailing list by sending a blank email to eroticanoir-subscribe@topica.com or visit her MySpace page at www.myspace.com/zaneland.*